Praise

"KD Mason takes his Southern California, v specials three-dimensic. ...meets the menacing Giles Endroit aboard *Gendroit*, a yacht with ominous technology, and it intensifies as Edso's romantic pursuit of the mysterious Jennifer leads to an unexpected climax. This book is a cliffhanger, and I could not put it down until the last page."
—Vin Wenners, Rye Beach, NH, Attorney at Law and avid reader

* * *

"Being an enthusiastic reader of KD Mason, I was delighted with the new twist of sending these unique East Coast characters to the West Coast to solve their mystery. I recognized many key settings and found it a comfort to place myself with them. Once again, this talented author leaves the reader with an ending that cries out for the next book!"
—Mary Ann Lafleur, Laguna Beach, CA, Retired Teacher and Principal

* * *

"Kudos to KD Mason for his latest entry in the Jack Beale mystery series. I was hooked by the story right from the first page! The story unites unfinished business from a previous mystery with new adventures on the West Coast—and what a fast-paced, intriguing ride full of unexpected twists and turns it is! As the characters come face to face with the dark side of humanity, we quickly realize that their escape from this evil is not guaranteed. A must read."
—Richard "Sandy" Stevens, Monroeville, PA but a NH native at heart.

* * *

"KD Mason takes readers to a heightened level of adventure in this new book. Having lived on both coasts, I enjoyed the characters and settings, which often felt comfortingly familiar. KD's gift for making readers feel like part of the suspense is unsurpassed! Get ready for yet another "I can't put this down" interlude with Max, Sylvie, Jack, and all of their friends and enemies who keep us on edge and warm our hearts."
—Paula Moore, North Port, FL whose heart remains in Rye, NH

* * *

"KD Mason continues the gripping saga of his character Jack Beale and his friends, in another layered, satisfyingly cozy mystery that is nearly impossible to put down."
—Mia Heintzelman, Las Vegas, NV, Author of "It's got a ring to it" and "Shades" and the upcoming Mixed Signals Series.
Visit miaheintzelman.com for more information.

Other Titles by K.D. Mason
ALL BOOKS ARE AVAILABLE ON KINDLE

HARBOR ICE
NOW AVAILABLE AS AN AUDIO BOOK
ON AUDIBLE.COM, ITUNES STORE, AND AMAZON.COM

CHANGING TIDES

DANGEROUS SHOALS

KILLER RUN

EVIL INTENTIONS

UNEXPECTED CATCH

BLACK SCHOONER

JESSICA'S SECRET

CANCELED OUT

CALIFORNIA
RECKONING

CALIFORNIA RECKONING

K.D. MASON

To Everyone
at Voyagers'
thank you and
Enjoy!
KD Mason

The author may be reached through www.kdmason.com

California Reckoning is a work of fiction. All of the characters, places, organizations, and events portrayed in this novel are either products of the author's imagination or are used fictitiously, and any resemblance to any actual persons, living or dead, business establishments, events, or locales is entirely coincidental.

Recipe for Zuppa di Pesce alla Napoletana reprinted with permission of Mary Ann Esposito and Peter E. Randall Publisher from *Ciao Italia, My Lifelong Food Adventures in Italy* p. 56

Recipe for Nellie and Joes Famous Key Lime Pie reproduced with permission of Nellie and Joes Famous Key West Lime Juice.

ISBN-13 978-1795323888
ISBN-10 1795323884

Cover and book design: Claire MacMaster | barefoot art graphic design
Copy Editor: Renée Nicholls | www.mywritingcoach.net
Back cover photographer: Richard G. Holt
Proofreading: Eileen Frigon, Nancy Obert, Deb Merrill, Candace Stevens

Printed in the U.S.A

California Reckoning *is dedicated to my wife, children and their families*

Nancy
Kyle and Laila
Kara, Scott and Lilly

* * *

THANK YOUs

As always, there are so many people who have provided help, advice, support, comments and opinions during the process of writing a book, some directly and others indirectly, that it is impossible to thank each person individually, so please know that I am forever grateful.

However, I must single out one special person—Edso Harding for his generous support of the NHSPCA by becoming, for the second time, the high bidder for the opportunity to have his name used for a character in one of my books, first in Jessica's Secret *and now, in* California Reckoning.

PROLOGUE

"SOMEONE'S AT THE DOOR," she hissed.

"Get rid of them," he called up from the cellar.

He listened from halfway up the stairs and heard angry voices, followed by a sharp "Ow!" Then the door slammed shut.

"Come on! We have to get out of here," she said, as she began heading down the cellar stairs.

"What about her?"

She cut him off. "Doesn't matter. It'll look like an overdose. We have to get rid of him. After he's gone for good, we can make it look like he killed her."

* * *

"Excuse me sir, we have a problem. They just called. They're in the boat heading for the dump point, but they don't have the woman. Someone came to the door and they had to flee immediately."

"Who? What?"

"It was hard to hear clearly, but I got the sense that they were confident that she was dead and it will look like an overdose."

"But they don't know for sure."

"No, sir. They don't."

"Didn't they understand what had to be done?"

"I am certain that they did. I explained it to them myself."

"In that case, it is now up to you to make sure that decades of work will not be put in jeopardy. Too much is at stake and we are so close. Do you understand?"

"I do. We'll leave immediately. *Last Chance* is fast and we'll easily meet up with them."

He paused, the look in his eyes left no doubt as to his intent, then he spoke again. This time his voice had the tone of a warning growl. "Just so there is no misunderstanding, there can be no evidence that they ever existed. None. The boat either."

"I understand," she said.

"Good. Remember, I will be watching."

CHAPTER 1

TO SAY THAT THE LAST YEAR had been tumultuous would be an understatement. Sitting at her desk, Courtney refolded the letter, stuffed it back into its envelope, and dropped it on her desk. She spun her chair around until it was facing the window, then looked out over the harbor. After a few moments, she interlaced her hands lightly, raised her index fingers like a steeple, and rested them against her lips.

"I think this will be perfect," she thought.

Then she said softly, "We deserve it."

Saying those words made it feel so much more real.

She continued to stare out the window, thinking about all that had happened over the past several months. Sylvie had wormed herself into their lives once again, but this time, it had been different. This time she had been the one pursued. This time she had been the one needing help. This time she had actively recruited Jack's help, giving him little chance to decline. Worse, Max, Patti, and Dave had also been sucked in. During that race, the difference between survival and death was no more than a snap of a finger. Had that slip on a random patch of ice happened a split second sooner or later, things may have turned out differently. Courtney knew that Max was still upset even though she wouldn't admit as much.

Her thoughts were interrupted by a knocking on her door. She recognized the voice that followed: "Knock, knock."

Courtney pivoted her chair around in time to see Max's face peeking in as the door was pushed open.

"You wanted to see us?"

It was late afternoon. Max and Patti were scheduled for the evening's shift, and Courtney had left word downstairs that they were to come up to the office as soon as they arrived.

Courtney adopted a stern tone and expression. "Yes. Is Patti with you?"

Max stepped into the room, with Patti right behind her.

Patti said, "Hey Court, I'm here. What's up?" However, as soon as she got a glimpse of Court, the smile on her face disappeared, replaced by concern. "Everything okay?"

"Come in. I have something to talk to the two of you about."

"This can't be good," she heard Patti whisper to Max.

Court motioned toward the two chairs in front of her desk, and they sat down quickly. Each of their faces reflected the same severe expression that Court had placed on hers. Each was obviously trying to figure out what was wrong but finding no clue.

"First, let me say that I want you to know that I will always be eternally grateful to you all for all you have done for me." Then she paused.

Max's eyes locked onto Courtney's face as if she was fighting increasing panic. She put one hand on her chest as if she was struggling to breathe.

"Courtney, what's wrong? I've never seen you like this!"

A quick glance at Patti revealed much of the same. She was frozen in place, her face was beginning to flush, and Courtney could see her eyes beginning to well up with tears.

Max took a deep breath and said, "Come on Court. Stop messing around."

Finally, Courtney took pity on them. She softened her expression and said, "What would you say to going on a little adventure with me?"

Both of her friends instantly relaxed.

"Define adventure," said Max.

"I was thinking that it might be good for the three of us to get away for a couple of weeks."

Patti looked confused. "You mean a vacation?"

"Exactly. We've, uh, you've earned it."

Max chimed in. "And where would this vacation be to?"

"I've never been to California. I kind of thought that might be nice."

"California," Patti said.

Now Courtney allowed herself to break into a big smile.

"California!" shouted Patti, as she leapt from her chair. "I've always wanted to go to California." All signs of the dread she had felt moments before were gone. Now, she looked like a child who was just told she was going to Disney World.

"What's the catch?" said Max. "Why?"

"No catch. But you guys saved me from Edso last year, and between that and what Sylvie just put you through, I thought we could use a break before summer begins."

"Oh my God," said Patti. "Cali. I can't believe it."

"Cali?" Max looked at her friend.

"That's what they say out there. There's a whole new language we'll have to learn."

Max gave her a slight eye roll, then looked at Court. "It's a big state. Any idea where? The north—San Francisco, or maybe wine country?"

"We all like wine," said Patti. "We could have our own Sideways experience."

"Sideways experience?" said Max and Court simultaneously.

"You know, like the movie."

They both nodded, then Court said, "Actually, I've been looking, and I think that maybe it would be fun to stay along the coast—maybe somewhere south of Los Angeles."

Patti's face lit up. "Really! O-M-G, maybe we'll get to see some stars." Then she stopped and stared at Max, inhaling deeply before exhaling, "Max, what if we see—"

Courtney cut her off. "Patti, slow down. You do know how many people live there, don't you? The chances of actually seeing someone you recognize is practically nil."

"Court's right," said Max. "Don't get too excited. To actually see a celebrity would be like finding a needle in a haystack."

"No. No, no. I can feel it. We are going to meet someone famous."

Max turned toward Courtney and said, "Just ignore her. Somewhere south of LA? Where?"

Court tried not to laugh. Patti was obviously making a list in her head of celebrities she was going to see.

"Well, I've been looking for a while. I found this great place, and I'll know tomorrow if we get it."

"Court, come on. Where? You can't just keep us in suspense!"

"Okay, it's in Laguna Beach."

"Laguna Beach?"

"I've heard it's really nice there—"

Before she could continue, Patti rejoined the conversation. "Did you say beach?"

Courtney smiled and nodded yes.

Suddenly, Patti stood real still, and her expression sobered. In a low, serious voice she said, "When?"

"When what?" replied Court.

"When do we leave?"

"Three weeks from today."

"Three weeks!" said Patti. "Do you know what that means?"

Court looked at her. Before Max could open her mouth, Court said, "No, Patti. I don't. What does that mean?"

"It means we have to get bathing suits. We live in New England. We have winter bodies, all white and pudgy."

"Hey! Speak for yourself," said Max.

Courtney just smiled at her friends and said, "We'll deal."

CHAPTER 2

"CAN YOU BELIEVE IT," said Patti. "We're going to Cali." She was practically dancing as she stood by the bar waiting for Max to make her drinks.

"Patti, take a breath, slow down." Max placed a third drink in front of Patti. It was in a large martini glass filled perilously close to the rim. "You spill those and I'll put your drinks in the slow pile."

"You won't. I know you. You're as excited as I am." Patti spoke in a singsong voice as she rearranged the drinks on her tray.

Max knew that she was right on both counts.

* * *

Several long hours later, Max saw Patti return to the same spot next to the bar.

"I'm all set," Patti said. "Come cash me out."

"Be right there."

As was usual, the dining rooms had closed well before Max was able to give last call. Patti waited as Max carried two glasses of wine and the check to the last couple in the bar.

Returning with the check and some cash in her hand, she whispered to Patti, "Those two have been all over each other, all night." Then she added, "I don't think they'll even finish that last round before their hormones take over completely. Then we'll be out of here."

"No hurry. You need any help?"

"Nah, I'm all set. Trash is out; everything's restocked. Just have to lock the door and cash out."

"In that case, I'll have a glass of wine and wait with you."

Max knew her friend preferred white. As Max placed the glass in front of her, Patti asked, "What time did Court leave?"

"Before that couple came in. She just waved as she went out the door."

"Can you believe that she's taking us to California?"

"Yes and no. I mean, I can see it because she's like that."

"I know."

"But I never saw this coming, especially so close to the summer months, when all hell will break loose."

"No shit. You think she had a stroke or something?"

Max giggled. "I hope not, but you're right, the timing does seem a bit curious."

"I tried texting Dave to tell him, but he never checks his texts. Have you told Jack?"

"No. I figured I'd just surprise him when I got home. Dave gonna' be all right with it?"

"Probably." Patti shrugged. "You know how he is."

"Yeah."

"How about Jack?"

"Same. They'll probably spend even more time running and drinking beer while we're away. I bet they'll go out to eat every night or grill steak, steak, and more steak."

"Sounds about right. Though Dave'll probably pick up some extra hours, unless he's able to go fishing."

Max nodded in agreement. "And Jack'll probably be working on *d'Riddem*."

Suddenly, Patti nodded her head toward the couple. She whispered, "I think they're leaving."

The couple in the back stood. Then, like Siamese twins attached at the hip, they walked arm in arm as one toward the back hall and bathrooms.

Patti whispered, "Thank God I just heard *two* doors."

Shortly after, Max heard them giggling, then the sound of the back door. They were gone.

"If you'll clear the table, I'll cash out, and we'll be out of here," said Max.

* * *

In less than ten minutes, Max was turning the key in the lock.

"Thanks for staying with me."

"No problem. Can you believe that we're going to Cali in three weeks?" Patti was getting all bubbly again.

"I know."

Then, in a more serious tone, Patti added, "She won't change her mind, will she?"

"She won't. Go home. We'll begin planning tomorrow."

* * *

"Mrowh."

Max pushed the door shut. "Shhh," she said, looking up the stairs.

Cat was sitting at the top of the stairs, silhouetted by a faint glow of light behind her. Max could feel the intensity of her gaze as she walked up the stairs.

"Hey, Cat," she said, as she reached out to scratch Cat's head. Immediately Cat stood and stretched, alternately arching her back and then stretching forward with her front legs as if bowing down in obeisance. As soon as her fingers touched Cat's head, the reply was loud purring and a barely audible "mrowh."

"You're not going to believe what happened tonight."

"Mrowh." Cat gave her a gentle head-butt, leaving Max no choice but to keep rubbing her head and ears.

Max sat down on the floor at the top of the stairs, and Cat climbed into her lap. Still purring loudly, Cat stretched up and rubbed against Max's cheek.

"Courtney's taking Patti and me on a vacation."

"Mrowh."

"That's right. We're going to California for a couple of weeks, so you'll be on your own with Jack."

Cat continued to insist that her ears and head be rubbed. The volume of her purrs increased, and she murmured another soft "Mrowh."

"Listen, I'm tired, so you have to let me get up."

As Max shooed Cat out of her lap, she stood and slipped out of her shoes, not wanting to make any unnecessary sounds as she moved about.

"Good night Cat," she whispered.

Cat had already settled on the couch.

"Mrowh."

CHAPTER 3

MAX COULD HEAR JACK'S SLOW, steady breathing as she tiptoed toward the bed. The floor was cold on her bare feet, and the room's temperature, even though well above winter cold, was not yet summer warm; she could feel goose bumps forming on her skin.

After brushing her teeth in the bathroom, Max pulled on one of Jack's long-sleeved running shirts—what he called a tech shirt. Lighter and softer than cotton, it was made of a special fabric designed to wick away moisture, and in almost-cold temperatures, it was the next best thing to not wearing anything at all.

Trying not to disturb him, she carefully slid under the covers. Like the floor, they were cold, and soon her entire body was cold. She sucked in her breath and shivered. Lying still, waiting for the bed to warm, she could feel the shadow of his warmth beside her, and without thinking, she edged closer to him until she could feel first her leg, then her shoulder, come in contact with him. He remained still. As she lay there listening to him sleep, and feeling the warmth radiating off him, memories of cool tropical nights began to dance in her head. The bed covers had begun to warm, but now she hardly noticed them as a pleasant warmth began to radiate outward from deep within. Ever so slowly she rolled onto her side and slowly slid one leg over his. Then, with her arm draped over his chest, she pulled herself into him.

Jack stirred. She could tell he was not yet fully awake, but he moaned, exhaled, and wrapped his arms around her, returning her embrace.

"You awake?" she whispered. "I have some news."

"Unhh," Jack exhaled, still more asleep than awake.

Max squiggled herself closer, and she felt him begin to respond to the pressure of her body against his.

"Max? What?" She could hear a sleepy half smile in his voice.

No longer seeking refuge from the cold, she now wanted more, but first she had to share her news.

"Courtney's taking Patti and me to California for a girls' vacation."

"What!" He was in full voice now.

"Court's taking Patti and me to California," she repeated.

"When? For how long?"

"Not for about three weeks, and we'll only be gone for a couple."

"She okay?"

"Why?"

"To leave this close to the busy season . . ."

"I know. We wondered the same, but she wants to do it."

"Come here," he said, pulling her up on top of him.

"Will you miss me?" she said. Her words were muffled as she nuzzled his neck.

"Why would I miss you?"

Max lifted her head, feigning hurt, and looked at him. Even in the near dark of the room, she could see him grinning.

She pressed her hips into his and felt his response With a slight lilt in her voice, she said, "Oh, I don't know."

His surrender was quick and complete. "I was just teasing. You know I'll miss you."

Max kissed him, and nothing else was said.

* * *

"So, California." Jack closed the door to the microwave to heat his morning cup of instant coffee.

"It still feels like a dream. Maybe it'll seem more real when I see Court today."

"Has Patti told Dave?"

"She texted him last night before we left Ben's."

"Why'd she do that? He never checks his texts."

"I know that. You either. That's why I didn't text you."

"I'm glad you didn't. I liked the way you told me much better."

She smiled. "I did too."

* * *

Patti was already at Ben's when Max arrived.

"You're early," said Max.

"I know. We have so much to plan, and I wanted to have time to talk before things got busy."

"What things? How'd it go with Dave?"

"Fine."

Patti's answer seemed a bit too nonchalant considering how excited she was about the trip.

"Fine?" repeated Max, studying her friend.

Patti's face began to pink up. "Yeah."

"What did he say?"

"He was good with it."

"With what?" Max could tell that Patti was getting uncomfortable. "How did you tell him?"

"I told him. That's all."

"I don't think so. You did the nasty and then told him, didn't you?"

"Max!"

"I knew it. And he's all fine with it."

She was in full blush. "Yes. He's fine with it."

"With what?" Max continued teasing. "The trip, or his little surprise?"

"Stop. He's fine with the trip, and yes, he did like the way I told him. Now, can we talk about the trip? We have a lot to plan."

"Okay. Where do you want to begin?"

"Isn't that obvious? We're going to the land of beautiful people, and we're staying at a beach."

Max understood her implication, but it was easier to play dumb.

"We need sunscreen. That's easy."

"Max, get serious. We have winter bodies—New England winter bodies. We need swimming suits."

"Okay. We need suits, so?"

"One piece or two? That's important."

"We should have both. When I was in Belize, I had both. That way you're ready for whatever."

"I suppose."

"Patti, stop worrying so much."

A third voice joined them. "Come on, you two! Time to get this place open."

Both jumped, and Max spoke first. "Court, how long have you been there?"

"Long enough to listen to you two worrying about nothing. I'm the one with issues."

"You are not," said Patti.

"We can discuss this later. Now, let's get going." She turned and walked away.

"Issues?" whispered Patti.

Max just shrugged.

CHAPTER 4

"SO, JACK, WHAT DO YOU THINK about this girls' vacation?" asked Dave.

They were thirty minutes into their run. The trails in Maudsley were clear, although in some places the footing was a bit soft, and in a few of the shadiest spots off the trails, Jack could still see remaining patches of snow.

"Sounds like fun."

"More like trouble if you ask me."

"You're probably right. But it's still nice of Courtney."

"Is Max acting as nutty as Patti?"

"How's that?"

"Patti is freaking out over swimming suits. Bikini versus one piece. What the hell is the big deal?"

"Oh, that. Yeah, Max is a bit insane."

"I mean, who will they be trying to impress? Each other?"

"I don't think that's the point."

"So what's the point?"

"If I knew the answer, I'd be a millionaire. Just accept it."

"I suppose."

There wasn't much talking for the rest of the run as the pace increased.

"That was good, thanks," said Jack, as they finally slowed to a stop.

"No. Thank you," said Dave. "It was good. Good idea to run here today."

"What're you up to the rest of the day?"

"Not much. I was thinking that I might pull out my fishing stuff. Maybe while they're gone, I'll get in a fishing trip. You?"

"I think I'm going to stop by *d'Riddem* since I'm down here."

"When's she going in?"

"It'll be a while, but I need to look at the project list."

"Anything major?"

"I don't think so. But you know boats. Just when you think everything's all set, something goes wrong."

"True. Glad I got rid of my boat. It was small, but it was still a pain in the ass sometimes."

"I think Max is off tonight. You guys want to get together later?"

"I'm in, but I'll have to check with Patti."

* * *

"I'd like to propose a toast to Courtney," said Jack, "even though she's not here." He lifted his beer. They were at Dave's, enjoying takeout from the Wok.

"To Courtney," said Max.

Patti raised her beer and said, "To Courtney."

Dave just smiled and reached across the table, adding his bottle to the series of clinks as they sealed the toast.

Toast finished, Dave downed his beer. Then, as he got up for another, he said, "So, how's the hunt for swimsuits going?"

Jack barely managed to stop himself from laughing. He knew Dave already had the answer but couldn't help himself. His friend was like that.

Patti flashed Dave a look that said, "Watch what you say."

Max spoke quickly, and Jack knew from experience that she would try to head off a fight by changing the subject. "It's going well. You gonna' go fishing while we're gone?"

However, Dave pressed on. "Jack and I were discussing which kind of suits would look best on you while we were running today."

Now it was Jack's turn to glower at Dave. "Really? I don't remember that."

"You know, itsy bitsy or teenie weenie."

"I really don't remember having quite that conversation," said Jack.

To his dismay, Max immediately switched to Dave's trouble-making side. "So, Jack, what did you decide I would look best in?"

"That's not fair. You two are being complete a-holes. Dave and I were talking in general terms only."

"But, if we go to the beach while on vacation, and we will, which should I wear?"

"That's up to you. But remember, I won't be there to defend you, so you'll be on your own when all those cute California surfer boys try to pick you up."

"No one's picking anyone up."

"Except Courtney," interjected Patti. "We've all heard the stories about her on vacation. This'll be our chance to see her in action."

"Patti, that's an awful thing to say!" Max pretended to look shocked, and they all started laughing.

"But seriously, girls, and strictly for my own enlightenment, what kind of suits *do* you prefer?" said Jack, trying to keep a straight face.

"You'll just have to wait and see," said Max.

* * *

Max and Jack were halfway home when she said, "So, what kind of suit do you really think I'd look best in?"

Jack looked over at her.

"Watch where you're going," she said, pointing toward the road.

"That's not fair."

"What's not fair? It's a simple question. Bikini or one piece?"

"Max, you'd look great in either. I'd probably say the bikini. It'd be easier to get you out of—"

She cut him off. "Jack, you pig. That wasn't the question."

"You asked. But seriously, you'd look great in either."

"Thank you, but you're not really being much help."

He shrugged, and they rode the final miles home in silence. As the truck came to a stop and Jack killed the engine, he turned to Max and said, "Okay. Either would be great, but you know the ones that have ruffles over the boobs. Those are ugly, so no ruffles."

"No ruffles. That's it?"

"No ruffles. Unless I see it on you, I can't say what would look best."

She pulled on the door handle. "You're impossible." Then she slid out of the truck.

As she walked toward the door, Jack came up beside her and put his arm around her waist. "Seriously, you'll look great in whatever suit you choose—even if it has ruffles."

"Mrowh."

Cat appeared at their feet as they reached the door, and as soon as it was pushed open, she raced inside and up the stairs.

"Mrowh."

Jack said, "Clearly, she agrees."

CHAPTER 5

"HEY, JACK."

Jack had been down at the commercial pier catching up on the local gossip. He was about to climb up into his truck when he heard Tom's voice. He stopped and looked around to see where his voice was coming from when he saw Tom walking toward him. He was not in uniform.

"Day off?" asked Jack.

"Yeah. Cooking dinner tonight. Came down to see who was in and what they might have."

"I think you're shit out of luck. Everyone just left. Most of the boats are in; no one had much."

"Well, it was worth a try. How's Max?"

"She's good," said Jack. "As a matter of fact, Courtney is taking her and Patti to California in a couple weeks for a short vacation."

"California? This close to summer?"

"I know. Surprised me, but that's what she's doing. She feels they need a break after all that happened over the winter."

"Sounds like nothing but trouble."

"I agree."

"Well, I've got to get going," said Tom and he started to turn away, then, before Jack could say good-bye, he stopped and turned back. "Hey, Jack, you remember the name Giles Endroit?"

Jack looked at Tom wondering where that came from. He shook his head no. "Why?"

"Just curious." Tom shrugged, then turned and began walking away.

"Hey, Tom. Hold up."

He stopped and Jack walked over to him. "You're not getting off that easy. Who's Giles Endroit?"

"You remember all that Francis House stuff a few years back?"

"I do." Jack paused obviously trying to remember the details.

"He was behind some group which secretly tried to buy up all the area around the harbor?"

"That's right. I remember. And I think Max and I even met him in Belize. I think he was an author." Jack paused again, "I'm sure of it. Max and I did meet him when we were on vacation in Belize. Early one morning I was walking the beach and I stopped to admire a large catamaran that was tied to a dock. Turns out it was his. We talked, and he told me that he was an author—cheesy beach reads as he described it. I think Max still has several that he signed."

"Wow. And that's what you remember—cheesy beach reads—after all that ended up going on around here?"

Jack grinned sheepishly. "Give me a break. Is he back?"

"No. But his name came up in a Homeland advisory."

Jack must have looked puzzled.

Tom said, "I get these weekly advisories from Homeland. They're mostly pretty vague and general in content, unless there's a specific threat."

"And?" said Jack.

"The latest one didn't list any specific threats, mostly references the rise of white supremacist groups and what to be on the lookout for."

"But you said Giles is mentioned."

"He is."

"So, that sounds kind of specific to me."

"It does, but his inclusion is more as background than as a direct threat."

"So, he's a white supremacist?"

"It doesn't say that specifically, but there must be some evidence of that for his name to be listed."

"And why are you telling me this?"

Tom shrugged. "Thought you might be interested. I mean, you did have a connection to him."

"That's thin."

"I know, but I thought you should know."

"So where is he?"

"Again, nothing specific, but I got the impression that he's on the West Coast."

"Where on the West Coast?"

"Didn't say specifically, but my guess is in the southern part of the state."

"Great. Courtney, Max, and Patti are going out there in a few weeks. Just our luck they'll run into him."

Tom grinned. "Wouldn't that be interesting."

Jack shook his head. Grimly, he said, "No. It wouldn't."

Tom raised his hands. "Whoa, Jack, take it easy. Southern California is a very big place, and the chances of the girls running into him are infinitesimally small."

"I know, but I can't help but worry now that I know he's on a watch list."

"Jack, stop. You're acting just like them when they get into conspiracy theory mode. I simply wanted to let you know."

Jack relaxed. "Sorry, you're right. It's ridiculous to think that they could ever run into him."

"Exactly."

Jack took a deep breath and then said, "White supremacists? What's with that?"

"Well, you've seen the news. Racists, white supremacists, alt-right, neo-Nazis, call them what you will, they've always been around—it's just that now they're emboldened by the political climate and are coming out from under their rocks."

"Anything to be worried about around here?"

"Yes and no."

"What do you mean by that?"

"Well, if you mean something like a physical attack on infrastructure, I don't think so. At least, not at the present."

"Infrastructures?"

"You know, things like pipelines, power plants, roads, bridges—that kind of stuff. Goodness knows there's a lot in this area: Navy Yard, the bridges over the Piscataqua, the nuke plant, et cetera."

"So if they're not going to be destroying stuff, then what?"

"As you know, those people have a way of stirring up a lot of social unrest, and most of them aren't smart enough to know that they're being manipulated. Think about this: doesn't it seem that they're being emboldened as their warped ideas are being voiced by more and more elected officials?"

"I suppose." Jack paused a moment before continuing, "Okay. So if this Giles Endroit is on the other side of the country, what's he got to do with what's going on here?"

Tom shrugged. "Again, I have no idea, but you know as well as I do that there are people in this town that like it lily white and want to keep it that way."

Jack nodded in agreement.

"As a side note, did you know that back in the early twentieth century, Maine had one of the highest concentrations of Klan membership in the country?"

"I did not know that."

"It did. There weren't a lot of blacks around New England, so it was mostly a reaction to the great influx of Catholics and white minority groups, like the Irish and French Canadians."

"But that was ages ago. How worried should we be now?"

"Hard to tell. These days, I'm sure there are more than enough frightened, gun-crazed people around to take care of all the worrying."

"That's so reassuring."

"Come on Jack, work with me. These notifications always look at things in the worst possible light. Reality is, I don't think we have much to worry about. I mean, while there are many possible targets in the seacoast, I'm confident that they are being well watched."

"I suppose. So should I tell Max?"

"I can't tell you not to."

"So, yes."

"I didn't say that, but working at a place like Ben's, they must hear an awful lot of gossip. If they hear anything, I'd hope that they'd say something."

"I'm sure they would."

Looking at his watch, Tom said, "I've got to get going."

"OK, but listen, Tom, keep me posted if you hear anything that's more than just speculation."

"Deal."

"Talk to you soon."

CHAPTER 6

EDSO GLANCED AT THE CLOCK ON HIS DASH. He was almost at the marina. The drive down from his home in Newport Beach to San Diego on the Five was jam-packed with traffic as usual. The two hot hours spent in near gridlock conditions were more than enough time for him to repeatedly go over in his mind the letter he had received notifying him of his grandfather's passing.

"Three months!" he said out loud. *"How could it be that my grandfather died three months ago, and I have only just learned of it?"*

He knew the answer, but it still mystified him. The day before, he had received a letter from a San Diego law firm. Its text was spare: no details, no explanation.

> We regret to inform you of the passing of Otto Jäger. His final wish
> was that three months after his passing we were to send to you the
> enclosed note. Our condolences.

He immediately contacted the firm, but they weren't really able to offer him any additional information. He simply learned that his grandfather had come into their offices one day and requested that they send the note to Edso three months after they received notice of Otto's death. A generous retainer was paid, and that was it. He shouldn't have been surprised. That was so like his grandfather: always secretive, always in control.

Edso glanced down at the note on the seat next to him. He didn't need to read it. Just looking at it was enough to remind him what it said. It had been in a sealed envelope with his name written on its face in his grandfather's hand. Tearing it open, he had found a small card that merely said *Kona Kai Marina* followed by a string of numbers and letters: *52143-F14-K7.*

He wasn't sad. He wasn't angry. He didn't know exactly how he felt, other than some guilt for not having kept in touch. After their departure from New England they had gone separate ways, and they had had no contact until the letter arrived. Even though his grandfather had kept his feelings private, Edso had known that he was shaken by all that had happened—especially the loss of his beloved yacht, *Vorspiel.*

"Walk away. You don't have to do this," a voice in his head kept saying, but he knew he wouldn't.

He could hear his grandfather's words. *"It is your duty. Family honor demands that when I am gone, you must continue my work."*

His grandfather was like that, always had been. He demanded one hundred percent loyalty and blind obedience. But now, Otto was gone, so there was no one Edso had to answer to, and yet, he couldn't not obey.

* * *

Coming off the highway, he glanced again at his grandfather's note. Knowing the man's penchant for cryptic instructions, he guessed that the numbers would be gate codes and slip locations. What he didn't know was why. Glancing at the GPS on his dash, he saw that he still had more than a mile to go, and a raft of memories filled his head.

After his parents had died, his grandfather took him in, and he spent his childhood in a never-ending series of boarding schools and exclusive summer camps. Then, when he graduated, his grandfather insisted that he come to live with him on his yacht. It was a good life, and over time, as the yachts grew in grandeur, Edso became more and more involved in his grandfather's business dealings. And while he didn't always agree with Otto's activities, he never challenged him.

As the gatehouse to the marina's parking lot came into sight, Edso slowed and noted that the address on the paper agreed with the GPS's announcement that he had arrived. Expecting to have to stop and explain to a guard with a clipboard why he was there, he rehearsed what he would say, but the gatehouse was empty. Without hesitation, he drove straight through and began a slow meander up one aisle and down the next until he reached the end of the parking lot. He pulled into the only empty spot, turned off the engine, and just sat a moment. He looked at the note again. He knew what it said. He had read and reread it so many times he had it memorized, but still he felt compelled to look at it again. In the distance, past the hundreds of slips filled with every conceivable type of boat, he could see several mega yachts.

For a moment, he remembered the excitement that he had always felt whenever they arrived in a new marina. It was a mixture of his curiosity about who he would meet and what he would experience, and he would try to imagine what the people already in the marina were wondering about who he and Otto were and why they were there. Theirs was not always the largest yacht, but it was always noticed and admired, and he easily parlayed that into an active social life.

52143-F14-K7. He took one last look then climbed out of his car and slipped the note into his pocket. Looking around, he saw an information board near the edge of the parking lot. He walked over and stood in front of it. The board was a large map of the marina with all of the amenities noted as well as the dock names and numbers. There were three clusters of docks. The largest group was in the center and called *Kona Kai*.

"Probably the original marina," he thought.

To its right was another slightly smaller set of docks labeled *Kona*. To the left, closest to the ocean, was the third collection of docks, which was labeled Mega Yacht Facility and the docks were all labeled K. It had the least number of boats, but there were far fewer mega yachts than more modest-sized yachts. Consulting the note once again, he concluded that the first few numbers must be the combination to open the gates that gave access to each set of docks, and the second and third sets of numbers he assumed were specific slip locations.

"Typical of Grandfather to leave a note with no explanations or

instructions," he thought. The one thing he was sure of was the fact that his Grandfather always had a reason for whatever he did.

The Kona Kai set of docks had the only dock labeled F, so he decided to start there. Standing in front of the gate that led to dock F, he pressed the first button on the keypad. But before he could punch in the full code, the gate moved ever so slightly.

He froze as a memory from his childhood flashed through his head. *He was ten years old. It was during one of the rare times when there was a short break between the end of the school year and the beginning of summer camp. He was staying on his grandfather's yacht. They were in a marina somewhere in the Mediterranean, and it was clear that his grandfather was more interested in conducting business than entertaining a young boy. One morning, he had seen his grandfather leave. Curious, he began exploring the yacht. He was just putting his hand on a closed door's handle when he felt a presence behind him. He turned and was startled to see one of the crew standing behind him. He panicked and turned to run, but that crewman grabbed him by his arm and pulled him back. He fought to get away, but the grip on his arm was unforgiving, and the more he struggled, the tighter it became. When he started to cry out, the crewman's other hand clapped over his mouth, stifling any sound. The crewman bent down and hissed, "Silence! What do you think you're doing?" As much as Edso wanted to respond, he couldn't because of the hand covering his mouth. It was so tight that he could hardly breathe, and fear and tears filled his eyes.*

Edso took a deep breath to clear that memory. He turned and looked around. He was alone. Facing the gate, he gave it a push, and it swung open. After one more quick look around he walked through. The gate swung shut behind him, and when he heard the lock engage, he stopped and looked back at it. A confirming pull verified that it was locked, and for a split second he wondered how it was that it had been unlatched.

He turned and looked out over the marina and was struck by the lack of activity. Considering it was mid-afternoon and the weather was perfect, that, along with his experiences with the two gates, left him feeling a bit uneasy. Trying to identify the source of his unease, he realized that it was the silence. He didn't hear any gulls squawking; there were no engines running, nor halyards slapping against masts. As he stood there, he thought he could hear a faint, almost whining, hum. He looked up, didn't see anything, and immediately realized that he had forgotten his sunglasses. And then the sound was gone. Knowing how sound does funny things near water, he thought to himself, *"Probably the highway."*

Picturing the map of the marina on the information board, he knew that the central gangway ahead ended at docks E to the left, and F to the right. On the way to F, he would first pass docks A and B, which were opposite each other, and then docks C and D.

The crang of his footsteps on the aluminum ramp seemed exceptionally loud considering the perceived silence. Stopping at the bottom of the ramp, he pulled the scrap of paper from his pocket and looked at it again. The address hadn't changed, and the string of numbers and letters remained the same. As he began walking toward dock F, he heard the soft quacking of ducks. Stopping, he looked down and saw a small flotilla of ducks gliding toward him, their progress barely disturbing the surface of the water. He smiled, thinking that his footsteps on the ramp must have been like a dinner bell. When it became clear that he was not going to feed them, they turned and paddled away.

When Edso reached the end of the gangway, he stopped. Looking left, down dock E, he could see that a large yacht was tied up at the end. He turned right and began walking down dock F. Numbers were painted on the dock's deck indicating the slip number. Slip 14 was halfway down on the outer side.

It was empty. As he stood looking at the vacant space, a voice called out, "They left yesterday."

He turned toward the voice, which had come from behind him.
hen he turned, the sun blinded him for a moment, and he had to

raise his hand to shield his eyes. Sitting placidly in the slip nearly opposite the empty number 14 was a classic sport fishing boat. The hull was painted pale blue, and all else was sparkling white except for the varnished mahogany trim and the gleaming stainless tower rising high into the sky. There was no doubt that its form defined its function. From the raised bow sweeping aft in a gentle and pleasing reversing curve leading to the low stern with a fighting chair mounted near the transom, it was a boat built for but one purpose.

"They're gone, left yesterday," the voice repeated what had already been said. It was a deep, gravelly voice and came from a man whom Edso guessed may have been in his sixties. He was sitting in the fighting chair, with his legs stretched out and his feet resting on the transom of the boat. His shirt was unbuttoned, exposing a pale white torso, which provided a sharp contrast to his deeply tanned face and arms. From under the sweat-stained baseball cap on his head, white curls escaped, and he had a smile that was somewhere between mischievous and all-knowing.

Edso asked, "You said they left yesterday? Any idea when they might return?" He really wanted to ask who they were, but he didn't want to raise suspicions.

The man tipped back his beer, draining the last drops from the can. Then he tossed it toward a bucket that already had others in it. As the empty clanked into the bucket, a loud belch followed.

"Sorry 'bout that," he said with a prideful grin. "Join me for a beer?"

Edso really didn't need a beer, but he decided that it might be the best way to get the information he wanted.

"Sure. Thanks."

"Come aboard." He motioned to Edso as he pried himself out of the fighting chair and made his way to the door that led inside his boat. By the time Edso had climbed over the transom, his new friend had returned with two beers.

"Name's Clyde," he said, as he handed Edso a beer.

"Edso."

Neither made any effort to shake hands.

Clyde looked at him, his expression puzzled.

"It's an old family name."

"Kind of like that car."

Edso was used to that, and he didn't try to explain. He just nodded, opened his beer, and took a sip. "Think they'll be gone long?"

"No idea. Boat was here yesterday before I went out. By the time I returned, they were gone. Friends of yours?"

"Never met them."

Clyde's expression demanded a better answer. Edso tried.

"My grandfather passed recently, and he asked me to come here, to slip F14. I'm assuming they must be friends of his. That's just the way he was. Always kept us guessing."

Clyde settled back into the fighting chair. "My old man was like that sometimes. Never really understood him."

Edso sat on the transom, not quite opposite Clyde, but close enough. "So, who are they?"

He shrugged. "Never really talked to them. A hello every now and then, but that's about it. Three of them, two guys and a lady. Never could figure out just what their relationships were, but she was definitely in charge. Looked like a real hard case."

"What kind of a boat?"

"Not sure what you'd call it. One of those modern designs, you know, all shiny white fiberglass, not a pure fisherman, but not a trawler either. Had a fly bridge, but no tower. Looked fast, even just sitting there. Not my cup of tea, but there aren't many of us who'll put up with an old classic like mine."

"I never would have known."

Clyde looked at him kind of funny.

"Your boat. She's beautiful. I can't believe she's all that old."

He smiled. "Thanks. She's my pride and joy. Nearly fifty years old, but she's been almost completely rebuilt over the last few years."

"Pretty sweet. Hey, thanks for the beer, but I've got to get going." Edso dropped his can into the bucket where he had seen Clyde throw his last empty.

Clyde made no effort to get up, but he did lift his now nearly empty can in a salutation as Edso climbed over the transom onto the dock. "Good luck."

"Thanks again for the beer. Oh, I forgot to ask. Do you know what their names are?"

Clyde shook his head no. "Like I said, never really talked to them."

"How about their boat's name?"

"*Last Chance.*"

"Thanks," said Edso. He turned and walked back to the main dock. Once there, he pulled the paper out of his pocket and looked at the numbers again. F14 was a bust, but maybe he'd have better luck with K7.

CHAPTER 7

AS EDSO WALKED BACK, he regretted again that he had not worn his sunglasses. The sun had begun its descent to the horizon and was now more directly in his eyes. As he walked toward the main gangway, he kept his head turned slightly to the left and held up his right hand, which allowed him to better see where he was going. When he reached where the central gangway bisected docks E and F, he decided to continue on toward the large yacht. Memories of *Vorspiel* flashed in his head, and he had to see it up close.

Edso's pace slowed as he remembered how much of his life had been spent on his grandfather's yacht. The freshest memories were the most bittersweet, and Courtney was foremost in them. He wished that she had not been central to his grandfather's failed quest. When he had first met her, she had been only an assignment: to be used, and then cast aside once her usefulness had been exhausted. But something about her had been different. He had found that he cared for her, and that had become a problem. From the moment Otto had taken him in as a child, the man's mantra was "No matter what happens, nothing is more important than family."

Only after his grandfather's scheme began to unravel, and he had chosen Courtney over family and she was safe, did he abandon her and rejoin his grandfather. His grandfather never fully forgave him for that, and it was part of the reason why they had separated as they fled west.

* * *

"Hello. Is there something I can help you with?" The voice startled him, and he must have jumped slightly as he turned. Facing him was an attractive woman in khaki slacks and a polo shirt with the name *M/V Wonder* stitched onto the shirt just above her left breast. Not quite his height, she had short, dark hair, lively eyes, and a warm smile. In each hand, with little effort, she held a canvas tote filled with groceries, confirming the impression that she was fit and strong.

His memories of Courtney instantly vaporized. "I'm sorry," he stammered, "I was just admiring your beautiful yacht."

He couldn't take his eyes off the woman.

"Yes, she is pretty special. However, the owner doesn't like strangers hanging around, so I must ask you not to linger here."

Ignoring her request, he said, "Before my grandfather passed, we lived on a yacht very similar to yours. We lost her in a fire, and I think that losing her may have been what eventually killed him."

Politely, she said, "I'm sorry for your loss, but I have to get back on board. I have dinner to prepare." Then, almost as an afterthought, she added, "If you could please move on, it would be appreciated."

Although her words left no doubt that their conversation was over, he was intrigued. As sure as she had deftly dismissed him, he was equally sure that he had heard a well-disguised hint of warmth in her voice.

She smiled, turned, and began walking up the gangway.

"Hey," he called out. "I didn't get your name."

She looked back, still smiling, but said nothing as she disappeared from view.

"I'll see you again," he thought to himself.

He stood there a few moments more, looking up at the *M/V Wonder.* At one point, he thought he saw a curtain move.

Edso finally turned and smiled, convinced that she had been watching him. Now he was more curious than ever.

The sun continued its slow descent toward the horizon, and the sky was beginning to change colors. All the way back to the gate he thought about her, running through several scenarios for meeting her again.

As he approached the gate, he thought he could hear the same faint whirring sound that he had heard earlier. Looking around, he didn't see anything, so he quickly dismissed the sound as an air conditioner or some other piece of unseen equipment. Besides, it was much more interesting to focus on the woman he had just met.

When the gate clinked shut behind him, he turned right and began walking toward the third and smallest cluster of docks. The sign over the entry gate announced the Mega Yacht Facility. Inside he could see that nearly all of the dock space was taken, which would explain why the *Wonder* was tied on the end of dock E and not tied up in the MYF. He punched in the same combination he had used earlier, and the gate clicked open.

He strode down the ramp. At the bottom, he turned left and followed the main gangway, which ran parallel to the shore. Off of the main gangway were three fingers jutting out to the right, each with one or more mega yachts tied up. Remembering that all of the finger docks were labeled K, he knew that space 7 would be the outer side of the furthest dock.

When Edso reached the end of the gangway, he turned right intending to continue down toward K7, but what he saw made him stop. All he could do was stare.

He had never seen a yacht quite like the one that loomed over the entire outer side of that dock. It was tied port side to, and its hull and superstructure were like that of any other luxury yacht, only instead of being white, black, or blue—and gleaming in a state of shiny perfection—it was all gray. Stacked atop its superstructure was an impressive display of domes and antennas, not unlike what was common on all super yachts: radar, sat-phones, and radio. However, something felt different. Moving closer, it took him a few moments to realize that the yacht wasn't painted gray; it was built of unfinished aluminum. All of its windows were tinted a silvery gray, giving it a mysterious, almost sinister, aura.

As he walked down the dock, he could see that her topsides bore the scars and imperfections of a vessel hard used. *"Research vessel?"* he wondered. He checked his piece of paper again. It was the right location, *"Why had his grandfather sent him to this strange looking yacht?"*

There were no name boards, or anything that would allow him to identify the yacht. No gangway, no steps, no stern platform. It looked like the only possible way to board the yacht was through a watertight door set amidship and high enough that if opened it would be several feet above the height of the dock. The problem was that he saw no way of getting anyone's attention.

"Where's a doorbell when you need one?" he thought grimly.

CHAPTER 8

THAT'S WHEN EDSO HEARD AGAIN a low humming sound, although this time it seemed much closer. As he listened, he became certain that it was not coming from one of the boats. It filled the air and defied all his attempts at locating it. First, he tried turning slowly in a full circle in an effort to determine its direction. No luck. Then he looked up and scanned the sky. The sun was nearing the horizon now, and the sky was in full color. Yellows were turning orange, oranges were turning red, and reds were becoming purple. As he looked up, marveling at its beauty, he thought he saw something flash by out of the corner of his eye.

He turned his head just in time to see a dark shadow hover above and then disappear onto the top deck of the gray mystery yacht. Silence immediately followed. It happened so fast that as he tried to process what he had seen, he began to doubt that he had seen anything. He considered the possibility that it was a drone, but all the drones he had ever seen had distinctive, high-pitched whines and were not solid objects. The object he had just seen looked like a flying Weber grill, yet he knew that this was just plain silly.

The lights on the power pylons that were positioned strategically along all of the docks came on. The water's surface had lost the colorful sheen of sunset and was now all but devoid of color. The sky, while not yet dark, was in the last stages of twilight, and a few of the brightest stars were becoming visible. He looked over at the *M/V Wonder*. She was lit up like a small city, and he found himself temporarily distracted from the situation at hand as he wondered what was for supper.

When Edso had lived on *Vorspiel,* he had always found this transition time from day to night exciting, especially in port. It was a time of role reversal. During the day, yachts, while grand, were just magnificent objects, closed off to all but the speculation and fantasy of those not on board. However, as the sky darkened and lights came on, those silent objects came to life as if by magic. The play of light and shadow created depth where before there had been none. Lit windows now became portals, allowing teasing glimpses into those intriguing inner worlds and their most private secrets.

Looking back at the mysterious gray yacht, he initially found no such access. Its windows remained dark. However, as he stared, he realized that what he had thought was the evening's light reflecting off the glass was actually a faint glow emanating from inside. When a shadow seemed to move across one of the windows, he convinced himself that someone was on board. Curious and emboldened, he decided to try knocking on that watertight door.

Knocking wasn't going to be easy. The yacht was held off the dock by a series of large-diameter fenders, making it a stretch to even touch the topsides, let alone knock on them. He was beginning to shift his weight and lean forward when several loud raps emanating from behind the door startled him. Abruptly he stopped his forward momentum, shifted his weight back, and resumed his motionless position on the dock.

The door swung open, and a soft red light emanated from within. A silhouette filed the space and a voice said, "Mr. Harding. Thank you for coming. Your grandfather told me you would. I've been expecting you."

Edso could not see clearly the person who had greeted him, but the accent was familiar. He had heard it his entire life. While the words were English, the accent was not. It was European in origin, a hybrid, a mash-up with French dominating. "You've been expecting me? How? My grandfather's dead."

"Come aboard. He would want you to," he said, and extended his arm to help pull Edso on board.

"Oh, what the hell," thought Edso. He allowed the man to grab his

hand and pull him into the gray yacht.

As soon as Edso was inside, his host released his grip, turned, and without a word pulled the door shut. It closed with a soft thump that could be felt more than heard as the rubber gasket compressed. Immediately, the man grabbed the large wheel that was in the center of the door and spun it. That spinning extended a series of latches, and as soon as they were fully extended, the wheel abruptly stopped spinning, and the yacht's watertight integrity was assured once again.

In the seconds that it took the man to secure the door, Edso looked around. They were in a corridor that extended fore and aft. It was wide enough that two people could walk side by side comfortably. The walls and ceiling were painted what he presumed to be gray, but the red lighting made it difficult to tell. A black, non-skid rubberized coating was underfoot. The only decor was the rows of piping mounted high on the walls. Red lights in vapor-proof globes were spaced in short intervals the length of the corridor and at each end was a watertight door like the one he had been pulled through. He had never seen a yacht like this, and he wondered what the rest would be like.

Door secure, his host turned and faced him. Standing in the doorway was an older man. Average height and powerfully built, his hair was white, his skin was dark, and his eyes were close set and shone with an intensity that reminded Edso of his grandfather. His wide smile and welcoming manner seemed a stark contrast to the mysteriousness of his boat.

With the door secure, his host now turned and faced him. "Come," he said, and he began striding toward the door at the forward end of the corridor giving Edso no choice but to follow.

CHAPTER 9

THE DOOR AT THE END OF THE CORRIDOR was similar in function to the one that Edso had used to enter the yacht, but its form was completely different. This time, as they approached, Edso heard a slight hissing sound, followed by a distinct but soft click. Then it swung open. Ahead was a stairway leading both up and down. As soon as they were on the stairs going up, the door swung shut. With a similar hissing sound followed by another barely audible click, it closed and sealed itself.

At the top of the stairs was yet another door, and well before they reached it, Edso heard another barely discernible hiss and click. Then it swung open.

His host slowed, turned slightly, and said, "There are sensors that cause it to open automatically as you approach. Makes it so much easier if you are carrying things."

Several seconds passed after they were clear of the stairs before the door closed automatically.

His host turned toward him again. With a big smile and a sweep of his arm, he said, "Welcome to my home. We are standing in the main salon. Her name is *Gendroit*. She is approximately thirty-five meters long with a beam of almost eight. Certainly not the largest yacht—actually she is quite small by some standards—but she is more than sufficient for my purposes. She has a cruising range of over thirty-five hundred nautical miles and can accommodate up to ten guests in addition to the crew."

Edso had no words as he looked around. As in many large yachts, the main salon occupied almost the entire deck, but this was like nothing he had ever seen before. The severe and obviously well used exterior had given no clues that inside she would be so striking. The light bamboo floors and the clean, uncluttered, but not completely spare decor

47

imparted a feeling of serenity without losing energy and excitement. To Edso, it felt more like being in a modern art gallery than on a yacht, because for its full length, large sliding doors and stationary windows opened the space up to the outside. Stepping into the center of the salon, he could see all the way forward a large oval dining table set athwartship, its curve mirroring the curve of glass that served as the forward end of the salon. The panoramic view out over the bow was spectacular. A single vase with a bouquet of bright red California poppies in the center of the table provided the only splash of color necessary.

Between the entry into the salon and the dining table, on the port side, was an open kitchen area featuring stainless steel and marble. Edso concluded that the actual act of cooking on this yacht was as much a part of the dining experience as enjoying the meal. Looking aft, he saw several groupings of chairs and small tables and a set of doors that led outside to the aft deck.

"She is beautiful," Edso said. "Can I ask you something?"

"Of course."

"When I was outside on the dock, it was difficult to tell if any lights were on inside. I'm assuming they were, but I see no window coverings. How is that possible?"

His host smiled. "Let's finish our tour, and I'll answer all of your questions."

"One more question?"

"Yes?"

"You know me, but I have no idea who you are. Can we start again?"

"You may call me Giles."

"Giles," he repeated. "Okay, Giles. Is there a last name?"

"Endroit. Come, let me show you the bridge deck."

Edso understood that he wasn't going to get any more information, at least not at the moment, so he said, "After you." Then he followed Giles to a door on the starboard side that was located between the kitchen area and the seating aft. Giles didn't touch anything, but the door softly opened. Soft red light poured out, and Edso realized that it was an elevator. Giles stepped aside, motioned Edso to enter, and then followed. The door softly shut behind him. Inside, it was eerily quiet and still, and then the door opened again, revealing another room. That, too, was bathed in red light. Giles quickly stepped out and said, "Welcome to her heart," as they stepped onto the bridge deck.

Edso had been impressed with what he saw on the deck below, but now he was totally floored. At the forward end was the helm station. In front of a single raised seat, arranged in an arc within easy view and reach, were all the electronics and controls necessary for the control of the yacht. But that was only the beginning.

The entire bridge deck looked like every picture he had ever seen of NASA's Mission Control Center in Houston. Each side was lined with banks of consoles with monitors, lights, switches, and gauges.

"Wha—" Before he could finish his question, Giles cut him off.

"This is where it all happens."

"What happens?"

"I'm sorry. I forget that your grandfather told you nothing. I consider *Gendroit* to be a research vessel, although there are those who would probably think otherwise."

"Research? What kind of research?"

"Scientific research."

"That doesn't really explain much."

He shrugged. "She has been built to monitor and test some of the newer technologies in communications and unmanned flight."

Edso went silent and stood there looking around at all the equipment, trying to understand exactly what Giles had meant by communications and unmanned flight. "Sounds like you are running some kind of a spy operation."

"I wouldn't call it that, but we do monitor things that most people know nothing about."

"Unmanned flight? Do you mean drones?"

He didn't reply as Edso stared at him.

"I'll take your silence as a yes. Do you use them to help you with these monitoring activities?"

Giles surrendered and answered Edso's question by saying, "Yes, actually, we do. It is quite remarkable what you can do with them."

Edso stared at Giles as the image of the flying Weber grill flashed through his head.

"When I first arrived this afternoon, I thought I heard a low-pitched humming sound. Later, on the other side of the marina, I thought I heard it again."

Giles' face remained blank.

Edso continued on, mainly talking to himself. "When I finally found your yacht, I thought I heard that sound again, only this time there was more of a whooshing quality to it. As I looked around, I thought I caught a slight movement out the corner of my eye. At first I didn't see anything, then I did."

"What did you see?"

"I don't know. I guess that if I had to describe it, I'd say it was a flying Weber grill."

Giles chuckled. "I've never heard that before," he said.

"So you know what I saw."

"I do. It was one of the many projects I am testing."

"A drone."

"Yes. But not like any drone you've seen before." He chuckled again. "I guess that in form it does look kind of like one of those grills."

"But any drones I have ever seen are quite noisy, like a swarm of mosquitoes, and they are mostly made up of propellers."

"And that's what's wrong with most drones. They are noisy and fragile."

"And yours isn't."

"Let's just say it's different."

Edso nodded, wondering what kind of drone would need such a control room, or whether this was for something more.

Giles said, "Now, I don't know about you, but I'm hungry. Let's go down and enjoy a nice dinner, have some wine, and get to know each other a little bit more. I assume you have time?"

As much as Edso wanted to see and hear more, his was stomach rumbling.

"Sounds like a plan."

CHAPTER 10

EDSO FOLLOWED GILES BACK INTO THE ELEVATOR. As before, after a few seconds of eerie silence and stillness, the door seemed to reopen almost as soon as it had closed.

The main salon had been transformed. Soft music played in the background, and other than a brighter glow coming from the kitchen area, the lighting had been dimmed.

Edso could hear someone working in the kitchen area, and Giles' next words confirmed it.

"My chef is preparing dinner for us. While we're waiting, let's get to know each other better. Come."

Edso followed Giles, who paused at the kitchen to speak with a young man in a chef's toque. The chef pointed at a saucepan on the stove, and Giles leaned over and looked into the pan. Without a word, the chef handed Giles a spoon, which he dipped into the pan to sample its contents. He smiled and clapped the chef on the shoulder before continuing to lead the way to the dining table.

On the table were two wine glasses and two bottles of wine, one still corked and the other uncorked. There was also a carving board with an assortment of cheeses, meats, and olives. Next to that was a small basket of bread. Giles took the seat on the starboard end of the table and motioned for Edso to sit to his left, giving him the view out that forward glass wall.

"Wine?" The question was more of a formality because Giles had already started filling both glasses before even asking the question. He lifted his glass, motioned for Edso to pick up his, and said, "To your grandfather—and the future."

Edso lifted his glass, nodded toward Giles, and took a sip. He said, "May I?" and reached for the bottle. The label was unfamiliar, and his expression must have conveyed that fact.

"It comes from a small vineyard I own in Italy. Very little of its production ever sees the outside world."

Edso nodded, his curiosity satisfied, and he put the bottle on the table and took another sip. "Very nice. Impressive."

Giles picked up a large olive in his fingers, studied it, put it in his mouth, and then licked his fingertips. "Everything you taste and experience here tonight comes from properties I own."

He nudged the antipasto platter in Edso's direction. "Try one of these olives."

They were large and a deep, almost muddy, green. Picking one up, Edso bit into it, being careful of the pit. He had never tasted an olive with such a delicate balance of saltiness and subtle earthy flavors. There was a firm butteriness to its texture, and he couldn't help but smile.

"Good. Yes?"

"I can honestly say that I've never tasted an olive like that."

"The grove it came from is centuries old. The same family has been tending it for probably that long as well. The majority of the olives are pressed into some of the finest oil you will never find anywhere, but the best olives are selected by the patron of the family and are kept whole for the table."

"Now you are going to tell me that you are also responsible for making these cheeses and meats?"

Giles just smiled, nodded his head, and said, "Guilty as charged."

Edso ate a small piece of hard salami and followed it with a thin slice of cheese on a small piece of bread. "This is all so overwhelming. I really don't know what to say."

"Well then, have some more wine, and I'm sure that the words will come to you."

Edso took another sip of his wine and looked at Giles, who simply continued eating and drinking. All of a sudden, a feeling of unease washed over him. He felt like he was being manipulated toward an eventual seduction. He thought, "*Is this the way the women I brought on board* Vorspiel *felt?*"

The thought of Courtney made him feel worse, so he struggled to shake it off. "*No. Not possible,*" he told himself. He returned his focus to the table and bit into another piece of bread with a slice of cheese.

"It's good, yes?"

Edso stopped mid-chew and stared at Giles.

"The cheese," Giles said. "It is also made on one of my properties. But never mind that. You have more questions. I can tell."

"I do."

Giles poured more wine. "For now, let's discuss the boat. We will talk about your grandfather later."

Feeling like he had no choice, Edso nodded for him to go on.

"First of all, my *Gendroit* may look plain—even scarred and poorly maintained—from the outside, but I can assure you that is far from the truth."

"How so?"

"For me, beauty is in function. A cosmetically perfect exterior means nothing. How something works, especially if it works well, is true beauty. Even her outside appearance is truly beautiful."

"Fair enough. So earlier, I asked you about how, before I came on board, it looked as if no lights were on inside your boat, but they were, yet you don't seem to have any kind of window coverings. Could you explain that to me?"

"We have combined two very different technologies, but each with the same goal. Have you ever heard of dynamic glass? Another name would be electrochromatic glass."

"Not sure."

"It's a specially constructed glass that, when connected to an electrical current, can change from clear to opaque. We found a way to modify it so it becomes opaque only when looking at it from one side, remaining clear from the other. On *Gendroit* we married that technology with that of one-way privacy glass, which needs to be light on one side and dark on the other. The outside of our windows and doors is treated to look like the rest of *Gendroit's* structure—gray—making her look windowless. During the daylight hours we can see out, but outside, all people see is a gray surface, and no one can see in. Then inside, we used the dynamic glass. This means that at night, with the flick of a switch all becomes opaque if you are trying to look in, but remains clear when looking in the opposite direction. As you noticed tonight, there is still a faint glow coming from inside, but we're working on that. And there you have it."

Giles sat back, popped another olive in his mouth, and smiled as if that was all that needed to be said.

"Impressive. What about that drone?"

Giles sighed, but before he could answer, a member of the crew materialized and announced that dinner was about to be served. He topped up their wine glasses, emptying the first bottle, then walked off with the antipasto platter and the empty bottle in hand.

That interruption ended the potential tug-of-war that Edso now anticipated between his desire to know more and Giles' intention to enjoy a social evening.

"Perfect timing," said Giles, as he began to uncork the second bottle of Chianti. Then he glanced at Edso, whose frustration must have been showing.

"Edso, be patient," he said. "I understand your curiosity, but there is a time for business and a time for pleasure. Now it is time for pleasure. I've had my chef prepare us dinner. Let's enjoy that first, and then we can talk of more serious matters."

Giles turned back to the wine. "As you perhaps guessed, I have an affinity for Italy."

The cork came out with a reassuring pop.

As if on cue, at the pop, the crewmember, who had cleared away the antipasto, returned with two small, flat bowls filled with hot water and a slice of lemon. Watching Giles dip his fingers in the bowl and wash away the olive oil, Edso did the same. The crewmember handed each man a towel, and as soon as they had dried their fingers, everything was cleared away.

Moments later, the chef placed a large bowl in front of each of them. The air was immediately filled with rich, thick aromas carried by the steam coming off of the bowls.

"Thank you," said Giles. "It smells divine."

A small nod of the chef's head signaled the acceptance of the compliment. Then he turned and retreated.

Edso inhaled deeply and studied what had been put in front of him. In the bowl, on a thick-cut piece of toated bread were large shrimps, scallops, squid and clams, all in a tomato and wine broth.

"Zuppa di Pesce alla Napoletana,"said Giles. "Neapolitan Fish Soup."

"I've had different fish stews, but never anything that smelled or looked like this," replied Edso.

"Everything was caught fresh today. Please, *mange*," he said, motioning for Edso to start eating. "It's best when it's hot."

As Edso sopped up the last of the broth with a piece of freshly baked bread, he said, "That was fantastic. Thank you."

Five minutes after the table was cleared, the crewmember who had cleared the dishes returned with two small salads and announced, "Insalata di Rucola, Radicchio, Romana,"

"Wonderful," said Giles. "It's a traditional salad of Arugula, Radicchio and Romaine Lettuce. It will aid in digestion."

Edso was sure that he was too full to even try a bite, as delicious as it looked. But out of politeness he took a bite, and before he knew it, he had cleaned his plate.

CHAPTER 11

SALADS FINISHED, THE TABLE WAS CLEARED quickly and efficiently.

"Thank you," Giles said to the steward. "We'll have coffee and dessert later."

Then, looking at Edso, he sipped the last of his wine and said, "Now, we can talk business. You have questions?"

"Yes. But first, dinner was wonderful. Thank you."

Giles nodded, acknowledging the compliment. Then he said, "So, what can I tell you?"

"I do want to know about my grandfather. But first, tell me about the drone."

"Ah, yes. The drone. It's a prototype that I am developing. It is for relatively near-range work, say up to fifty miles. But, more important, it is nearly undetectable."

"Undetectable? Fifty miles?"

"We are developing a new stealth technology, if you are thinking of those small toy drones that people use for photography, well this has much more capability."

"You need to explain."

"When you arrived at the marina, was a guard present?"

"I didn't see one."

"That's because I sent him away, and the drone gave me eyes on your arrival. When you were at the gate, was it locked?"

"I assumed it was, but when I started to punch in the code, it swung open before I could even finish. Then it latched when it closed."

"The drone did that."

"The drone did what?"

"Unlocked the gate and then relocked it. With the drone, I can control almost any kind of electronic device."

Edso was stunned and said nothing for a moment. Then he said, "That was the low-pitched humming sound I heard?"

"It was."

"I heard that sound again when I was on the other side of the marina."

Giles smiled.

"Why did my grandfather's note send me over there, when you are over here?"

"We did that so that I could make sure that you were not followed."

"We?"

"Your grandfather and I. This was all planned quite some time ago. It was his death that triggered it."

"You're losing me."

"I'm sorry. Let me try to explain. Your grandfather and I had known each other for a very long time."

"How did I not know this?"

"You'd have to ask your grandfather. Yes, I know that's not possible, but I can guess that he was trying to protect you."

"Protect me? From what? And, why you? Until tonight I never even knew of your existence."

"He wanted it that way."

Edso's confusion was growing by the minute.

"Your grandfather and I shared many of the same beliefs. There is a certain natural order in the world that is proper and righteous. Hitler and his failed Third Reich tried, but he thought he could achieve success quickly by using a hammer to impose his will. Look what happened. Stalin did much the same in Russia. He and his successors lasted longer than Hitler, but then ultimately they failed. China is following in their footsteps and seems to be learning from past mistakes. We're not sure yet if they will succeed, but they give us hope—although ultimately they will prove problematic. What we have learned is that if we are to impose our vision on the world, it must be done slowly and subtly. Not unlike touching someone with a feather. It tickles, but they get used to it. Eventually they don't even notice it. In our case, by the time they figure out what is being done, it will be too late."

"But all my grandfather ever did was search for some lost German gold in a misguided quest to clear his father's name. I always took it as an obsession born of his twisted upbringing."

"There is some truth in your assessment. It was what you were supposed to see."

Edso's confusion was turning to unease. "I'm sorry. You're losing me. What I was supposed to see? My grandfather was convinced that a woman named Courtney was the key. He enlisted me to seduce her into revealing what she knew, but that turned out to be nothing. He was still convinced that she had information, so he kidnapped her. I was afraid he might kill her, so I helped her escape. In the process his beloved *Vorspiel* was destroyed. Then we escaped."

"That's what he wanted you to see. Everything he did was to test you, to make sure that you would be able to carry on his work. That woman was part of his test."

"Test?"

"He knew you would fall for her, that you would try to save her, but he hoped that in doing so his enemies would be revealed, and that you would choose him over them."

Edso was dumbstruck.

Giles' gaze made it clear the seriousness of what he was being told. "Edso, did you ever think about why you weren't pursued and how easy it was for you both to disappear?"

"Things were pretty hectic and I never gave it much thought. But, my grandfather did say on several occasions that the Network would protect us."

"Did he ever explain what he meant?"

"No. But at the time we separated he reminded me to trust them."

Giles stared intently at Edso as if trying to decide how much to tell him.

"I'm getting a feeling that you might know something of this group," said Edso.

Giles nodded his agreement. "I do."

"And are you going to tell me?"

"Edso, you must understand that you and your grandfather disappeared with the help of many people who share similar views. Most prefer to exist out of the public eye, but as in any organization, there are those, like your grandfather, whose views are more radical and in-your-face. While I have never shared his loyalty to the evil creatures that he so revered, we did agree on the final desired result."

"I know he revered Hitler and the Third Reich, and remained a Nazi until his death, and that he did have many friends of a like mind, but what you're telling me is that he was only the tip of an iceberg."

"Nicely put. That is correct. These people go by different names: white nationalists, nationalists, populists. Whatever the name, they share similar goals in varying degrees."

"Do you have any idea how crazy this all sounds?"

Giles shrugged. "Perhaps. But when you fully understand, it will all make sense."

He pushed away from the table, "Come, let's go back up to the bridge deck. I want to show you some of my *Gendroit's* capabilities."

Instead of walking toward the elevator, this time Giles led the way to the stairs. Passing the kitchen, Edso realized that they were alone. The chef and steward had quietly disappeared. He looked back one last time before following Giles into the stairwell. The lights by the dining table had already gone out, and those in the kitchen area were starting to dim.

CHAPTER 12

GILES WAS NEARLY AT THE TOP OF THE STAIRS by the time Edso started his climb. Edso was struck by how silent it was. He realized that *Gendroit* lacked the vibrations and sounds he usually felt or heard on yachts, no matter how large or luxurious, under way or moored. The extreme level of quiet felt unnerving.

As Giles reached the top of the stairs, the door whooshed open automatically. Fighting the urge to whisper, Edso said, "Is everything on sensors?"

He felt like he was shouting, the silence was so profound.

Giles stopped and looked back. "Yes. Now, come on." He motioned for Edso to catch up.

Edso noticed that the lights were already on in the bridge deck as he entered. As soon as he was clear of the door, it whooshed shut behind him.

"Why?" he asked.

"Why what?"

"The doors, and I'm assuming the lights . . ."

"Pretty cool isn't it?" said Giles. "I could set them to manual, but why? It's much more fun with sensors."

Edso shrugged. *"Can't argue with that,"* he thought. Then he added, "True. It is cool."

"Precisely. So, here we are."

Once again, Edso was impressed by his surroundings: the helm was forward and aft, consoles filled with electronics filling the rest of the bridge deck area.

Giles stepped in front of a console that was set athwart and separated the helm from all those other consoles. He flicked a switch, and the console lit up. Many small red lights, each next to a switch or a button, came on. Several screens began to glow a pale green, and what must have been the master screen rose up from behind the console until it effectively became a partition. In the center of the console was a joystick controller, not unlike the ones Edso had seen in high-end video games.

Giles explained, "Each of the other stations you see has a very specific purpose. It would be too chaotic to try to monitor each one individually, so each is tied into this master console. As data comes in and is refined into actionable data points, it is sent here, where better decisions can be made."

"So what kind of data are we talking about?"

"It could be as simple as a video feed from the drone. That's how I followed you around the marina. Then, using the drone, I was able to manipulate the locks on the gate. There's no shortage of options. After you came in, I could have disabled the keypad, denying access to anyone else through that gate. I could even shut off power in the marina—in its entirety or selectively—if I wished."

"You're kidding."

"No."

"What else?"

"Besides what I can do with the drone? Communications monitoring, both incoming and outgoing, satellite and land based, electronic interference, ship profile, radar, sonar, audio infiltration, pretty much whatever you can imagine, we can do."

"Sounds like you've built a spy ship? Does anyone know what you're doing?"

"If you mean the government—no. They have no idea."

"How can you be sure? Clearly they'd be enraged to find that you were sticking your nose into things."

"They do it. You would not believe all that those initial agencies do."

"Initial agencies?"

"You know, alphabet initials. The FBI, CIA, NSA, and others."

"But we know about them and what they do."

"Let me stop you right there. You have no idea what they do."

Edso was dumbfounded. But before he could reply, his grandfather's friend continued.

"Whatever you think you know about their activities is what they want you to know. They always tell you enough to satisfy your curiosity, but I can assure you that there is so much more that you will never know about."

Giles was smiling now. In fact, his smug look reminded Edso of a grade schooler giving a report before the class and knocking it out of the park.

"But you aren't a government agency. So why all this?"

Once again, Edso looked briefly around the bridge deck. When he returned his focus to Giles, he realized the man's expression had changed from gleeful excitement to dead seriousness and he spoke slowly and directly.

"Weren't you listening?" He stared straight into Edso's eyes, and Edso shivered. Only once before in his life had he felt this way, and it scared him.

He could almost hear his grandfather's voice as Giles said, "Because it is now our time. It has begun, and this . . ." he paused and swept his arm around the room, "will make it happen."

The menacing tone seemed to linger in the room, and Edso desperately sought a distraction.

"So tell me about this drone," he finally blurted.

Giles suddenly smiled, and Edso was relieved to feel the tension drain from the room.

"Come."

Giles turned, and with Edso following, he walked aft to the last console in the row on the port side of the deck. He flicked a switch and it came alive with red, green, and amber lights. There was one large monitor, about the size of a thirty-six-inch television, in the center, in front of which there was a joystick controller. He seemed satisfied that all was as it should be, and said, "Let's go see my baby."

Giles moved toward a door in the back of the bridge deck. Like all the others, it opened automatically with a soft whoosh and then swung closed after they were through.

The night air felt good to Edso. He took a deep breath and looked back at the *Wonder*, all lit up like a small city.

"She's beautiful, yes?" Giles said, following his gaze.

"Yes, she is." Edso felt his face turning red, not sure whether he was referring to the yacht or the woman he had met.

Giles added, "And you're wondering what her name is. Come."

Edso followed Giles up another flight of stairs to the fly bridge. Smaller than the deck below, its extreme aft end went only as far as the enclosed part of the bridge deck and overlooked the open end below. Forward was an abbreviated helm station, sufficient for driving the boat in the best of conditions, but Edso could see that if the weather deteriorated, it would not be practical. Above it was a stout mast mounted with the impressive array of domes and antennas that would feed information below. Halfway between the stairs they had just climbed and the helm station, sitting in a custom cradle, was the drone. It was larger than he had expected. As he stared at the dark shape in front of him, he estimated it to be about five feet across and three feet high. It appeared to be smooth all the way around. He could see no propellers, cameras, antennas, nothing. It was just a "Weber grill"–shaped object.

Giles walked around it, releasing the straps that secured it to the cradle. Once it was free, he walked forward to the helm station, opened a door in the mast holding up all the electronics, and took out what looked like a TV remote.

"Stand back," he said.

Edso took a step back and recognized the sudden faint hum. The "grill" moved slightly and then silently rose off the cradle and disappeared into the night sky.

CHAPTER 13

"HOLY SHIT," WHISPERED EDSO.

"What do you think?"

"Holy shit," he said again, only this time he said it louder and looked at Giles.

"Yeah, I know what you mean. I still get that same feeling, and I've flown it hundreds of times."

"How . . . ? What . . . ? I mean, holy shit." Edso was now stammering excitedly.

Giles smiled. "I could count on one hand the number of people who have ever seen what you just witnessed. Needless to say, they have all been impressed."

Then he pointed back toward the stairs. "Come. I want to show you what it can do. Let's go back down to the control center and see if we can find out your lady friend's name." He turned, replaced the device he had taken from inside the mast, and began walking back toward the stairs.

At first, Edso didn't move. Then he closed his mouth and pulled his eyes away from the sky.

Giles paused at the top of the stairs. "Come on. There's nothing more to see here."

By the time Edso reached the bottom of the stairs, the door was whooshing shut. As he approached, it whooshed open for a second time for him to pass through. As it began to whoosh shut, he caught himself turning his head back to watch it close. Then he smiled, almost in embarrassment, at how he was reacting to something that was really quite common back on shore, but here, on this mysterious yacht, automatic doors seemed so strangely exotic.

Giles was already sitting at the second console he had activated.

His right hand was on the joystick, and he was looking intently at the screen.

"Look here," he said.

The screen was split into two images. The one on the left was nearly dark, but as Edso studied it, he realized that he was looking down on the dark shadow that was *Gendroit*. In sharp contrast, the other image was clearly the *M/V Wonder*, all lit up like a Christmas tree.

"Now watch." Giles moved the joystick slightly. Slowly, almost imperceptibly, the images began to change. The shadow that was *Gendroit* began to shrink and fall away as the brightly lit *Wonder* moved closer. "While I could have preprogrammed her to do what we want automatically, it is much more fun to do it by hand. First we'll circle around our target, and then we'll park and see if we can't find out her name."

Giles flicked a switch, and the images on the screen changed size. The dark side now took up only one third of the screen, while the brightly lit *M/V Wonder* took up the remaining two thirds. Deftly he guided the drone around *Wonder*.

"How high are you?" Edso asked.

"Five hundred feet," Giles said, pointing at some numbers on the bottom of the screen. "See. Altitude, Lat./Lon., Speed. Orientation, Distance from target."

"You're kidding."

"I'm not, and even at several thousand feet, the pictures would be as clear."

Edso watched as Giles guided the drone around the yacht. The *M/V Wonder* was truly a beautiful vessel.

"Dinner was delicious."

Edso jumped when the voice came out of the console. The sound quality wasn't as clear as the images they were watching, but it was still clear enough for him to understand what was being said.

"Is that . . . ?" Edso leaned in, his head cocked while studying the screen. All that remained visible was the well-lit yacht.

"Yes. That's the owner."

"And you know this, how?"

"I recognize his voice."

"You recognize his voice?"

Giles nodded, and the corners of his mouth turned up in a smile.

"How . . . ?" Then Edso added, "You've done this before."

"Practice makes perfect. Along with the high-def cameras, there are directional mics and other sensors, and . . ."

"You're shitting me?"

Giles smirked. "I'm not. It's really quite remarkable what *Eva* can do."

"*Eva?*"

"Yes. I named her *Eva—Eva Braun.*"

"Hitler's mistress?"

Giles chuckled. "Yeah."

A woman's voice came over the speaker, "For dessert, I've made key lime pie."

"With the chocolate crust?"

"Is there any other?"

Edso watched as Giles pressed several buttons and flipped a switch. "Let's see what thermal imaging tells us." The screen on the console flickered, and the larger portion of the screen changed from the clear view of the yacht to one of a variety of shapes and colors. The *M/V Wonder* was mostly blues and greens with some areas showing red, orange, and yellow.

"There," Giles said, pointing at two bright shapes. "That's him," and as the second shape began to move, he said, "And there goes your friend."

The moving shape faded from sight, then returned. There was a cool spot in her hand.

"That must be the pie," said Giles, pointing at the screen.

The man's voice came over the speakers again. "Thank you, Jennifer."

"Jennifer," thought Edso.

"There you are," said Giles. "Her name is Jennifer." Then, he turned from the console and faced Edso. His tone changed. "Your grandfather told me about your appetite for women. I don't care what you do or who you do it with—just know that our cause is all that matters, and it will be defended at all costs."

Edso took his eyes off the screen and looked at Giles. The expression on his host's face said much more than his words, and a chill washed over him again.

"I think it's time to bring *Eva* home," said Giles, returning his attention to the console.

With a flick of a switch, the screen was filled again with the image of the *M/V Wonder* in all her lit-up glory. Giles had just grasped the joystick when Jennifer came out of the yacht and stood by the railing.

"Wait," said Edso, as she looked up, straight into *Eva's* cameras.

"She's pretty," said Giles.

"She is."

"The look on your face! Edso, you do know that she can't see or hear us."

"Of course," Edso said, but as he continued to stare into Jennifer's eyes, he couldn't help but wonder.

CHAPTER 14

EDSO'S ATTENTION REMAINED FIXED ON THE SCREEN as Giles guided Eva home. The ever-changing numbers on the bottom of the screen told the digital story of what he was watching. Giles' skills at maneuvering Eva back onto her cradle from down within the bridge deck were impressive. As soon as she had set down, he flicked several switches, and all the lights and screens went dark. Abruptly he got up. Then, without a word, he walked to the door, which whooshed open obediently, and disappeared outside.

"He's quick, for an old guy," thought Edso, as he followed.

As before, there were no lights on the flybridge deck, but none were needed. Light from the area surrounding the yacht—streetlights and cars in the distance, the low lights on the marina docks, and, just behind, the *M/V Wonder,* which was still lit up like a Christmas tree—was more than sufficient. Giles was already pulling a cover over the drone by the time Edso reached him.

"That was quick."

Giles looked proud that he had impressed his guest. "Let's go back down. I'm ready for some coffee, and maybe a little dessert."

He made it all sound so casual, but Edso recognized that everything about this evening had been carefully orchestrated.

Back on the bridge deck, Giles led him to another set of stairs, and they went down to the deck area aft of the main salon. Edso walked to the stern rail and leaned on it, looking in the direction of the *Wonder.*

Giles joined him.

"I must compliment you on that demonstration. Quite impressive."

"Yes, but compared to what else we can do, Eva is a mere toy. Now mind you, she is an effective and deadly toy, and she serves a purpose."

"And my grandfather's purpose was . . . ?"

After a very long pause, Giles began speaking softly, with a wistful quality to his voice. "Like I said, Hitler had it right; he just moved too quickly. His impatience and impulsiveness set us back, but now we are again moving forward and this time we won't be denied. Your grandfather was fully on board with that."

"I'm not sure I understand what you are saying. Hitler was a delusional madman."

"No doubt. But in the beginning, he understood that racial purity is key. Unfortunately, as he became ever more powerful, he was surrounded by more and more sycophants. Most of them were mentally deranged thugs, and things began to spin out of control."

"He thought he could conquer the world."

"That's the point. He thought he could conquer the world by *brute force*. That will not work, especially today with the kinds of weapons available, so a new way has to be employed. We just have to make sure we keep the same underlying principles."

"So you're saying that my grandfather's twisted ideas of racial purity are still valid."

"Exactly. It comes from a fear of others, either real or imagined, and a thirst for power. Those who have power want to remain in power and the simplest way is to create and maintain that fear."

Giles watched as Edso thought about what he had just been told.

"Edso, that fear that has been preached for years by the right wing media has finally borne fruit and now, with a whole new power structure in Washington, our time has come. There is still a lot to do, but we are beginning to reap the benefits of our efforts. First and foremost, the appointment of conservative judges will assure the advance of our agenda over the decades to come. And you, because of your grandfather, will be a part of this historic movement."

Giles paused, as if to let his words sink in.

"In time, and with patience, the world will be ours. Now enough of this serious talk, let's go inside and have coffee and some dessert, and end the evening on a lighter note."

Giles touched Edso's arm as if to nudge him along as he turned from the rail and walked toward the door into the salon. Edso followed, and as they approached the door, it whooshed open, light spilling out from within. Again, Edso was amazed at how there had been no indication that lights were on inside, and yet they were. As soon the door whooshed shut, he turned and looked back. He could clearly see the *M/V Wonder* in all its lit-up glory.

"Our glass technology still amazes you, yes?"

"Yes."

"There is much else we are working on, but that is for another day. Come. I smell coffee, and I'm sure a wonderful dessert will be waiting for us."

The coffee was strong and rich, and it served as the perfect complement to the Chocolate Cake that was served.

"How did you like the Torta di Caprese?" asked Giles as Edso finished his cake.

A ship's clock chimed eight bells, midnight. Edso hadn't realized how late it had become.

"That cake was delicious, as was dinner," he told his host. "This has been an eye-opening evening. However, it's late, and I must get going."

Giles had not invited him to stay, nor had Edso expected him to do so.

"Yes, it is late. We shall have to do this again," said Giles, rising from the table. He led the way, and as they reached the doorway just past the kitchen area, the door whooshed open. Giles opened the watertight door, and cool night air rushed in. Edso faced his host. "Thank you for your hospitality. This evening was most enlightening."

Giles' smile began to fade and his voice became serious. "I look forward to seeing you again. Never forget that your grandfather was a great man." Then he paused and looked at Edso even more intently. "Few people have seen what you have seen tonight and your silence is non-negotiable. Never doubt that anyone who puts us at risk will be dealt with severly." He grabbed Edso in a bear hug and whispered in his ear, "Have a safe ride home."

Edso leapt to the dock, and as he landed, he heard the door clang shut. He turned and looked up at the dark, lifeless grey yacht. Had he not known differently, he would have imagined that no one was on board.

* * *

Edso walked quickly away from the *Gendroit*. It was eerily quiet, and his light footsteps felt as loud as a hammer on wood. For a moment he even considered taking his shoes off, but he decided that that would be silly. Only after he reached the main dock did he pause to look back. He could see the dark silhouette of Giles' mysterious gray yacht, a stark contrast to the glow of the *M/V Wonder*. He held his breath and listened to the night. There was no reason to expect that Giles would reactivate Eva, but he listened anyway.

The air was still. He did not feel even the faintest hint of breeze against his skin. He walked on and didn't stop until he reached the bottom of the ramp. There, he looked out over the water. For a moment, he felt as if he were looking down into an endless depth, because the water's surface had become a perfect mirror, reflecting every detail of the world above. That perfection lasted but a moment before it began to distort. The disturbance seemed to be coming from a forty-foot sailboat tied to the dock near the ramp.

It was too small to have a regular slip in the Mega Yacht Facility. *"Probably a transient,"* thought Edso.

An errant halyard had begun to slap softly against its mast. *"Odd,"* he thought, *"with no wind."* Returning his gaze to the water, he considered another possibility: perhaps unseen movement on board the boat was causing it to rock. His encounters with Courtney flashed through his head, and he could feel his face warming. Then, his thoughts turned to Jennifer. *"Could be,"* he thought, grinning slightly.

At the end of the ramp, he stopped and looked over at the *M/V Wonder*. She no longer lit up the night. Only a few small security lights lit the side decks of the yacht. He saw no other lights that would indicate that anyone was still awake.

"Jennifer," he mouthed her name. He liked its feel as it rolled off his tongue. "Jennifer," he repeated. His voice was barely above a whisper, and yet in the silence he felt like he was shouting. His body grew even warmer as he remembered how she had looked up into Eva's cameras. "You don't know it yet, but we will meet again—soon."

Out of reasons to linger, he returned to his car. The guard shack was still empty as he drove out of the parking lot. He slowed to a stop and waited for the automatic gate to lift. Still in shock over all that had happened in the past few hours, he realized he needed some time to think. The gate lifted, and he drove through.

"Grandfather, what have you gotten me mixed up in?"

CHAPTER 15

"HEY, MAX," SAID JACK, as he walked into the bar at Ben's.

"Jack, what are you doing here? I thought you were going to work on *d'Riddem* and I wouldn't see you until dark."

"That was the plan," he said, his tone subdued.

"You all right?" she said.

"Yeah, I went over, but didn't get much work done. Mostly just stared at stuff."

Max looked at him, "You want a beer?"

"Please."

She went out back to draw him a beer. Returning with the beer, she was about to ask him for details when the register began its chukka-chukka-chunk as an order scrolled out, followed by Patti walking in.

"Hi, Jack. Max, on that margarita, she wants salt on one side of the rim and sugar on the other."

The shadow that passed over Max's face seemed to express her feelings perfectly as she turned to make the drinks.

"You excited?" Jack said, looking at Patti. He knew what the answer would be because he had talked with Dave, but he had to ask.

"O-M-G, I am so excited."

"How's the swimsuit hunt going?" He knew that answer also, but like Dave, sometimes he just couldn't resist stirring the pot.

"Awful," she answered. "Nothing fits right. I'm all fat and lumpy."

Max turned toward them. "Patti, you are not. You look great, and those bikinis you tried on yesterday at Drift were fabulous."

Patti looked at Max and seemed to force a smile. "Thanks. You're a good friend, but a lousy liar."

Max set the half-salt/half-sugar margarita on the bar. "Here, take this and stop bitching. You looked better than I did."

74

Patti picked up her tray. As she walked off, Max called out after her. "Just don't slosh it! If the salt and sugar wash off the rim, you'll have to bring it back."

She turned and faced Jack.

"What?"

"You went to the boat, did nothing and came home. What's going on?"

"Before going, I stopped down to the harbor. Ran into Tom."

"What's he up to?"

"Cooking dinner. His day off and he was looking to see who might have some fresh fish. No one was around so we just shot the shit for a bit."

"And?"

"Do you remember the name Giles Endroit?"

Before she could answer, her register came to life again, and she turned for the slip. Jack watched as she efficiently took three beers from the cooler and made two frozen drinks.

Finished, she turned back to Jack, "He's that author we met in Belize?"

"Exactly."

"And wasn't he involved with all that Francis House stuff?"

"Oh, you're good."

"So why do you ask?"

"Tom gets these bulletins from Homeland Security about possible threats."

A shadow of concern passed over her face, so he quickly said, "No, it's all right. They come weekly and are mostly repetitive—the same general info each week."

"But this one was different, wasn't it?"

"Kind of. His name was mentioned."

"Giles?"

"Yes."

"So why's his name on a security bulletin?"

"Wasn't any specific reason, but it seems that the report mostly concerned white supremacist groups."

"So he's a—"

"It didn't say specifically, but his name was mentioned in conjunction with those kind of groups."

"So why'd Tom share this with you?"

"Max, I don't know. Maybe just because he'd been around here once." Jack could tell that she wasn't buying his explanation in its entirety. "Thanks for the beer."

"Jack. I asked you why."

"He just wanted us to keep an eye out. Or an ear out. Let him know if you hear any weird stuff here, that sort of thing. But I want you girls to be careful on your trip, too. Tom got the impression that he was on the West Coast, specifically in southern California."

"Southern California? And you're worried about us."

Jack sipped his beer silently.

"Aww. That's sweet."

"Hey, guys." It was Patti. "Looks like all my tables will be leaving in the next few minutes, and I'm getting cut. I just called Dave, and he's coming down for a drink and a bite to eat. Jack, you eaten?"

"Not yet."

"You want to join us?"

He glanced at Max.

"Go ahead," said Max. "I'm here until closing. You've got to eat. Go on."

"We'll just eat here," said Patti. "Maybe you can join us for a few minutes if you get a break."

Max's register began to rattle. As she turned away to look at the order, Patti said, "Jack?"

"Sounds good to me."

"Good. I've got to go finish up. Dave'll be here soon."

As she walked away, Max looked at Jack. "Can I ask you a favor?"

"Sure, what?"

"Don't say anything about this Giles Endroit stuff."

"Why?"

"I think it would just freak Patti and Courtney out." Jack could hear the concern in her voice. "Jack, please. The fact that Tom received a Homeland warning about something on the West Coast, especially something that was tied to Rye, would only get them completely unglued."

"Fine," Jack agreed. "And I didn't mean to freak *you* out. Remember, this was quite a long time ago. I'm sure we'll all be fine."

CHAPTER 16

"I THINK MAX HAS LOST HER MIND," Jack told Dave a week later.

They hadn't run together for nearly two weeks, so when Dave had called an hour ago to see if Jack was up for a run, Jack couldn't get ready fast enough. With the ensuing warm days, Maudslay was a totally different experience. The brown and gray trees and trails that had been accented with snow now had the bright, lemony-limey greens of new leaves, which created an atmosphere that felt as ripe as it looked.

They were into their second mile. The pace remained easy and conversational.

"I know what you mean. Patti is still totally obsessed with this swimming suit problem," said Dave.

"Makes no sense. Max has probably brought home over a dozen suits, asking for my opinion every single time. I give it and she calls me a liar. Points out that the color's not right, or that it pinches here or there, makes her butt look flat, is too revealing or doesn't cover enough, blah blah blah. Then she returns them and it all begins again."

"Same. That's why I'm here. She's out shopping again, and I want to avoid being at home for as long as possible. Kind of give her time to settle down before I have to tell her how great she looks."

"Maybe it'd be better if we just told them that all of the suits are ugly."

Dave laughed. "Yeah, right."

"You're right, bad idea. Best just to not be there."

They ran in silence for another mile. Dave went ahead for a bit but then stopped to let Jack catch up. When Jack finally reached him, Dave said, "You okay?"

"I'm good. Hold up." Instead of picking up the pace again, Jack began walking.

"You sure you're okay?"

"No, uh, yes. I'm fine."

"So, what's going on?"

"If I tell you something, can you keep quiet about it?"

Dave stopped, and Jack could see the panic in his friend's eyes. "Don't tell me Max is knocked up."

Jack broke into a huge grin. "No. God no!"

"Oh man, you had me going for a minute. So, what's up?"

"Why would you even think that?"

"I have no idea."

"I saw Tom a week ago. Actually, it was the day you and Patti came over to Ben's for dinner."

"What's new with Tom?"

"Well . . . he had some information, and I'm not sure if we should worry or not."

"What kind of information?"

They began running again, slowly, and it took another mile for Jack to explain.

"You'll let me know if you hear anything else, though, won't you?" said Dave.

"Absolutely. I'm sure it's nothing."

As the trail narrowed to single track, Dave took the lead. "Let's get this over with."

Jack had to be content to follow his friend. It wasn't long before the run became competitive, and every time Dave picked up the pace a bit, Jack responded, staying close behind his friend.

When they finally broke out of the single track, Jack pulled even, and they ran side by side all the way back to their cars.

"Oh, man," Jack wheezed. "That was work. Thanks."

"It was good."

"I haven't run that fast in a while."

"Me neither."

Jack walked away from their cars as he worked to catch his breath, while Dave went to his car, popped the trunk, and began rummaging around inside.

"Beer?" he said to Jack, as Jack returned.

"Sure. I'll be right there." He walked to his truck and got a towel from his bag. Then he joined Dave for a cold beer. "Thanks."

Dave raised his can. "Well, here's to swimsuits. Good luck to us."

"Yes. We'll need it."

Jack tipped back his beer and took a long sip. Lowering the can, he chuckled.

"What's so funny?"

"I was just thinking. You know how wound up the girls are over this swimsuit stuff. I don't think it would be such an issue if it weren't for the fashion industry promoting the importance of having a perfect tan and the ways that swimsuits will show it off. The fact of the matter is, we—at least I— really don't care much about Max having a perfect tan. Aside from the fact that with her red hair, she mostly pinks."

"What the hell are you talking about?"

"Tans. Who cares? It's the white spots that we're really interested in."

"You're bad."

"Guilty. But it is true."

"No argument here."

"Another?"

"Thanks, no. I'm all set."

CHAPTER 17

AFTER THE RUN, Jack spent most of his afternoon puttering about in his shop. When he returned to the apartment, he realized that Max was still out with Patti and Courtney, searching for that elusive perfect swimming suit. He was sitting on the couch, sipping a beer and reading his latest sailing magazine, when Max walked up the stairs.

"Oh, good. You're here. I think I found it!" Max announced excitedly, as she hurried past and disappeared into the bedroom.

"Great," he said, without looking up from his magazine. He had heard that line too many times to get excited again.

Moments later, he heard her return from the bedroom. "Jack. What do you think?"

Based on her tone, he felt compelled to look. He raised his eyes from the magazine's pages, said nothing for several long moments, then slowly put down his magazine, never taking his eyes off of her.

"Well?" she asked again, her face reflecting her excitement.

He remained silent. Then, still staring, he said softly, "That's it."

"What's it?"

"The suit. It's perfect. I'm really glad you don't have any time left to change your mind. And with the bikini you tried on yesterday, I'm not even sure I should let you go."

"Really?"

"Yes, really. That's it."

Jack motioned for her to spin around, slowly, so he could take one more close look. She turned slowly, mimicking moves from professional models, all the while turning her head and looking at him to gauge his reaction. The suit was a one piece. The material clung like a second skin, and while its cut wasn't extreme, it perfectly accentuated her body. It had a tropical leaf pattern in subtle shades of green and blue. In a word, it was stunning.

"Come here."

She walked toward him and he held out his right hand, never taking his eyes off hers. With locked eyes, she reached out and took his hand, allowing him to gently pull her in, guiding her to sit in his lap. Sitting sideways, her right side against his body with her right arm draped around his neck, she sank into him. Jack reached up with his left hand and gently touched her shoulder, while his right came to rest on her thigh. His heart was beginning to pound in his chest, while her breathing was becoming more shallow and rapid. Looking up at her, he could see that a soft pink flush was spreading over her neck and chest. Seconds felt like hours. Max shifted her hips slightly and looked down into Jack's face.

"What?" she whispered. The answer was unnecessary because he knew she could feel the what, and she leaned down to give him a kiss. Her lips were warm, and he could feel her body's warmth as he held her. His left hand slowly nudged the swimsuit's strap off her shoulder while his right hand caressed her leg. As the strap fell off her shoulder, he nudged it further, exposing her breast while their kiss deepened.

Time seemed to slow as those first soft touches became caresses. With the increasing intensity and urgency, conscious thoughts ceased to exist as baser instincts took over.

* * *

"Mrowh." Cat's voice broke the silence.

Jack lifted his head to see what Cat was talking about. Max was perfectly still and draped halfway over his body, her skin still wearing the flush of their recent exertions.

"Hey, Max," Jack whispered. "I think Cat likes your new suit."

Max rolled her head over to look. Cat was sitting on the suit, staring at them.

"It really creeps me out that she sits there watching us. What do you think she's thinking?"

Jack looked over at Cat again.

"No idea, but you're right. It is a bit creepy. Think she enjoyed the show?"

Cat's expression remained unmoved, but her eyes told a different story.

"She's definitely thinking something."

"How about we give her something more to think about?"

Max pulled herself on top of Jack, and kissed him softly on the lips as her hips pressed into his. "Let's."

* * *

"I'm hungry, you?" said Jack.

"I am. Do we have anything here?"

"Not really. Why don't we go over to Ben's. It's close."

"Fine by me."

Max slid off both him and the bed. As Jack watched, the deepening shadows softened her form. He smiled when he noticed that Cat had obviously grown tired of watching them and gone elsewhere. As he looked out the window, he saw that the sun was nearing the horizon, and while the sky was still painted in oranges and reds, the blues and purples were poised to take over.

Picking his clothes off the floor, he pulled them on, walked out of the bedroom, and found that Max was ready and waiting for him.

"Ready?" she said.

"Ready."

By the time they reached Ben's, having chosen to walk, the sun had set and little natural light remained in the sky. The number of cars in the parking lot numbered less than twenty. As Jack reached for the door handle, Max slid between him and the door, wrapped her arms around his neck, and kissed him.

As quickly as she had embraced him, she pulled away, turned, and reached for the door handle.

"Let's sit at the bar. It's too cold to sit outside," she said, as she pulled the door open.

Jack followed her in, smiling. "Sure."

JACK HAD HIS USUAL BURGER, and Max ordered the Mussels, which came in a unique sauce with turmeric and fennel.

"How's your burger?"

"Good," said Jack, as he wiped his mouth.

"What do you think about the new bun?"

"I like it. What's it called?"

"Brioche."

"It's good," he said, as he took another bite. Swallowing, he asked about her mussels.

Max was sopping up the sauce with a piece of bread. "Oh my god, I love this sauce. The mussels are good, but . . ." Her words were muffled by the sauce-soaked piece of bread she had just stuffed into her mouth.

"I told Dave."

"Told Dave what?"

"About what Tom told me."

"When'd you do that?"

"The other day, when we were running in Maudslay."

"What'd he say?"

"You know Dave. Not much, really. Just asked me to keep him informed if I heard anything else."

"Do you think he told Patti?"

"He was more concerned in dealing with her swimsuit insanity."

"Jack!" She playfully slapped him on the shoulder and acted offended.

"His words, not mine."

"Yeah, right."

"Listen, I'm just glad that you found one."

She understood his implication. "It was a process. You don't understand how important that decision is."

"No. You're wrong. I understand perfectly how important it is."

Before Jack could say anything else, Courtney walked in.

"Hey, guys."

"Court," said Jack. "Did you hear the good news?"

"What news?"

"Max found a swimsuit."

His statement was followed by another slap to his shoulder. "Brat," said Max.

Court chuckled. "I was with her, Jack. I know."

"You all packed?"

"Just about."

"Hey Court, where exactly are you staying? I haven't been able to get a specific answer from Max."

She turned to Max and said, "I thought I gave you that information."

"If you did, I wasn't paying attention."

"We're staying in Laguna Beach. I'll send you a link to the place. It overlooks the beach, but there's a short walk to get there."

"You're getting a car?"

"Of course. We already have a long list of things we want to see and places we want to go."

"But will you?"

"Will we what?"

"See anything," said Jack. "I've seen pictures of the parking lots they call freeways out there. You may get in a car and just sit."

"You are being such a jerk. It won't be like that."

Max broke in. "Stop it, Jack." Then turning toward her friend, she said, "Court, don't tell him anything more. He'll just have to wait until we return to hear all about our adventures."

"I've got to get going," said Court. "This restaurant doesn't run itself, you know."

"Love you, Court," said Jack, as she walked off.

As soon as she was out of sight, Jack said in a voice just above a whisper, "You will call me and let me know what you're up to, won't you?"

"Awww. That's sweet. You're worried," said Max.

"I'm not sure worried is the right word, but, well . . . okay, yes, I am worried. I know you three, and if there's trouble to find, you'll find it."

"You're worried about what Tom told you."

"Am not. Odds of running into that guy are slim to none. I'm referring to all the other kinds of trouble you can get into."

"So you're worried that we'll be picked up by handsome, rich men who will whisk us away on their yachts."

"That's not funny. We just went through that with Court."

"I know, and that's exactly why it won't happen. This trip is all about us—just the three of us."

"Well, I can still worry. I've seen you in that new swimsuit."

Max blushed. "You have nothing to worry about."

* * *

"Knock, knock," Jack said, as he rapped on the doorframe to Tom's office.

"Jack."

"Got a minute?"

"Sure, Come in. What's up?"

"You hear anything else about what you told me the last time we talked?"

For a second, the look on Tom's face reflected his confusion. Then he said, "You mean that Homeland notice?"

Jack nodded.

"You're worried about the girls. They're leaving soon, aren't they?"

"Tomorrow. And no, I'm not worried; I'm just curious."

"You're worried."

Jack said nothing.

"No. I haven't heard anything else. I don't think that you have anything to worry about, at least where Giles Endroit is concerned." He paused. Then he grinned and added, "But all those Hollywood types with their perfect hair and teeth and their expensive fast cars—now that I'd worry about."

"You are such an asshole," said Jack. "Thanks. I'll see myself out."

"Don't worry, Jack. They'll be just fine," Tom shouted after his friend.

CHAPTER 19

"I CAN'T BELIEVE WE'RE REALLY HERE," said Patti, as they stood waiting to pick up their bags.

The flight to John Wayne Airport was uneventful—long, but uneventful—and they were on the ground just after noon. Max's friends thought she had gone soft in the head when she pulled out *Moonlight on the Beach* and began reading during the flight, but she defended herself by explaining that it was the perfect vacation book. She didn't hide the fact that the author had signed the book, but she didn't point it out either. Nor did she mention that Jack had told her that the author was mentioned in a Homeland Security notice that Tom had received and that he was presumed to be in the LA area.

"With a little luck, the traffic won't be too bad," said Courtney, as she led them from the baggage claim to the car rental desk.

"What kind of car are we getting?" asked Patti.

"You'll see," was the cryptic answer, but Courtney delivered it with a smile.

"Is anyone hungry?" asked Max.

"I thought that we'd stop on the way," said Courtney.

"Anyone ever heard of In-N-Out Burger?"

Court said yes, but Patti said no.

"They're supposed to be fabulous. Maybe we'll find one on the way," said Max.

The rental process was quick and efficient, and after a quick bathroom stop, they walked straight to the car pick-up area. The day was warm, the sky was nearly cloudless, and as at all airports, there seemed to be a continuous breeze.

"I hope the car is air-conditioned," said Patti, as she put on her sunglasses. Her blonde curls shone in the bright sun, and with her carefully chosen sunglasses, she could have been a movie star.

"Here we are," said Courtney, checking the paperwork to make sure that they were standing by the correct vehicle. It was a cherry-red convertible, and its top was already down.

"Oh. My. God. Court, you are the best!" gushed Patti when she saw it. "It's perfect."

"Patti, you get the back seat. I want Max to help me navigate," said Court.

Luggage stowed, Patti climbed in. Playing the part of a starlet, with her arms outstretched and resting on the back of the seat, she cocked her head back. "I am so excited I don't even care if my legs are crammed in like sardines."

"Where to?" asked Max.

"We're going to take the Pacific Coast Highway south. I got directions from the car guy, and I think it's pretty simple, and he said there was an In-N-Out Burger in Costa Mesa, which is not too far out of the way."

Court fiddled with the GPS and soon a small, blinking red dot identified them on the screen. It was simple—west to Newport Beach, and on the way, In-N-Out Burger, then south on the PCH.

* * *

"Oh, my God!" said Patti as they climbed back into the car. "Those burgers were to die for. Too bad Jack isn't here, being our burger aficionado."

"I'll send him the pictures I took," said Max.

The drive to Newport Beach didn't take too long. The traffic was no worse than driving down to Boston via Route 1 by Saugus and Revere.

"Hey, isn't this cool. We're on Route 1, just like at home," said Patti. They had just made the turn onto the Pacific Coast Highway. Driving south, Max saw Newport Beach Harbor on the right, and it seemed to go on forever. Even when she couldn't actually see the water or any boats, there was no doubt that it was there.

"So, are you going to tell us about where we're going?" asked Patti.

"I already told you," said Court. "We're staying in Laguna Beach."

"I know that, but where?"

"You'll see. Be patient."

"We're in Corona del Mar," said Max, looking at a tourist brochure she had picked up in the airport. "We just passed the Sherman Museum and Gardens."

Patti looked in the direction Max was pointing. "What's that?"

"It's a botanical garden known for its orchid collection, and according to the brochure, it's also the repository of many documents from California's early history, when it was a part of Spain. It might be fun to visit."

"I've heard they have a really nice restaurant there. We'll have to put it on our list," said Courtney.

The road wound along the coast, not at sea level like so much of Route 1-A at home, but high above the water. To the left, the landscape climbed steeply.

"Check out those amazing homes," said Max. "They seem to be hanging onto the hillside."

"Is that Gilligan's Island out there?" said Patti with a giggle.

"Patti, are you serious?"

"Come on. Do you really think that I don't know that Gilligan's Island is made up? I was just checking to see if you were paying attention. Besides, you couldn't see Gilligan's Island from shore. That was the whole problem; they were out in the middle of nowhere. That's Catalina."

And with that she began singing, "Twenty-six miles across the sea, Santa Catalina is a-waitin' for me."

Courtney and Max joined in, "Santa Catalina, the island of romance, romance, romance, romance . . ."

"We should go there," said Court.

"Oooo, yeah. Courtney's on vacation. Ready to go to the island of romance," said Max.

Courtney flashed her a look, then they all started laughing.

It wasn't long before resorts, gated communities, restaurants, and shops began to fill in along the road. The road no longer ran above the immediate coast. Instead, it dipped down, and suddenly the beach was right there on their right.

"Welcome to Laguna Beach," said Court.

Max and Patti looked around, pointing and commenting on every little thing.

Just past the center of town, as the road began to climb and turn away from the water, Courtney turned right onto a small street marked with a sign that said *Dead End*. The closely spaced houses that lined the street were all perfectly maintained. Small, carefully manicured yards, some of which were no wider than narrow strips of grass with carefully manicured flower beds, separated the homes from the road and from each other. The closer they came to the end of the street, the size of the homes and the space between each one increased. The landscaping provided more and more privacy until it was replaced by a high wall that hid the homes behind.

A low stone wall marked the end of the street, which was wide enough to allow cars to turn around. Ahead, Max could see only sky and ocean.

Courtney stopped at the wall, and Patti clambered out of the convertible. Instantly her camera was pasted to her face, and Max could hear a steady *kchick, kchick, kchick* as Patti kept pressing the shutter button.

"So, why are we here?" asked Max.

Courtney smiled but said nothing. Instead, she shifted the car into reverse and began backing up.

Patti seemed not to notice they were leaving her behind.

"Uh, Court . . . Patti?" said Max.

"Oh, she'll be fine."

CHAPTER 20

BEFORE MAX COULD SAY ANYTHING ELSE, Courtney shifted into gear, turned the car through a gate in the high wall, pulled over, and shut off the ignition. Patti came running up from behind. Max looked over and saw her friend's jaw drop.

"Welcome to your West Coast home!" said Courtney with a note of triumph in her voice.

Max looked at her friend, then at Patti, then back at Court. "You're kidding?" she said.

She smiled and said, "No, I'm not."

As Court climbed out of the car, Max and Patti stared in silence. Whatever Max had expected, this wasn't it. The stone wall that hid the home from the street was the only concession to the Spanish architecture that seemed so prevalent in many of the homes they had seen on the ride from the airport. What actually stood in front of them appeared to be a small cottage. Its green, painted exterior had a kind of beachy, New England feel to it.

"What do you think?"

Max answered first. "It's cute."

"Looks kind of small," said Patti.

Max moved over and bumped Patti with her elbow. "Shhh!"

"I think you'll be surprised," said Courtney, who was still smiling. "Come on. Let's go in."

Courtney led the way, opened the door, and waved her two companions inside. Nothing they had seen outside had prepared them for the interior. Straight ahead, through a wall of sliding doors, they could see an outdoor patio.

Patti headed straight for the doors.

"Max, look at this," she said excitedly, as she pulled open one of the doors and went out.

By the time Max had reached the door, Patti had already crossed the patio and was standing at the glass-paneled railing that surrounded the patio, waving for her to hurry up. Instead of rushing across the patio, Max stopped and looked from left to right. Over the far right end of the patio, a large white sail was stretched, providing shade for an outdoor bar and a teak table with seating for six. Away from the shade cover, in the center was a gas grill, and next to that, a grouping of over-stuffed patio furniture surrounded a gas fire pit. On the left side, Max could see an opening in the railing and the beginning of what appeared to be a stairway.

"Max," Patti called out again.

As Max crossed the patio to join Patti, all she could see was Pacific Ocean ahead.

"Did you see that?" exclaimed Patti.

"I think so."

"There," Patti said, pointing. "It's a whale!"

"There's a whole bunch of them," said Max. Turning, she called out to Court to join them.

"There are whales spouting and jumping all over the place," said Patti.

For the next few minutes, the three friends stood and watched the show out in the ocean. Max could hear laughter and squeals. Looking down, she saw that fifty feet below was a sandy beach with a dozen or so people playing Frisbee.

"Oh, Court, this is amazing," said Max.

"I must say, it's better than I imagined. There should be some champagne in the kitchen. Anyone want some?"

The vote was unanimous, and she left to get it.

"Pinch me," said Patti. "I think I've died and gone to heaven . . . Ouch! I didn't mean for you to actually do it."

"Do what?" Courtney's voice interrupted.

"Nothing," said Max.

"Here." Courtney held out a tray with three glasses. The champagne was cold, and condensation dripped from each glass. Patti lifted her glass and said, "A toast. . . What happens in Cali, stays in Cali!"

Rims were clinked and champagne sipped.

"Come inside," said Court. She turned toward the door, and Max and Patti followed.

"The kitchen is there," she said, pointing right. Then, turning and pointing left, she said, "The bedrooms are down that hall. We each have our own, with private baths, and each opens out onto the patio. Mine is the far one."

"Oh my god! This is amazing," said Patti.

"How did you find this place?" asked Max, but Court had already disappeared back into the kitchen.

Max took the first room, leaving Patti in the center. Patti said, "I'm not even going to bother unpacking. I'm going out to explore the neighborhood. Anyone want to come?"

When Max and Court declined, Patti promised to be back in an hour. Max and Court decided to sit out on the patio overlooking the ocean, where they finished the champagne and made up shopping lists.

"This is amazing. How did you ever find this place?" Max asked again.

"A friend hooked me up."

"A friend? Who?"

Courtney just smiled, and Max knew that she wasn't going to get an answer to that question.

"Oh, I see," she said, giving Courtney an all-knowing kind of look. "So, in other words, you're not going to spill the details."

Courtney said nothing.

* * *

An hour later Patti walked in.

"See anything interesting?" Max called out.

"I did. I went down to the beach and got some great shots. Then I walked up the street back toward town. There's a really cute bar just around the corner, and as I came back I met one of our neighbors. Older guy, seemed really nice. Told me that this cottage was originally owned by a big movie star in the thirties. It was the only place out here, so it was very private, and there are many stories of some pretty wild parties."

"Well, there won't be any wild parties here in the next few weeks," said Court.

"I never said there would be," said Patti.

"So, Patti, you ready to go?" asked Max. "We've got shopping to do."

Patti lowered her sunglasses back onto her face and sighed. "It's a tough life," she said, "but someone's got to do it. Let's go."

CHAPTER 21

EDSO SHIFTED HIS CAR INTO NEUTRAL and turned off the ignition. Finally home. Because of the late hour, the drive from San Diego to Newport Beach had taken only an hour, but he recalled very little of the actual journey.

He let his head fall back against his seat's headrest and closed his eyes. As his muscles relaxed, he felt the tension of the long day leaving his body. Slowly, moments from his time in San Diego drifted through his memory, starting with the initial quest to find the right yacht. First there was Clyde, with his belches and beers, talking about his neighbors on the absent yacht, *Last Chance.* Then there was that standoffish steward of the *M/V Wonder,* who had asked him not to loiter by the yacht. Thanks to Giles and Eva, Edso now knew that her name was Jennifer. He wondered if Jennifer had realized that she was being watched. No matter. What he did know was that he had to see her again.

* * *

"You saw him."

"I did."

"And?"

"And I told him that the owner didn't like people hanging around the yacht. He left, but I could tell he was interested."

"In the yacht, or you?"

"Probably both," she said matter-of-factly.

"What else?"

"He walked off when I went on board. I watched him walk to the *Gendroit.*"

"Did he know you were watching?"

"No. I was inside, and I used the ship's camera system."

"Good."

"There's something else."

"What?"

"After dark, Endroit showed him the drone."

"Did you see it?"

"I didn't, but I knew it was there."

"How, if you didn't see it?"

"I knew."

"Be careful."

She ignored that last comment. "I think we should head up to Newport Beach with *Wonder* and see if we can't rattle his cage a bit more."

"Good idea. I'll join you soon and we'll go." The line went dead.

She dropped the phone overboard and exhaled. Then she whispered, "You may not know it yet, but we will be meeting again—and soon."

* * *

Sleep didn't come easily to Edso. Whenever he closed his eyes, all he could see was Jennifer's face looking up into the drone's camera. As irrational as it was, there was something in her eyes that convinced him she knew she was being watched.

He sat up with a start. Sunlight filled his bedroom, and a light breeze ruffled the curtains. Outside he could hear the ever-present sounds of leaf blowers and other machines of outdoor grooming. A glance at the clock confirmed that his day was starting much later than normal. Swinging his legs off the bed, he sat for a moment before standing. He pulled on an old pair of shorts and dragged himself into the bathroom. A glance into the mirror confirmed that a shower and a cup of Maria's coffee were badly needed before he could face the world.

Coffee came first. He didn't know what kind it was or what Maria did to brew it, but as usual, it was exceptional. As the coffee cleared his head, his thoughts turned to Otto. He and his grandfather had parted ways shortly after leaving New England. Until yesterday, he hadn't known that his grandfather had continued to keep tabs on him.

"So like him, always needing to be in control," he thought to himself.

Filling his cup with more coffee, he turned and stepped outside. His house was right on the Corona del Mar Bend, where each house filled to near entirety the lot that it was on. From the street side, most were unassuming, with garages visible. The waterside was another story. The houses were constructed to take full advantage of the view, with mostly glass walls and outdoor patios, and each had a private dock for direct access to the water. He looked right, toward Balboa Island and Newport Harbor, where he could see that the day's activities were already in full swing. Looking left, he could see that the ferry to Catalina Island was just making the turn as it exited the channel on its daily run to the island. He looked down at his own boat, which was tied to the dock that came with the house. Only thirty-five feet in length, it was quick and comfortable, perfect for fishing, coastal cruising, and the occasional seduction.

"Maybe I'll have to make another run down to San Diego," he mused as he thought of Jennifer again.

CHAPTER 22

IT DIDN'T TAKE LONG for the friends to establish a routine. Most days, Patti got up first. She usually grabbed her camera and headed out in search of that perfect picture. She explained to Max that the early morning light on the West Coast felt different to her, and she was determined to capture its essence. Eventually, Court and Max would get up and head out together in search of coffee. By mid-morning, all the friends were back at the house, where they decided as a group what to do for the rest of the day.

They spent the first few days enjoying sun and beach time in the morning, followed by an afternoon in the car exploring the area, and then cocktails and dinner in some interesting restaurant. Courtney always treated because she claimed that she was doing research for ideas to take back to Ben's.

One night they were just finishing the rare dinner at home when Courtney said, "What do you say to heading up to Newport Beach Harbor tomorrow?"

"Sounds like fun," said Max. "I've heard they have these cute little electric boats you can rent and tool about in."

"Sure," agreed Patti. Then she added, "This morning I met someone down on the beach. We got to talking, and he said we have to take at least one day and go out to Catalina Island."

"He?" Both Max and Court interrupted her at the same time.

"Nothing to get excited about. There was this pelican on the beach and I was trying to get close enough for a shot, but he kept moving."

"The pelican or the guy?"

"The pelican."

As soon as she said that, Patti blushed, realizing that they were teasing her.

"I must have looked pretty silly, all hunched over chasing this bird around, trying to get the perfect angle for the shot. Anyways, all of a sudden there was this voice from behind me. It startled me because I thought I was alone. I jumped, and the pelican took off. When I turned, there was this guy standing there, and he was kind of laughing at me."

"And? What was he like?"

"I don't know. I really didn't get a good look at him."

"But you did have a conversation about Catalina Island."

Patti's face turned redder. "Look, I'll admit he was good looking, but who isn't out here?"

"What was his name?"

"I didn't ask."

"Patti, what's wrong with you?"

"Nothing. He was nice, but not my type. Besides, there's no reason to think that I'll ever see him again. And what would Dave say?"

"Good point," said Max. She decided to change the subject. "So, we going to Newport Beach tomorrow?"

"Absolutely," said Courtney as she opened another bottle of wine— after all, planning was thirsty work.

* * *

The next morning's revival began slowly, but after much iced water and many cups of coffee, the girls were finally ready for their adventure. Courtney was wearing navy shorts and sandals with a sleeveless white shirt with little anchors on it. Max wore boat shoes, the light tan shorts that Jack liked so much, and a short-sleeved emerald green shirt that did not button to the neck, leaving the top quite open and flirty. They were outside on the deck, standing by the railing looking out over the Pacific, when Patti finally emerged.

Patti had on a floral-patterned sundress with bejeweled sandals. A wide-brimmed sunhat sat atop her curly blonde hair, and once again, she looked every bit the part of a starlet from an earlier time. All three were wearing sunglasses, which were less a fashion statement than a necessity after the previous night.

"Look at you," said Court, as Patti joined her and Max out on the patio.

"Do you think the hat is too much?" she asked.

"Not at all," said Max, smiling.

"We ready?" asked Courtney.

* * *

The top was down on the car, and the Beach Boys were blaring from the radio. Over the rush of the wind, Max shouted, "Is anyone else hungry?"

There was no answer from Patti, who was sitting in the back seat, but Courtney said, "I thought we might have lunch at the Sherman Gardens. It sounds really nice."

"Oh, good. I was hoping we might go there sometime," said Max. Turning, she looked back at Patti. She was sound asleep, her head tilted to one side, mouth open, her hat on the seat, held tightly in her hand.

Max tapped Courtney on the shoulder and motioned for her to look back. Adjusting the mirror, Court looked back at Patti and smiled.

The car lurched slightly as they turned into the garden's parking lot, waking Patti. As Max turned back, she saw her friend look around with a sense of momentary confusion as her brain tried to catch up with her eyes.

"We're here," Courtney announced, as she turned into an open parking spot that was opposite the entrance.

"It looks beautiful," said Max, twisting around and looking into the garden through the arched entrance.

Patti simply took a deep swig from her bottle of water. Then she reached for her camera and sunhat and opened the door.

* * *

"Oh, my god," said Patti. "This is amazing." She lifted her camera.

Standing just inside the entrance, Courtney held out the map that she had been given when she paid their admission. Directly in front of them was a large, open area with a fountained pool, and a central garden area with paths that led to other sections of the garden. Even with the large number of couples, families, and individuals strolling about, the atmosphere was that of calm and serenity.

"The Cafe Jardin is over there," said Courtney, pointing to her left. "Shall we eat first then walk around?"

"Yes, I'm starving," said Max.

Patti had already wandered off, her camera glued to her face.

"You go see about a table. I'll go after Patti," said Max.

By the time Max had convinced Patti that what she was photographing would still be there after lunch, Courtney had been seated. As soon as Max caught her eye, she waved them over. The table had a white umbrella for shade, and it was next to the perennial garden.

"Good job, Court. This is absolutely lovely," said Max.

Patti's face had frozen into a perma-smile, and she nodded in enthusiastic agreement.

Glasses of chilled rosé accompanied an appetizer of homemade country pâté, which they shared. For lunch, Patti ordered the Dungeness crab cake, Max went for the grilled chicken chef salad, and Court had quiche Lorraine and a cup of soup.

"This salad is delicious. I love the greens and the dressing is . . . I don't know what it is, but it's delicious," gushed Max. "You think we could make something like this at Ben's?"

They discussed each dish with equal enthusiasm.

After lunch was finished and cleared, their server returned and asked, "May I suggest our lemon tart with berry sauce for dessert?"

Max groaned and said, "I'm too full." In fact, all three declined, and Court asked for the check. Then they spent the next hour wandering through the gardens and displays, with Patti documenting every moment.

* * *

"Thank you, Court," Max and Patti chimed simultaneously as they climbed back into their car.

"You ready to go boating?"

"Boating?" said Patti.

"Remember last night, at dinner, Max mentioned those electric boats?"

"Yes."

"Well, they're called Duffy electric boats, and my friend who got us the cottage has some connections. I called them this morning, and made reservations for a sunset cruise. I thought I'd surprise you."

"Really?" said Max.

"Yes. We need to be there in a couple of hours."

"It takes that long to get there?" Patti asked.

"No. Actually, they're really quite close by. The boat rental place is out on Balboa Island, a company called Voyagers. When I made the reservation they told me that parking could be a challenge and suggested getting an Uber. But first, we need to get groceries. You can't have a proper sunset cruise without food and drink. I checked and there's a Whole Foods not far from here, so I thought we could go and get our picnic stuff, leave the car in their parking lot and Uber over from there."

CHAPTER 23

WHEN THEIR UBER DRIVER dropped them off, they were met by a man wearing a bright red shirt with the company name embroidered on the left breast, tan Bermuda shorts, and classic leather boat shoes. He looked at all three of them and broke into a huge smile. Then, focusing on Courtney, motioned toward the bag in her hand and said, "Welcome. You must be Courtney. Let me take that."

She smiled, and Max saw her beginning to blush.

"Why yes, I am Courtney," she said. "How'd you know?"

He winked at her. "We were expecting you. Go on into the office and Andrea will check you in while I take your stuff down to the boat." He gathered all the bags they were carrying and disappeared around the side of the building before she could say anything else.

"I think Court has an admirer," whispered Patti to Max.

"Shhh," replied Max, nudging Patti as they followed Courtney into the office.

"You're all set," said the woman named Andrea a few minutes later. She smiled broadly and handed Courtney her credit card. "Brad is waiting for you down at the docks. He'll be your captain today. When you go back out, walk around the building, and I'm sure you'll find him."

Max and Patti followed Courtney out of the office.

"Brad. His name is Brad," said Patti, her voice low and conspiratorial.

Courtney rounded the corner first. As soon as she was out of sight, Max said to Patti, "Stop. You're being a brat."

Patti looked at her and stuck out her tongue.

They rounded the corner. There were several boats tied up at the dock. It looked like the beginning of a Disney ride. Each of the boats was gleaming white, with a red-and-white-striped surrey top that covered the entire boat. Cushioned bench seats went all around the inside of the boat. In the front was a small table, and in the back of the boat was the helm station.

"There, down at the end," said Max, pointing toward the last boat in line, where a man was waving at them.

Courtney led the way.

"Good evening and welcome," It was the man who had greeted them when they arrived. His smile was disarming.

"You must be Brad." Court returned his smile.

"I am, and I will be your captain tonight. I hope that you don't mind that I went ahead and set the table for you."

Max glanced down into the boat, where the table had been set with the food they had brought with them. Not only had he set out their food, he had added wine glasses to the table. There was also an ice bucket, condensation dripping off its sides, and inside were the two bottles of rosé they had brought.

"You didn't have to do all that," said Court.

"It was my pleasure. My instructions were to take very good care of you."

Courtney blushed.

"First the cottage, and now this," Max thought. *"Courtney had better be planning a special thank you for her friend."*

While Brad helped Courtney on board, Max found herself staring at him. He was tall and thin, but not in a skinny way. Possessing a classic southern California tan, he was obviously fit and athletic.

Patti leaned in toward Max and whispered, "He's gorgeous."

"I bet he's a runner; look at those legs," Max whispered back.

"Ladies." The sound of his voice brought Max back to the moment.

One after the other, he helped Max and Patti step down into the boat. Then, while Brad busied himself with casting off, Courtney lifted one of the bottles of rosé out of the ice. "Time for a toast."

At the moment they clinked glasses, their boat began to move silently away from the dock.

* * *

"This is too cool," said Max. Patti put her wine on the table and began documenting everything with her camera.

Brad expertly steered the boat through the crowded mooring field. The silence of the electric boat was a new sensation for Max, almost like being under sail, but even quieter. Courtney moved aft and sat near Brad. Max leaned back on the seat with one arm stretched out on the gunwale and the other holding her glass of rosé.

"Smile," said Patti. Her camera clicked and whirred, as she photographed Max. "You look like some kind of a forties starlet," she teased.

Max stuck out her tongue at her friend.

Brad steered the boat around Harbor Island, under the Pacific Coast Highway, and into the Back Bay area. "If you are into kayaking," he said loud enough so all could hear, "this area is one of the largest coastal wetlands areas in Southern California. This marina and resort is the only commercial development in this area. If any of you would like to go kayaking, I can take you."

"Hey, Court. Why don't you come join us before we eat everything," called out Max.

Court began to get up and move forward to join her friends, then she turned and asked Brad, "Would you like anything?"

"Nah, thank you for asking. I'm good."

"I bet he is," thought Max. Taking a look at Court's face, she thought, *"And Courtney knows it, too."*

Max handed Courtney a glass of rosé. Several times she caught Courtney glancing back at Brad as he reversed course back to the harbor.

Passing under the PCH bridge again, they turned right and rode up the east side of Lido Isle. At the end of the island, they turned and passed under the Lido Isle Bridge. Then they continued south along its western side, passing mooring field after mooring field until they reached the main channel.

"What's that?" asked Patti, pointing, as they continued down the main channel.

"All that land is a narrow peninsula," said Brad. "You're looking at Balboa Village." He pointed toward a large white building. "There's an amusement area called the Fun Zone, and the ferry terminal to Catalina Island. Going out to Catalina is a great day trip. On the other side is the Balboa Pier and a great beach—good surfing spot, too. I can see that the ferry just got back."

"Hey, Court, what do you think?" said Patti.

"About what?"

"Going to Catalina."

"Could be fun."

"Look at that yacht," said Max, interrupting. Then she shivered as she thought to herself, *"Looks like the one Edso used to kidnap Courtney."*

"The *M/V Wonder*," said Max, staring at the yacht as they cruised closer.

"What did you say?" said Courtney.

"Its name. The *Wonder*. Hey, Brad, you ever seen that yacht before?"

"No. We don't get huge numbers of those really big yachts here. They mostly go to San Diego or Long Beach. She's good looking, though. Looks like she's moored there. Probably just a short stopover. It happens."

The conversation went back to visiting Catalina Island, and Courtney returned to sit near Brad.

Max couldn't take her eyes off the yacht.

"Max, what do you think?" said Patti.

"Huh? About what?"

"Catalina. Going to Catalina."

"Oh, yeah, it'd be fun," she said, still staring at the yacht.

"What're you looking at?"

"Nothing in particular."

Max turned from staring at the yacht and held out her glass. "Patti, may I have some more wine?"

"Sure."

After Patti poured the wine, Max took a sip, then twisted around to look at the yacht again.

"What's the deal with that boat?" said Patti.

"Oh, I'm sorry," said Max, turning back. "Nothing. Nothing really."

Patti looked at Max, not completely believing her friend. She then leaned over the table and looked up at the yacht, trying to see what seemed to be so interesting to Max.

"I told you, there's nothing. It's just a beautiful yacht."

Max helped herself to another cracker with cheese. Giggles and laughter became more frequent as they had more wine. The sun was setting, and the sky turned amazing shades of pink and orange. Brad steered a course that took them as close to the entrance to the harbor as possible, then crossed back across the main channel as lights on shore began to come on. Ahead, and to their left, they could see the Ferris wheel all lit up as it spun around, giving tourists and locals alike a spectacular view of the harbor and the sunset.

Max saw that the *M/V Wonder* was now lit up as brightly as the amusement park. She wasn't sure why, but she found it fascinating. "Who has that much money?" she asked to no one in particular.

Brad must have heard her. "Between Hollywood stars, dot-comers, and sports stars, the amount of money in this area is insane. That yacht I saw you looking at is really quite modest. Get down to San Diego or up to Long Beach, and you will see dozens that will make that one look insignificant."

As Brad steered a course close to and parallel to Balboa Island, Max was only able to get brief glimpses of the *M/V Wonder*.

"Hey, Brad, any chance you have any binoculars?" asked Max.

"Sure," he said, and handed a pair to her.

Max lifted them and looked in the direction of *Wonder*. She was able to get only brief glimpses of the yacht, but it was enough to keep her interest.

"Still looking at that yacht?" asked Patti.

"Yeah."

"Why? You've seen yachts before. What is so interesting about that one?"

Max didn't answer.

Then, as they passed one gap, she caught a glimpse of a smaller boat pulling up next to *Wonder*. She almost dropped the binoculars, catching them just before they hit the bottom of the boat.

"That's impossible," she murmured under her breath.

"You say something?" asked Courtney.

"No. No nothing," she mumbled.

Then she quickly readjusted the binoculars' focus and zoomed back in on the yacht.

CHAPTER 24

"MAX. WE'RE BACK," said Courtney, as Brad brought the boat gently to the dock.

Lowering the binoculars, Max continued to stare at the yacht as her two friends climbed out of the boat, joining Andrea who had come down to meet them, on the dock.

"Hey, Max! You coming?" Courtney called out.

Max turned and looked toward the dock. "Coming," she said. Then she looked at Brad. "Thank you. It was wonderful." Realizing what she had just said, she then quickly added, "No pun intended," and giggled. She handed the binoculars to Brad and thanked him again.

"No problem. It was my pleasure." He winked.

Max, still giggling climbed out of the boat.

"You ladies have a wonderful evening," said Brad as she joined her friends.

"Ready?" Max said to Courtney and Patti.

"What was that all about?" asked Court.

"Nothing. And no, I wasn't hitting on your boyfriend."

"What? He's not my boyfriend," said Courtney, feigning outrage.

Lowering her voice, Max said, "I saw how you were looking at him."

Court gave her a playful slap on the shoulder. "You are such a brat. Hey, where's Patti?"

"Over there," said Max, pointing down the dock.

Patti was standing by the edge of the dock with her camera lifted to her face and pointing out over the water.

"Hey, girlfriend. Don't you have enough pictures?" said Max, as she and Court walked toward Patti.

"Coming," she said lowering her camera.

The three friends walked back toward the boat to say their good-byes to Brad and Andrea.

"I called an Uber for you to take you back to your car," said Andrea.

"You didn't have to do that," said Court.

"I know, but we were asked to take special care of you. We hope you had a fun ride."

"It was great, and so were you. Thank you again," said Court. Then she turned to join her two friends.

* * *

"Okay, confession time," said Patti, as they walked into the cottage. "Come on—outside." She walked to the door to the patio and motioned to her friends.

Max followed, but Courtney turned toward the kitchen. A few minutes later she joined Max and Patti, who were sitting by the fire pit, with a bottle of wine and three glasses in hand.

Patti lifted her glass and said, "A toast. To Courtney and her mysterious friend who arranged for this amazing day."

Rims were clinked and Courtney said, "You're welcome." Then she took a big sip and smiled.

Max looked at her, expecting more, but all she got was a smile.

"You're not going to tell us about him, are you?" said Patti, after a few awkward moments.

Courtney merely took another sip.

"Okay then, Max, what was so interesting about that yacht?"

Max took a sip and smiled, trying the same tack that Courtney had used for avoiding the question.

* * *

Patti picked up her camera and began scrolling through the pictures she had taken. Finally she said, "Actually, I got some great shots of that boat." Looking at Max she said, "Were you interested in the boat or the people on board?"

She held out the camera to Max so she could look at the photos. The first shot was of an attractive woman in some kind of uniform leaning on the railing, her attention focused on what was obviously a boat that had come alongside the yacht. The second was a shot of the boat that she was looking at. A man was on board, and he was looking up at her. Max sat in silence as she scrolled through the dozens of pictures that Patti had shot. Several times she paused and studied an image.

"What do you think?" Patti said to Max, as she stopped scrolling and looked up.

"Nice pics," said Max, still unwilling to offer any explanation. She handed Patti the camera.

"I was watching you. I think you recognized someone on that boat."

Max remained silent.

"Can I see?" asked Courtney, as she reached for the camera. Scrolling through the images, she suddenly stopped and inhaled sharply. The color drained from her face.

Patti grabbed the camera from her and looked at the image she had stopped at. "Someone you know?"

Court's answer was barely audible. "Yes . . . No . . . It can't be."

Visibly shaken, Courtney got up, walked over to the railing, and stood looking out over the Pacific.

Patti faced Max, turning the camera so she could see the picture. "You know who this is?" asked Patti.

Max took the camera from Patti and looked at the image that Court had stopped at. It was one of the man on the smaller boat. He had turned, and Patti had caught his face.

"Edso," whispered Max.

"Edso?" said Patti.

"Yes. Remember? He was the guy who kidnapped Courtney. His yacht burned, and he disappeared with his grandfather."

Patti looked down at the picture again. "I do remember, but I don't think I ever saw him. Wasn't his grandfather some kind of a Nazi or something?"

Max nodded yes.

"Oh, my god. Poor Court." She looked over at Courtney.

"What do you think we should do?"

"I don't know."

CHAPTER 25

A BELL WAS RINGING. What was it? A warning? An alarm? Jack pried his eyes open and looked at the clock next to the bed: 2:00 a.m. The bell rang again. He wasn't dreaming. It was his phone that was ringing. Picking up the phone, he managed to grunt out a "Hello."

"Jack. Are you awake?"

He recognized Max's voice, which was all it took for him to become fully awake. Before he could even form the words necessary, in his mind he was having multiple conversations. Had something happened? Were they safe? Was there an accident? What? Finally his mouth caught up with his imagination.

"Max? Do you have any idea what time it is? Is everything okay?"

"Jack, listen, we're fine. I'm sorry for calling you at this hour, but it's important."

"So, you're all safe."

"Yes. We're fine."

"So what's so important that it couldn't wait for a more civilized hour?"

"I saw him."

"Saw who?"

"Edso. I saw Edso."

Jack said nothing for what seemed an eternity. "You're sure?"

"Patti has pictures. We were on a boat ride around Newport Beach Harbor. I had borrowed some binoculars, and I saw Edso talking to an attractive woman on a huge yacht."

"Slow down, Max. Tell me again what you saw."

He could hear her take a deep breath, and then she repeated the story, this time with more detail.

"Can you send me the pictures Patti took?"

"As soon as she's up."

"Max, be careful. Don't do anything foolish."

"Jack, please have a little faith. He's the last person any of us wants to be anywhere near. I just thought you should know."

"You're right. Thank you for calling me, despite the time."

"I'm sorry. Love you."

"Love you too. Send the pictures."

"I will. Next time I'll call at a better time."

* * *

The phone had also woken Cat. She ambled into Jack's room just as he hung up. Then she jumped up onto the bed. She was purring loudly and pushed her head under Jack's hand, looking to get her ears rubbed.

"Hey, Cat, you won't believe what just happened."

"Mrowh." She continued to insist on having her head rubbed.

"That was Max. She saw Edso."

Cat pulled back from her head rub, sat, and looked at Jack. It was as if she understood exactly what he was telling her.

"Mrowh."

"I know. She's going to send me the photos that Patti took. Then, we'll go see Tom."

"Mrowh."

"Not we as in you and I, but we as in me."

Cat mrowed one more time and then jumped off the bed, leaving Jack alone with his thoughts. Four hours later, when his alarm went off, he was surprised that so much time had passed. Sleep had seemed elusive because of the constant stream of conversations that spun through his head as he processed what Max had told him, but the alarm confirmed that he must have slept.

It took Cat's insistence on breakfast to drive him out of bed. While Cat ate, Jack stood in front of the window looking out over the harbor, sipping a large mug of coffee. What Max had told him seemed so improbable he had begun to wonder if it hadn't all been a bad dream. Still, that was unlikely. He was sure she saw what she said she saw. More to the point, what did it mean? Was Edso merely pursuing another woman, or was it some other sinister plan? That vague idea nagged at him, and knowing Max, Courtney, and Patti, he was worried.

* * *

Shortly after 7:00 a.m., Jack knocked on the door to Tom's office.

"Jack. Come in. What brings you by so early? I've only been here myself for ten minutes."

Without even saying good morning, Jack started telling Tom about Max's phone call.

"She's sure?"

"Yes."

"And you?"

"She's sending me the pictures that Patti took. I have no reason to doubt her. Of course, until I can see for myself, I'm leaving open the possibility that she's wrong. Honestly, I hope she's wrong."

"As soon as you get those pictures, will you forward them to me?"

"Of course. What do you think it could mean?"

"Impossible to say. Like you said, it could be quite innocent. But then again . . ."

Tom grew silent.

CHAPTER 26

AFTER CALLING JACK, Max found sleep hard to come by. She couldn't stop thinking about what she had seen. What was Edso doing there? Was he simply trying to pick up yet another pretty woman? He certainly had the track record for it. Still, considering Courtney's devastating experience, and what little she knew of his troubled past and his wack-job grandfather, it was hard not to think that something more was going on.

Shortly before sunrise, Max gave up trying to sleep and decided to get up. The tile floor was cold, and she shivered. Pulling a blanket off the bed, she wrapped herself in it and went to the kitchen to make a cup of coffee. Hot coffee in hand, she went out onto the patio to watch the arrival of a new day. She snuggled into one of the cushioned chaise lounges on the deck, her blanket pulled close, creating a cocoon of warmth. The aroma of her coffee mingled with the fragrance of the gardens that surrounded the patio. The sky was just beginning to lighten as she took her last sip of coffee before her eyes closed.

The next thing she felt was a hand gently shaking her shoulder. Someone was calling her name. Not fully conscious, she slowly opened her eyes and realized that the sun was now up, though not yet high enough to bathe the patio in sunlight.

"Max," she heard her name again. It was Patti.

"Patti."

"How long have you been out here?"

"I couldn't sleep. I talked to Jack last night after you went to bed."

"He must have loved that, time difference and all."

"Yeah, I didn't think of that. I think it was two o'clock in Rye."

"Ooo, yeah, that's not good."

"I told him about seeing Edso, and I said I'd send him all the pics you took. Can you do that for me?"

"Sure, no problem. I'll do it right now."

As they walked into the cottage, Max still wrapped in her blanket, Courtney was just coming out of the kitchen with a cup of coffee.

"You guys are up early. What's with the blanket?"

"I couldn't sleep so I went out to the patio, where I fell sound asleep. Patti just woke me up," said Max.

"She called Jack last night. I'm going to send him the pictures I took of Edso yesterday," added Patti. She turned and walked toward her room.

"That coffee smells good," said Max.

"I made a whole new pot."

"You're a savior. Court, we need to talk."

After refilling her cup, Max joined Courtney out on the patio.

"I can't believe he's here," Court said. "I couldn't sleep either. Had I known you were out here, I would have bundled up and joined you."

"I can't imagine what you must be feeling."

"I'm not sure what I feel."

"Part of me wants to confront him."

"Me too, but then I'm not sure what I'd say. Maybe we should just forget about him," said Court.

"Now, you know that's not going to happen. How could you just forget that you saw him? Especially since he was obviously hitting on some other woman."

"We don't know that that's what he was doing."

"We don't, but I bet he was. Who do you think she was?"

"I don't know. But maybe we should try to find her and warn her."

"Now there's an idea."

"What's an idea?" Patti walked out onto the patio. "I sent the photos to Jack."

"Thank you," said Max.

"So? What idea were you talking about?"

"We were talking about what to do about Edso. Court suggested that we should try to find the woman on the boat and warn her about him," said Max.

"Bad idea," said Patti. "Very bad idea."

* * *

Sipping his morning coffee, Edso stood on his patio overlooking the harbor. Seeing the *Wonder* leaving her mooring, he swapped his coffee for some powerful binoculars and watched as she steamed toward—then past—him on her way out of the harbor. He didn't see any sign of life on board until just before she began the final right turn out of the harbor, pointing her bow toward Catalina Island. At that moment, Jennifer stepped into view. She walked to the stern rail, leaned on it, and looked precisely in his direction. As before, when she had looked up into the drone's camera, he was certain that she was looking directly at him. Even though he knew this was an impossibility, the thought excited him.

He smiled as he anticipated the lunch date on Catalina Island that he had convinced Jennifer to accept. Last night's gamble had paid off. Taking his boat out to the *M/V Wonder* after spotting her in the harbor had been the right thing to do. As he had come alongside, she had been standing by the rail and seemed genuinely pleased to see him. How fortunate that she had just happened to be on deck enjoying the night! Granted, she had not been pleased enough to invite him on board, which would have been the icing on the cake, but she had agreed to a lunch date out on Catalina Island.

"Baby steps," he told himself. "Soon you'll have her."

Glancing at his watch, he realized that there was no need to hurry. He knew his boat was faster than the *Wonder* and he didn't want to seem too eager, so he picked up his coffee cup from the table, leaving the binoculars in its place, and went inside for breakfast.

CHAPTER 27

AS JACK WALKED BACK TO HIS TRUCK after his visit with Tom, he tried to estimate how long it would be before Patti would send him the photos. With the difference in time zones, he figured that it wouldn't be for another couple of hours. Part of him wanted to go for a run, but the rumble in his stomach reminded him that he had not yet had breakfast.

Parking his truck at Paula's, he realized that in just a few short weeks, parking spots would become much harder to find. The bell on the door to Paula's clingled as Jack pushed it open and walked in. Letting the door close behind him, he stood for a moment and looked around. Several heads immediately turned toward him to see who had just arrived. Since the summer season was still several weeks off, most of the tables were filled by locals. Rye Harbor being such a small town, he knew most of the folks having breakfast.

Beverly waved hello from behind the counter and signaled for him to take one of the empty seats there. As he walked toward her, she placed down a menu and started filling a cup of coffee.

"Good morning, Beverly."

"Morning, Jack. Max still away?"

"She is."

"When'll they be back?"

"About a week."

"They behaving themselves?"

"I can only hope. I talked to Max, and it sounds like they're having a good time."

"I'm sure. Give you a minute?"

"Yeah, sure. That'd be fine."

She walked off, leaving Jack sipping his coffee. The more he thought about what Max had told him, the more concerned he became, not only about Edso's appearance, but also about what Max, Court, and Patti might do.

* * *

Jack pulled into the drive at his apartment but remained in the truck, mulling over his conversations with Max and Tom. Noticing Cat, who was sitting in a sunny spot behind Courtney's cottage, he thought to himself, *"Wouldn't it be nice if life could be as simple as sitting in the sun, chasing bugs, and hunting mice?"*

He finally pulled on the door handle, pushed the door open, and slid out of the cab. As he walked toward the apartment door, Cat sauntered over to greet him.

"Mrowh."

Bending down to scratch her ears, he said, "Well, Cat. What say we go see if Max sent us those pictures?"

"Mrowh." Cat turned away and walked back toward her warm spot, completely unconcerned. He imagined her saying, "No. Not my problem. If you need me, I'll be over there in the sun."

Jack walked up the stairs. With each step his anxiety increased, but he couldn't bring himself to hurry. He wanted to delay for as long as possible what he knew would inevitably be a big problem.

He opened his laptop, and the screen came alive. Clicking on mail, he waited and watched as new emails were loaded. There it was. He saw Patti's name show up in the inbox with the subject "Photos." He paused for another moment, then pressed the key that would answer all his questions.

Click. The first photos were of Max and Courtney climbing on board a small canopy-topped boat. Wine and food had been set on a table in the center of the boat. Max was wearing tan shorts and an emerald green, sleeveless top that gapped open provocatively as they posed for the camera. He hadn't seen that green top before and was unable to take his eyes off of her. He smiled and, for a moment, forgot the reason for looking at the photos in the first place.

Still smiling, he began to scroll through the photos: boats, expensive houses, Courtney sitting by the boat driver, more boats, and more evidence that they were having too much fun. After dozens of images, the first shot of the yacht came up on the screen. Even at a distance, the yacht was impressive.

"M/V Wonder," Jack thought. *"Interesting name for a boat."*

The next few dozen shots were of the boat, but in only one could he see anyone on board. A uniformed crewmember was leaning on the rail, and the person appeared to be watching the girls pass by. The crewmember was partially hidden in the shadows, but he got the impression that it was a woman.

The final dozen pictures were taken from the dock at the conclusion of their cruise. Not yet fully dark, even though the sun had dipped below the horizon, lights from on shore and those of boats in the harbor, all reflecting off the water, created a festive atmosphere. Patti must have changed the lens, because the next sequence of photos of the *M/V Wonder* was shot through a gap between boats in the mooring field. The yacht was now lit up, and the crewmember was now clearly visible. His premonition was correct: it was a woman. Her dark hair was cut short, and he could tell that she was smiling broadly. She was looking down on a smaller boat that anywhere else would have been considered quite sizable. The man in the boat was looking up at her, and they were clearly conversing. As the photo sequence progressed, Jack became increasingly fascinated with her. Something about her seemed familiar. Yet as good as Patti's telephoto lens was, the distance still made it hard to see her clearly enough to determine why.

It wasn't until the final two pictures that Patti caught the man's face. The woman on the yacht was pointing at something, and he had turned his head away from her and looked straight into Patti's camera. Jack couldn't take his eyes off the image on the screen. It was Edso, plain and simple. Jack felt a moment of embarrassment for ever doubting Max.

"You son of a bitch. What are you doing there?"

A chill washed over him as his imagination took over and he briefly considered what Max, Patti, and Courtney might do.

Jack continued to stare at those two pictures of Edso, even after forwarding them to Tom. Something kept gnawing at him, and it wasn't until he stopped focusing on Edso's face that it hit him.

He knew the woman on the yacht. And that scared him even more than the fact that Edso had reappeared.

"Oh, my God," he said under his breath. "Do they know? But surely Max would have said something."

In a near panic now, he clicked back and forth between several of the pictures. *"It is you,"* he thought.

Then, in a soft voice, as if saying it more loudly would make bad things happen, he said, "Sylvie. What are you doing there?"

CHAPTER 28

"DO YOU REALLY THINK THAT'S A GOOD IDEA?" asked Patti.

"She has to be warned," said Courtney.

"But, I mean, I don't think we can just row out to that yacht and tell her that the guy she was talking to last night is a Nazi and a kidnapper."

"Why not?"

"Well, for one thing, we don't have a boat to get out there. Second, if we did get out to the boat, we couldn't just walk on board. They have security systems, and if she wasn't there, or even if she was, we'd probably get arrested."

"So, do you have a better idea?"

"Not really."

Max, who had been silent during this exchange, now spoke up. "If we could catch her on shore, we could talk to her."

"Brilliant! And how do you propose we do that?" said Courtney.

"Sarcasm noted. I don't know. Maybe we could go back to Voyagers and talk to Brad or Andrea. I bet they have a pretty good idea of what is going on in the harbor. Maybe they could call us if they see her going ashore."

"Oh, that's good. We'll just walk into their office and explain that we think the woman on that yacht might be in danger and would they watch it for us and let us know if she leaves the boat."

"When you put it that way—"

"What if . . ." Patti interrupted.

"What if what?" said Max.

"Well, I was thinking that maybe a way to get in touch with her would be to pretend that we are doing a photo essay for a magazine."

Max stared at her.

"That's not half bad," said Max.

"But, aren't most people who have that kind of money pretty private?" said Court. "To do something like that, we'd probably have to jump through all kinds of hoops."

"Still, it might be enough of an excuse to just go out to the yacht and 'knock' on the door," said Max.

"That's dumb," said Court. "I need more coffee."

As soon as she walked off, Max said to Patti, "I think it could work. We can't be from a well-known magazine; that'd be too easy to check. What if we were just from a small town back East, on vacation. We work for the local paper and we are writing about our adventures—you know, things we would never see or do at home."

Patti looked excited. "Ooo, I like it. We'd be like spies or something conning our way in, so we could warn them of grave danger."

By the time Courtney returned, Max and Patti were talking in hushed tones, feverishly hatching a plan.

"Okay, girls. What're you two cooking up?"

"Whatever are you talking about?" said Max, using a fake Southern accent and batting her eyes.

"Cut the crap. Give."

They did, and after an hour of discussion, Court agreed that it might be worth a try. But first, they needed a boat. They agreed that another visit to Brad and Andrea for some local knowledge and a boat was in order.

* * *

Brad wasn't there, and neither was the *M/V Wonder*, but Andrea was. She said, "I saw that yacht leave less than an hour ago,"

"You don't know where they were going, do you?" said Patti.

Andrea shrugged then said, "Why do you want to know?"

Before leaving the cottage, they had agreed to tell Brad and Andrea the truth. Max was the first to speak, and she did her best to explain the situation without sounding too deranged.

"You're kidding?" said Andrea.

"No. That guy really did kidnap me," said Courtney. "He's danger-ous and we just want to warn that woman on board."

"You said he was a Nazi."

"Well, his grandfather definitely was. The jury's still out on Edso, that's his name, but the specifics don't really matter. He's definitely not a nice person, and she needs to be warned."

"Who needs to be warned?"

Max, Patti, and Court all turned at the same time at the sound of Brad's voice.

"Hey, Brad," said Andrea. "You know anything about where that big yacht that was moored across the harbor last night might be going?"

"Why?"

For the second time, Max recounted their story, only this time it was even more abbreviated.

"Seriously?" said Brad. "That's crazy. No, I have no idea where they went, but let me call someone who might."

He disappeared into a back room and closed the door. A few moments later, he returned. "Okay. You were talking about the *Won-der*, right?"

The three friends nodded together.

"Word around the harbor is that they are headed for Catalina, maybe for a few days. My friend had no idea where they might go after that."

He had barely finished speaking when Courtney nearly tackled him with a huge hug. "Thank you, thank you, thank you," she said, without letting go.

"You're welcome, I guess," he said. Max saw his cheeks start to blush.

She finally let go of Brad, and Patti asked, "So, how do we get to Catalina?"

"Simplest is the ferry," said Andrea, "but it's already gone for today. You'll have to wait until tomorrow morning,"

Max's heart dropped. Then she said, "Andrea, Brad, thank you. Ladies, what say we get going? I could really use something to eat."

After handshakes and more hugs, Patti and Max headed for the door.

"Court, you coming?" Max said.

"I'll be right along. Meet you at the car."

"She so wants him," whispered Patti to Max.

Max grabbed Patti's arm and ushered her out the door. As soon as they were outside, Andrea joined them. "He's just saying goodbye."

The look on her face indicated to Max that this was not completely unexpected.

Andrea added, "I'm just going down the street to get some coffee. Good luck, and enjoy your stay here." She walked off, leaving Max and Patti standing in front of the office.

It was a few more minutes before Courtney came out and joined them. Acting as if nothing had happened, she simply said, "Shall we go?"

CHAPTER 29

"SO, WHAT'S THE PLAN?" asked Patti, as they climbed into the car.

"First, we're going to get tickets for tomorrow's ferry to Catalina," said Courtney.

The ferry terminal was located on the opposite side of the harbor on Balboa Peninsula next to the Pavilion. Courtney said little during the drive around the harbor. As they drove slowly down Balboa Boulevard toward the Pavilion, she asked Max to keep a lookout for a place to park.

Just as the cupola on the Pavilion came into view, Max noticed a red Toyota pulling out of a spot. "There!"

Court hit the brakes and yanked the wheel to the right, garnering an angry honk from the car behind. She gave an "I'm sorry" wave as the car went by, and from the back seat, Patti said, "Jesus, Court. You trying to get us killed?"

Courtney ignored her, finished wedging their car into the parking place, and then twisted around to face Patti. "Sorry." Before announcing, "We're here."

"Good job. How lucky was that?" said Max.

She smiled for the first time since leaving Brad at the boat rental. "That is a good omen."

"So what's the plan?" asked Patti. She still sounded a bit shaken.

"Tickets," was Courtney's one-word answer.

"And then?" said Patti.

"And then we'll get going."

"Since we're here, we can't not do a short walk-about," said Max. "I mean, besides the Pavilion on this side, on the other side I've heard the beach is amazing, and there's a huge pier out over the water."

"Okay," acquiesced Courtney. "But if we're going to do this, let's get going."

It was only a short walk to the Pavilion, and it didn't take long to get their tickets for the next day's trip.

"Okay, so now where to?" asked Courtney.

"To the beach and the pier," said Max.

Once outside, Patti spent several minutes taking pictures of the Pavilion; she even convinced a stranger to take one of all three of them in front. Then, photo shoot finished, they began walking back down the street that had led them to the Pavillion. But now, going in the opposite direction it led directly to the Pier on the other side of the peninsula.

Max said, "Did you know that the pier and the Pavilion were both built in the early twentieth century? I read about it in one of those brochures that came with the car."

As they neared the beginning of the pier, where it began to rise, Max saw a beautiful park that led down to the beach. As the pier rose above the sand, she could see in both directions the long, clean expanse of sand.

Reaching the end of the pier, they stood at the rail and looked out over the Pacific at Catalina Island as it rose out of the sea.

"Can you believe that it's twenty-six miles away?" said Court. Then she added, "Isn't that the distance of a marathon."

"It is. Jack and Dave would be impressed that you knew that," said Max. "Imagine, we'll be there tomorrow."

"It looks a lot closer," said Patti. "Kind of like the Isles of Shoals back home, but they're only six miles out."

"It's pretty high and definitely big," said Court. "The person at the ticket booth told me they have buffalo roaming, and each year there's a marathon out there."

Max said, "Enough marathon talk already. This is supposed to be a break from the guys! Anyway, I'm starving. Lunch at the Sherman Garden's again?"

Court nodded, and Patti said, "Sounds great."

* * *

It didn't take too long for the drive back to the gardens. As before, once inside, they were in a refuge of peace and tranquility in stark contrast to the traffic and crowds surrounding it. Seated at the same table as before, a bottle of wine was ordered and while waiting for it to arrive, Patti excused herself and went off on another photo expedition.

"Court, you've been awful quiet today. You okay?" asked Max.

"Honestly, no. Seeing Edso in those pictures really has me spooked."

"I can only imagine," said Max. Then a smile came over her face, "But more importantly, what's going on with this Brad?"

"What? Nothing."

She was beginning to blush so Max pushed a bit more. "Come on Court, I saw the way you were looking at him. He's cute and I think he's interested."

"I don't want to talk about it," said Court, now fully flushed.

Before Max could ask more, their server arrived with the wine. She poured their glasses and asked, "Shall I pour your friend's glass as well?"

"Yes, please," said Max.

After filling all three glasses she said she'd be back to take their orders as soon as their missing friend returned.

Conversation during lunch alternated between the serious, Edso, and the romantic, Brad.

* * *

As promised, Jack sent the pictures to Tom, who spent the next thirty minutes flipping back and forth between them. Finally he stopped and pulled open his desk drawer and took out a business card. After staring at the card for a moment, he dialed the number on the back of the card. A voice answered on the third ring and Tom introduced himself.

"Hello. This is Tom Scott from Rye Harbor, NH. . . . Tom. . . . Yes. I'm the Chief of Police in Rye Harbor. Several months ago we had that incident with the *Vorspiel*."

The conversation was short and as soon as the line went dead, Tom forwarded the two pictures to the email address on the back of the card. As soon as he had done his duty, he sat back in his chair and looked at the pictures again. He felt a bit strange that he hadn't told Jack what he was going to do with the pictures, but it had been made extremely clear to Tom that he was to remain silent.

* * *

"Jack."

"Max." They each said the other's name at the same instant. Then they said "You first," in perfect harmony. Jack paused first to let Max speak.

"You got the pictures? Did you show them to Tom? Isn't Edso a fugitive?"

"Max, slow down. I got the pictures. You're right. It looks like him. Is Courtney all right?"

"She's fine. Tom?"

"Yes, I sent them over to Tom. We got together this afternoon, and he's not sure how much he can do."

"What! What more does he need?"

"He said he needs more proof. Remember he never actually met Edso . . . Max. Stop. You know it's him, Courtney knows it's him. I know it's him, so how about we just cut Tom a little slack. He wouldn't say, but I got the distinct feeling that he was going to do something."

"Jack, that sounds like so much bullshit. I bet Tom knows something."

"Max I'm just relaying to you what he said. Would you feel better if I came out there?"

"No. It's our last week here. I'll be home soon enough."

CHAPTER 30

EDSO PATTED HIS POCKETS ONE LAST TIME, picked up his sea bags, and headed down to his boat. He was ready. Several hours had passed since he had watched the *Wonder* steam out of the harbor and point her bow toward Catalina.

Although it already felt like a hot day, he knew it would be much cooler out on the water. Climbing onboard, be glanced around the boat before opening the door to the cabin. His pre-departure checklist was hanging on the knob to the cabin door. Jorge had checked off all of the items, so Edso knew that the boat was ready to go and he wouldn't have to worry about anything. He unlocked the cabin and felt a rush of cool air. Jorge had left the air conditioning on and Maria, Jorge's wife, left a vase of fresh red California poppies on the table. He smiled at her thoughtfulness and gave the vase a slight push. It didn't move; it was held to the table's surface by a powerful suction cup built into the vase's base.

He tossed his sea bag on the berth then checked in the fridge. As expected, it was fully stocked with chilled wine, and a selection of cheeses, pâtés, and some chocolate-covered strawberries. A fresh baguette was nestled in the small hammock that hung above the counter. On the counter was a small bakery box. He peeked inside and found four chocolate croissants. The ice well in the well-stocked bar was full, and there was plenty more in the freezer. His level of confidence in having a successful date with Jennifer was as high as it could be, especially since Jorge and Maria had taken care of every little detail, as they always did.

He offered a silent thank you to the Network. When he and his grandfather had fled New England, the Network's help had allowed them to quickly and effectively disappear in plain sight. Then it had helped him relocate. Edso wasn't sure exactly how it worked or who was involved, but he had received a call about the house in Newport Beach. To anyone outside the Network, Jorge and Maria were his yard man and domestic. In reality they provided so much more, starting with security.

Edso left the cabin. Just as he was about to begin his departure routine, he saw Jorge standing on the dock. Jorge had already coiled up the shore power cord and was starting to remove the spring lines from the boat. He nodded at Jorge and gave him the thumbs up. Jorge returned the gesture, and Edso pressed, one at a time, the start button for each engine. Each roared to life and then settled into a satisfying soft purr. Jorge passed each of the dock lines to Edso and then stood by on the dock as Edso nursed *Verführer* away from the shore and into the channel.

Slowly, he motored down the channel toward the harbor's entrance. Out of habit, he glanced back several times at the Coast Guard and Harbor Patrol Stations. Both were conveniently located close to his home. When he had first moved in, their proximity concerned him, but Jorge had assured him that there were reasons for that and he should not be concerned. Over time, as he settled in, he appreciated the irony of hiding out right under their noses.

Clear of the harbor, he made the turn and pressed his throttles forward, feeling the power he had unleashed as his boat rapidly rose up to a plane. In no time, *Verführer* was cruising at over twenty knots, heading straight toward Catalina Island and Avalon Harbor. He engaged the autopilot and sat back for the ride, his only job to keep watch for other vessels that might be making the same run. The ocean was calm and flat, so there was little pounding or wasted energy as he flew toward his destination.

* * *

As the *M/V Wonder* picked up her assigned mooring, Sylvie was called to the bridge.

"He's on the way."

"Good."

"One more thing. I got a weird call this morning. Apparently some woman who's here on vacation recognized Edso from somewhere or other. She sent a photo of him to her boyfriend. The boyfriend then took it to a cop, who called it in to us."

"What? Say that again."

He repeated the story.

"Were you told anything else?"

"No. Seems a bit strange, doesn't it, but I got the sense that you'd know what it was about. Do you?"

Torn between feelings of confusion and alarm, Sylvie just stared at him for a moment. She scrolled through her memory for anything that might fit his words.

Suddenly, what seemed the most unlikely explanation flashed through her head. *"It can't be,"* she thought to herself. *"I've got to call Ken. This could seriously complicate things."*

CHAPTER 31

WITH EVERY PASSING MINUTE, Santa Catalina Island rose higher and higher out of the sea. As boat traffic to and from the island began to increase, Edso disengaged the autopilot and resumed manual control for the rest of the trip. Gradually, the features of the island became more and more clear, and soon the town of Avalon came into sight.

As he approached the harbor, he gradually cut his speed. When he reached the mouth of the harbor, he spotted the *Wonder* on a mooring. The procedure was to wait for a Harbor Patrol boat to come to him and assign a mooring. Rather than motoring over to the *Wonder* while he waited, he picked up his binoculars to see if he could locate Jennifer. He didn't, and neither did he have much time to look, because the Harbor Patrol boat arrived almost immediately. He was directed to a mooring about midpoint between Jennifer and the shore. As soon as he was securely moored, he called for a Shore Boat. He'd ask the captain to take him to the *Wonder*, pick up Jennifer, and then take them both ashore.

* * *

There was a knock on the door. "Sylvie, he's just arrived. The Harbor Patrol is directing him to his mooring."

"Thanks, I'll be right up," she said through the closed door.

She spoke rapidly into the phone. "Thank you, Ken. I owe you big time."

Ending the call, she quickly took off her uniform and pulled out a pair of wide leg culotte pants with a bright flowered pattern and a white, short sleeved buttoned shirt. After a quick glance in the mirror, she took off her bra and studied her reflection. She had to decide bra or no bra. She smiled and for a moment closed her eyes, gently sliding her hands over her breasts, trying to imagine what it would feel like to have

Jack's hands touching her.

"Stop it!" the voice in her head shouted. *"He'll be here shortly. Now, get yourself dressed and up on deck."*

The bra she had been wearing would not do, so she pulled several out of the drawer and considered her options. A lacy white one was the obvious choice. It was cut to reveal maximum cleavage, and the support was not so great as to inhibit any movement. Dressed, and with one more look in the mirror at the completed outfit, she assessed the result. With her back to the mirror, and twisting from side to side in front of the mirror, she strained to see the view from behind. Ultimately, she deemed it acceptable and sure to get his attention. Facing the mirror again, she twisted right and left. Then, after unbuttoning another button on her shirt, she twisted right and left again. Satisfied that the shirt gaped the right amount when she moved in certain ways, she pulled on a pair of black Chinese cloth shoes, left her quarters, and headed topsides. As a final touch, when Sylvie emerged on the aft deck, she put on a pair of sunglasses. They were dark and large, an homage to the late fifties and early sixties, and they would effectively hide her eyes from his.

Looking across the water, she could see the Shore Boat approaching. Edso was sitting in the back of the boat, one leg crossed over the other, leaning back, arms resting on the back of the seat. He appeared to be both relaxed and confident. She gave a small wave of acknowledgement—not too enthusiastic, but enough. He smiled and waved back.

She stepped down onto the *Wonder*'s aft swim platform to board the Shore Boat as it came alongside. Edso was smiling broadly as he offered his hand to her for boarding. Ignoring his gallant gesture, she gracefully stepped over the rail of the Shore Boat like she had done it a thousand times before.

"Hello, Jennifer, you look amazing."

"Thank you." She smiled, knowing in that moment he would be putty in her hands.

They sat down on the seat in the back of the boat, and immediately the Shore Boat pulled away from the *Wonder*.

From behind those glasses, she saw him give a quick glance at his watch before asking, "What would you like to do?"

"I'm good with whatever you would like to do."

"Have you ever been here before?"

"Believe it or not, no."

"Perfect. Hungry?"

"Not at the moment."

"Then we'll start with a helicopter tour of the island."

"You're kidding."

"I'm not. First, we'll tour the island, then we'll have lunch, and after that we can see where the rest of the day takes us. You game?"

"Game."

"It's just a short taxi ride to the Airport in the Sky. I've arranged for a helicopter to pick us up there."

The Shore Boat arrived at the dock, and they disembarked. A cab was waiting, and they headed right for the airport.

"You think of everything, don't you?"

"I try, but I do confess, I did have some help."

* * *

"I had no idea this island was so rugged," said Jennifer, as they soared above it.

"It really is amazing, isn't it?"

As the helicopter touched down back at the airport, Edso asked, "You ready for lunch?"

"I am."

"Then I know just the place to go."

"Where?"

"You'll see."

The same taxi that had brought them to the airport was waiting, and as soon as they were settled inside, without any directions from Edso, they drove off. The ride back to Avalon seemed faster than the ride to the airport. Driving through Avalon, they began to ascend again, and soon Jennifer saw a sign that said *Welcome to Mt. Ada.*

"What's this?" asked Jennifer.

"It used to be the home of William and Ada Wrigley, but now it is a small boutique hotel."

They were shown to a table on the patio that overlooked Avalon and the island.

"Oh, my god," said Jennifer. "This is incredible."

"I thought you might like it."

It was a long and leisurely lunch that lasted until well after all the other dining guests were gone.

"Edso, this has been a wonderful day, but I must get back to the *Wonder*. I still have work to do."

For a split second, she could see the disappointment wash over his face, but he hid it well. "I understand. But first, can I at least convince you to come out to my boat for a sundowner? The sunset is quite beautiful from out on the water. You won't be disappointed, I'm sure."

CHAPTER 32

SHE HESITATED A MOMENT before accepting his invitation, reiterating that she would stay only until the sun had set. She didn't want to let on that she would have been disappointed had he not invited her back to his boat.

"Welcome aboard," said Edso, as he helped her step out of the Shore Boat and onto his. "I realize that she isn't as grand as the *Wonder*, but she is quite comfortable and has all the necessities."

Sylvie looked around. Everything was gleaming white, immaculately cared for, and she couldn't help but wonder if he did all the work himself or if he had help.

"*Verführer—Seducer. That figures*," she thought, then said, "She's lovely."

He stared into her eyes and said, "Thank you for joining me today." While he opened the door to the cabin, she slipped off her shoes and tossed them under the helmsman's seat. As he disappeared below, she did a quick walk around the boat, noting what was where. He returned with two glasses in hand, condensation frosting the outside and leaving small drips on the floor.

"Thank you," she said, taking the glass he held out to her.

Noting her bare feet, he paused and smiled. "I was going to say that you should make yourself at home, but I can see that you already have. Prosecco?"

"Thank you for inviting me," she replied.

He lifted his glass in her direction, "Here's to many more such days."

She touched the rim of her glass to his, saying nothing, but instead lowering her eyes demurely, then looking back up at him she slowly touched her glass to her lips and took a taste. A drop of icy condensation fell onto her foot, causing her to flinch.

"Mmmm, this is good," she said.

"It is," agreed Edso, as he took a more aggressive sip. "I'll be right back," he said, and turned and went back below.

Curious, she followed him to the cabin door and looked in. His back was to her and he was squatting down in front of what had to be the refrigerator, from which he was removing small tubs and packages and putting them up on the counter above.

"Can I help?" she asked.

He looked back to where she was standing. "No, I've got it, but thank you."

She stepped into the cabin as he stood. "You sure?"

Edso turned and looked at her. "I'm just getting us something to go with our wine." Then, pointing at the vase of red poppies, he said, "Actually, could you take those outside?"

"What pretty flowers."

"They are," he agreed, before adding, "California's state flower is actually the golden poppy, but Maria always gets the red variety."

"Pretty," she said, picking up the vase. She was about to exit the cabin when he said, "After you take that out, could you come back in for something else?"

When she twisted around to look at him, her shirt gaped open, as she knew it would, and she had no doubt that he was enjoying the show.

"Sure. Let me put these flowers and my wine down."

When she returned, he had already set out on a wooden board with several varieties of cheese and what looked like some pâté. Without looking back he said, "Grab that baguette and a knife, will you?"

He nodded his head to the right, indicating where she could find the knife. Unlike on the *Wonder,* where the galley alone was larger than his entire boat, things were pretty close, and as she reached for the knife, she brushed up against him. He looked over and smiled.

"Sorry," she said.

"Nothing to be sorry about."

She took the baguette and the knife and moved outside, while he followed with the wooden board he had been setting up.

The sun was still above the island, but a shadow was creeping down the mountain toward Avalon. With each passing minute, as the sun got closer to the mountains, the sky began to change colors, and the waters in the harbor began to reflect those colors. Edso refilled their glasses, took the knife, and began to cut the baguette into thin slices. Next, he cut small slices from each of the cheeses and the pâté.

"Here, try this," he said, as he placed both some cheese and pâté on one of the bread slices.

She accepted his offering and took a bite. "Ooo, this is delicious."

Few words were exchanged during the next half hour as the sun dipped behind the island and the sky seemed to expand as it changed from the brilliant blue of the day into the pinks, reds, and oranges of the sunset. The water's surface began to reflect both the colors of the sky and the lights of the town as they began to come on.

"It's beautiful," she said.

"I'm sure it's nothing that you haven't seen a million times before, considering that you live on the *Wonder*."

"True, but it's not quite the same. There, I am always on call. Often I never get to see the sunset because I'm below preparing a meal or something."

"I hadn't thought of it that way."

Shortly after, the colors of the sunset were nearly gone, quickly being replaced by a dark gunmetal blue sky. Only a few stars were visible, and the moon had yet to rise. Lights were on in the town, and their reflections danced on the water's surface.

She broke the silence. "What do you do, Edso?"

He paused, gently swirling the wine in his glass. Then he took a sip, swallowing slowly.

"I'm not exactly sure how to best answer that. If you're asking if I have a job, the answer is no. If you're asking what I do with my time, I do many things."

"Do you have any family?"

"I don't. My parents died when I was young, and I was raised by my grandfather, who I just found out died recently."

"I'm so sorry. You said, *found out?* Does that mean you had lost touch with one another?"

"I guess. In so many words."

"How did you lose contact, if I may ask?"

"It's a long, complicated story that you certainly don't want to hear."

"Oh, but I do. He must have been quite important to you."

"Another time," he said quietly.

"Tomorrow?" she said, deliberately injecting a hopeful note into her voice.

"Maybe. How long will you be here?"

"Do you mean here-here, or here as in this general area?"

"Both."

"As far as I know, the *Wonder* is going to be spending the next few months between San Diego and Los Angeles. So yes, we'll be in the general area, and I expect at least one more night in this harbor."

"So, may I see you tomorrow?"

She looked at her watch. "I've got to get going."

"You didn't answer my question."

"No, I didn't, did I? Give me your number, and we'll see."

CHAPTER 33

"HOW'D IT GO?"

"Fine," said Sylvie. "He briefly mentioned his grandfather."

"That's a start. Anything new we can use?"

"Not really, pretty much what we already know. He wants to see me again."

"When?"

"Tomorrow. He gave me his number. I said I'd call him."

"And will you?"

"Yes."

* * *

The *Catalina Flyer* was well less than half full. Boarding had begun at 8:30 a.m., an hour after the three friends had locked the car and walked to the terminal. After boarding, they settled in on the second deck. The front half of it was enclosed, but aft it was open. Today, Courtney was the fashionista. The weather had been unusually warm, even for California, so she was wearing a white V-necked, sleeveless blouse over tan linen slacks. Her outfit was pulled together with not-too-high wedged sandals and a wide-brimmed floppy straw hat. Large-framed, dark glasses helped hide her face. Max wore cargo shorts, a plaid shirt with a ball cap, wraparound sunglasses, and running sneakers. Patti was wearing fashionably torn jeans, Converse Chuck Taylors, and a Ben's Place t-shirt. With a faded plaid shirt tied around her waist, a black backpack with gray trim on her back, and her camera slung around her neck, she looked every bit the part of a freelance photographer.

"Hey, look over here," said Patti, as she pointed her camera at her two friends. They were standing at the starboard rail, watching as the

Flyer moved away from the dock.

Max hammed it up, but Courtney only turned her head briefly. Ever since she had seen Edso talking to that woman on the yacht, she had been morose, and Max was worried about her. Now, facing the task of finding that woman and warning her, clearly Courtney was in no mood for levity. Max hoped that after the warning was delivered, they could finally get the vacation back on track.

Max nudged Patti. "Let's give her some space."

They moved to the port side of the boat.

"Look at those houses," said Patti. "Can you imagine what they must be worth?"

Max shook her head. "I can't."

As the *Flyer* made the turn out of the harbor and pointed her bows toward Catalina, the sound of the engines changed in pitch as the *Flyer* began to live up to her name. In no time at all, she was at full speed and seemed to be just kissing the water's surface.

"Hey, guys." It was Courtney. She had come up from behind to Max and Patti. "I'm sorry. Can we talk?"

"Of course," said Max.

"Over there, okay?" said Court.

Without answering, they moved to an area where no one else was sitting.

"You okay?" asked Max.

"Honestly, not really. Am I nuts?"

Max resisted the impulse to give a really sarcastic answer.

"No. You're not nuts," she said seriously. Then, after a pause, she added, "But we're totally crazy for going along with you."

That broke the tension, and they all laughed.

"Thanks."

"So, tell me again how we're going to do this?" said Patti.

"Well, first," Courtney said, "I'm sure that the yacht she's on will be easy to find. Then, we'll just have to find a ride out to it and hope that someone, preferably her, is on board and that they'll—she'll—talk to us."

"Just like that?" Patti asked.

"Just like that."

"Do you still want me to be a photo journalist?"

"I've been thinking about that. If we say that we're from an actual publication, or even a made-up one, that might be too easy to check, so I was thinking about this instead. Let's say that I'm an author working on a lifestyle book. Max, you're my secretary, and Patti, you're a photographer friend. In the book I'm working on, there's a yacht, and theirs is just what I was imagining, so can we talk to them about it?"

"That's pretty ballsy," said Max.

"You got a better idea?"

"Not really."

"Then it's settled."

There was no further debate, and for the rest of the trip they stood by the rail and watched as the island rapidly grew larger. Boat traffic around them continued to increase, and as Avalon came into sight, the sound of the engines changed as the *Flyer* began to slow.

"Look, there she is," said Max, pointing at the *M/V Wonder*.

"You really think we can pull this off?" asked Patti one more time.

Courtney said, "If we don't try, we'll never know."

The *Flyer* moved slowly toward the dock, and the passengers began to gather by the rail for disembarking. Courtney, Max, and Patti waited until most of the other passengers had walked off the boat before they followed.

"Well, here we are," said Max, as they stepped off the gangway. The air was warm and the sun bright.

"I read that there are water taxis called Shore Boats," Courtney said. "People use them to get to and from boats in the harbor. They're located at the Green Pleasure Pier. I don't think it's too far to walk. Ready?"

Because of the sun, the walk seemed much longer than Max had anticipated. When they passed by a golf cart rental place, Patti said, "Look. We could rent a golf cart. Wouldn't that be fun?"

"We're not renting a golf cart," Courtney snapped, wiping a bead of sweat from her forehead. "Come on, the water taxi place is down that pier that's just ahead."

Max felt like this would be a good time to nip the growing tension in the bud. "I could use an iced coffee." She pointed to Scoops Ice Cream shop.

"I could go for an ice cream," chimed in Patti.

Courtney frowned and kept on walking, but Max and Patti went in and placed their orders. Courtney came back and joined them just as Max was taking her first sip of a large iced coffee and Patti was digging in to a small bowl of ice cream.

"Hey, Court, you want something? This cool mint gelato is to die for," said Patti.

"I really don't feel like a whole ice cream." Then her expression softened, and she said, "But, may I have a taste of yours?"

"Of course."

"Oh, my. That's good."

Five minutes later, Court purchased a bottle of water, and they continued on toward the Shore Boats.

CHAPTER 34

EDSO WAS IN NO HURRY TO START HIS DAY. Lying awake in his berth in the early hours that followed the dawn, he listened to the sounds of the harbor. Occasionally, he closed his eyes and thought about the previous day. Jennifer was exactly the kind of woman he enjoyed. Strong. Independent. Mysterious. But, would she call? His mood alternated between confident and worried. When his phone did ring, his heart began to pound.

Out of habit, he checked his watch. It was not yet eight. He sat up and reached for his phone. The number on the screen was unfamiliar, but he was certain it was her. Surprised that she was calling so early, he decided that he wouldn't answer until after the fourth ring. It was better not to seem too eager, and he smiled as he quickly considered the possibilities of what her eagerness could mean.

As the phone rang a second time, he took a deep breath and exhaled slowly in an attempt to quiet his beating heart. When the phone rang for a third time, he took another deep breath and again exhaled slowly. His hand felt as if it was shaking like a leaf in a storm. He held it out and looked at it. It was rock steady. The phone rang for the fourth time, and he picked it up.

"Good morning."

"Edso."

It wasn't her. It was a man's voice, and for a split second he wasn't sure who it was.

"Yes," he said, trying not to sound flustered.

"How's Catalina?"

"It's fine."

The voice was familiar, but he was still dealing with the fact that it wasn't her.

"We need to talk."

"Giles?" he said, finally identifying the voice.

"Yes. How was your day with Jennifer?"

"It was fine. But how did you know—"

"I'm sending a boat out for you. Be ready in an hour."

The phone went dead.

Edso sat on the edge of his berth and stared at the phone in his hand. *"What just happened?"* he thought.

"Shit," he said, as he tossed the phone on the bed.

Even though he was now fully awake, he needed coffee. After brewing a pot, he poured a cup and stepped out of the cabin. The sun was out, as he knew it would be. The sky was nearly cloud free. The fleet of Shore Boats were busy going back and forth between the island and moored boats. He could see the *Wonder* sitting placidly in the outer reaches of the mooring field.

"What does Giles want?"

He had no idea, but he was pretty certain that it couldn't be good, especially since all he wanted to do today was see Jennifer.

At nine, just as the *Catalina Flyer* was arriving, a Shore Boat pulled up alongside Edso's boat. The captain of the Shore Boat silently motioned him aboard. The silence continued as Edso climbed in, and as soon as he was seated, the captain shifted into forward and drove toward the pier. As he laid the boat alongside, he spoke for the first time.

"At the end of the pier, a taxi is waiting for you."

When Edso approached the taxi, the driver opened the door wordlessly. Before climbing in, Edso looked around and saw the first wave of new arrivals from the *Catalina Flyer* walking toward them. Then, as soon as he was inside, the door clicked shut and the driver quickly walked around and climbed in. Without a word, he started the engine, shifted the car into forward, and pulled away from the curb.

"Where are we going?" asked Edso.

His answer was a stony silence.

"Fine, suit yourself," Edso mumbled under his breath.

Thirty-five minutes later, the taxi came to a stop at the Chimes Tower. Edso was pretty sure that he hadn't taken the most direct route.

As Edso stepped out of the car, the driver pointed toward the tower. Not sure what he was expected to do, he looked back at the driver, who pointed again. Next to the tower, he saw stairs that led down the hillside. Cautiously, he walked to the stairs, and after a moment's hesitation, he walked slowly down the steps.

He didn't see anyone as he reached the bottom of the stairs. Then, stepping around the corner, he saw Giles Endroit standing by the wall looking out over Avalon.

Without turning, Giles said, "Good morning. Thank you for coming."

"I didn't have much choice."

Giles turned and faced him, giving a slight shrug of his shoulders.

"What's with all this cloak and dagger stuff?"

"You remember what we talked about when we met on my boat?"

Edso nodded.

"Good. You must always assume that you are being watched. I came here to warn you, and understand, I wouldn't be here if the threat wasn't credible."

"Warn me of what? What threat?"

"One of our many sources has information that you may be in danger."

"In danger of what? By whom?"

"We don't have any details yet, but we suspect that it may have to do with that mess back East. A phone call was made by the police chief in Rye Harbor reporting that you had been seen."

"Seen?"

"Yes. Apparently someone got pictures of you talking to that woman on the yacht *Wonder*."

"Who?"

"We don't know yet, but whoever took the pictures sent them to the Rye Harbor Police Department. We expect to know more shortly."

For clarity, Edso repeated what he had just been told. "So, you're telling me that some random person out here got photos of me and knew to send them to the Rye Harbor Police Department. That's crazy!"

"It would seem so. Any idea who could have done that?"

"No idea. I didn't think anyone knew I was here."

"Someone obviously does, so be careful."

"I will. But, tell me, why didn't you just call me with this information?"

"I could have, but would you have paid as much attention to my warning had I just called? I suspect not. After all, you are pursuing that young woman, and I don't want you to get careless. Besides, meeting face to face is more secure."

"I see your point. So, what now?"

"Just be careful. It looks like you had a nice day yesterday."

"Stop. You were spying on me, too?"

"I wouldn't exactly call it spying. Let's just say that we have eyes everywhere and that we protect our assets."

"So, are you now going to tell me that she's off limits?"

"No, nothing of the sort. For the moment, we haven't found out anything about her that would cause concern. She looks to be a quite pleasant diversion. If I were younger, I'd probably be going after her myself."

After what Giles had just told him, Edso shouldn't have been surprised, but hearing it just made it seem so much more odious. He stared at Giles. "Are we through?"

Then, without waiting for an answer, he turned and began walking away.

As he turned the corner, he heard Giles say, "Remember what I said. Be careful. We'll be in touch."

CHAPTER 35

NOT TOO FAR PAST THE ICE CREAM SHOP, the three friends found the pier where the water taxis tied up. Max pointed at a small one with a sign that said *Shore Boat*.

Courtney walked up to the captain and asked, "Are you available?"

"Sure am. Come on aboard."

Courtney, Max, and Patti climbed into the water taxi while the skipper began releasing the dock lines. As soon as the boat was free, the skipper stepped back on board, pushing off at the same time. Shifting into forward, she guided the taxi from the dock and headed out into the mooring field. "Where to?"

"That big yacht out there," said Courtney, pointing at the *Wonder*.

"Friends of yours?"

"Not really."

"Are they expecting you?"

"Probably not."

Max sensed the captain's unease and quickly started the story. "We're on vacation from New Hampshire." She nodded toward Courtney and said, "She's working on a lifestyle book. I'm her secretary, and we've brought our photographer. When we saw that yacht, we thought it might be worth trying to get a completely unrehearsed, impromptu interview."

This additional information seemed to relax the captain a bit. Still, she shook her head. "That's not a good idea."

"Why do you say that?"

"People like that are mostly pretty quiet. And private. They often look at strangers as threats."

"I guess that makes sense. But if you don't want to be in the spotlight, then why have a yacht so enormous it draws attention to yourself?"

The Shore Boat captain shrugged. Max was just relieved that she hadn't insisted on taking them back to shore.

Then the captain said, "I see where you're coming from, but I think you're a bit naive. I see this sort of people all the time. Most are pretty nice as long as there is a clear limit to the exposure. For example, when they are on board my boat and I'm taking them ashore, they can be really nice and talkative, almost normal. However, as soon as I drop them off, the barriers go back up, and it's as if I don't exist. And then, some of the others are just complete dickheads. No matter what."

"Point taken," said Max.

"Can you at least just drive slowly around the yacht?" asked Courtney. "Maybe we can take some notes that way."

"Sure."

Maintaining a safe distance, they slowly cruised around the yacht. For the next few moments, the only sound was Patti's camera as she continued to document their adventure.

"I'm not sure there's anyone left on board," the captain said.

"Why do you say that?" asked Max.

"Just a feeling. Earlier this morning, I brought two people from the *Wonder* ashore."

Courtney turned away from looking at the yacht and faced the captain. "Two? Who?"

"No idea, but the way they talked, I'd bet on crew."

"Did they say where they were going?"

"Not really. The man did say he had to speak to the harbormaster. She said something about going to do some shopping for her family."

"Let's go back," said Court, as they finished their circumnavigation of the *M/V Wonder*.

Then the captain added, "The more I think about it, the more certain I am she definitely was crew."

Max said, "Why?"

"She said that she was looking forward to sitting down in a cafe and having someone wait on *her* for a change."

"She say which café by any chance?" asked Max.

"Sorry. Maybe you could try the Hotel Metropole. They have a marketplace complex with some nice cafés." She paused, then added, "Good luck. I don't think you'll have much luck with your interview even if you do find her. Most of those people really just want to be left alone."

"You didn't happen to hear her name, did you?" asked Courtney.

"I think it was Jennifer." She paused a moment, then said, "Yes, I'm sure. He called her Jennifer."

CHAPTER 36

BACK ON SHORE, Courtney grabbed a map and brochure of the area. As they walked along, Max read over the brochure, while Patti continued her documentation of their adventure.

"Hey, Court, what if we get lucky and find her?" asked Max.

"You know what. We're going to introduce ourselves and tell her what we know. No point in that whole lifestyle book fabrication anymore."

"But what if she doesn't want to listen?"

"She'll listen."

"And you know this how?"

"I just do."

The walk from the pier to the marketplace took less than ten minutes. Max was relieved to find that a breeze had cooled things down.

"This is too awesome!" Patti said, as they stepped off the street and into the marketplace.

Ahead was a wide, meandering, cobbled pathway that cut through the block and ended at the Hotel Metropole. Small shops lined the path, and many had their wares displayed outside on racks. The spots that were serving food had tables and chairs outside. Tropical plants in large pots and planted gardens with trees that formed a natural canopy made Max feel like she was stepping into another place and time.

Courtney said, "This is exactly the kind of place where I'd go if I wanted to get away. How about you two take that side and I'll take this side, and we'll meet in the hotel?"

"And what happens if one of us finds her?" asked Max.

"Depends on the situation. I think it would be best if all of us confront her together rather than individually."

"I agree, so text the others if you see her?

"If you can. If you can't, then you'll just have to wing it and follow her until it becomes possible."

"And if we get to the hotel without finding her?" said Patti.

"Then we'll figure something else out," said Courtney.

"Okay then, let's get going," said Patti.

CHAPTER 37

JACK WENT FOR A RUN but found no relief for his inner turmoil. *"Should I tell Max about Sylvie or not?"* He still was debating the issue an hour later as he followed Cat up the apartment stairs. He stopped dead in his tracks when a male voice said, "Hello, Jack."

He stood frozen for another few seconds as adrenaline flooded his body and his heart pounded. It wasn't Tom's voice, Dave was at work, and he wasn't expecting anyone else. He crouched, prepared for the worst.

"Jack," the voice said again.

This time he realized that it sounded familiar. Where had he heard that voice before? He looked up, straining to see as much of his place as possible without exposing himself too much.

"Who's there?" he said, trying to sound as normal as possible.

Then Ken came into his sight.

"Ken?"

"Hey, Jack. How've you been?"

Jack was still feeling the effects of the adrenaline rush, but now as he began to relax, he almost felt weak in the knees.

"You scared the shit out of me. What are you doing here?" he said, as he walked up the last few steps. Ken's smile appeared to be on the edge of laughter.

"Sorry. Have a good run?"

"I did."

They moved toward each other for a quick bro-hug.

"You didn't answer my question," said Jack.

"Want a beer? I picked some up on the way over. You like ESB if I remember correctly." Ken walked over to the refrigerator, opened the door, and pulled out two beers without waiting for Jack's answer.

"Uh, sure. So, again, what're you doing here?" Jack repeated. That first rush of relief that the intruder wasn't a threat was exchanged for wariness. After Courtney's rescue, the sinking of *Vorspiel* and the subsequent disappearance of Edso and his grandfather, there was no reason to expect that they would ever meet again. He knew what Ken was capable of, and he knew, or rather sort of knew, who he worked with— and now Ken wasn't answering his question.

"Here." He handed Jack a beer, extended his bottle toward Jack's, and touched Jack's bottle, making a soft clink in a one-sided gesture. No formal toast was offered, but the implication was clear.

"Thanks. So, now are you going to tell me what this unexpected visit is all about?"

Ken walked over to the window and looked out. Jack didn't move.

"I got a call from Sylvie," Ken said, with his back to Jack.

"Really?" said Jack, trying to sound surprised. He had suspected as much.

"But, I'm sure you already figured that out."

Jack took a long, slow sip of his beer. He had a bad feeling about what was coming next and hoped he was mistaken.

"I understand that Max and her friends are out in California."

"How'd you know that?"

Ken turned and answered with a look that said, *"You know I know, and how isn't important."*

Jack said, "Right."

"We know about Edso, and we're afraid that your friends may do something stupid."

"We. Who's we?" pressed Jack. "And stupid like what?"

"Like try to make contact with him, which wouldn't be a good idea."

"I agree."

"You have any idea what they might do?"

"I don't. I only spoke with Max yesterday. She told me about seeing Edso, and she sent me some photos that Patti took. It was definitely him all right. But she didn't say anything about what they might do."

"Nothing?"

"Nothing. And I told her to be careful. Tell me, what's Sylvie doing there?"

"What are you talking about?" Ken said. "She called me, that's all."

"Cut the crap, Ken. You've all but said she's out there. And I saw her. In the photos with Edso. Thankfully, I don't think Max noticed."

"Tell me about those pictures."

"You first. Why's Sylvie out there?"

After several minutes of stony silence, Ken relented. "All right. She's involved in an investigation of someone we've been after for a very long time."

"Edso? Or someone else?"

Jack could see that Ken was wrestling with how much to tell Jack.

"Our main target isn't Edso. But—tangentially—we believe he's involved."

"Go on," said Jack.

"As I'm sure you remember, his grandfather was an ex-Nazi and an avowed white supremacist."

Jack nodded. "Yes."

"So, the night when we rescued Courtney and his yacht burned and sank?"

"What about it?"

"I let Edso and his grandfather escape that night. But you knew that, didn't you?"

"I didn't know it for sure, but I suspected it. Why did you let them get away?"

"It's complicated. Suffice it to say that we wanted bigger fish and saw Otto and Edso as a way to go up the food chain."

"And how'd that work out?"

Ken shrugged. "Honestly, I still think that it was the right thing to do. But somehow they managed to disappear."

"Until now."

"Until now."

"You still haven't told me who you're really after."

"Giles Endroit. Perhaps you also remember him?"

"Giles Endroit?" said Jack. "You're kidding. Tom brought up this name a couple of weeks ago. Endroit showed up in a security bulletin. Tom insisted it wasn't serious."

Ken shook his head. "I can see how Tom might have had that impression, but let me tell you, it is serious. We think he's near the top of the white supremacist group that Edso's grandfather had ties to."

"That's just great."

"It gets better. He's out in the same area as Edso—and the girls. When you talk with Max, *tell her to stay away from them.*"

"I'll do my best," said Jack. "But those three have minds of their own."

Ken sighed and looked at his watch. "I was afraid you'd say that. Look, I've got to go. Keep in touch. Here's my number, but don't call unless it's an emergency."

CHAPTER 38

"COME ON, PATTI," said Max, giving her friend's arm a slight tug.

"See you in a bit, Court," said Patti, as she let Max pull her away.

"So, how'll we do this?" asked Patti.

"I think we should go in and out of every store. And to minimize the chance of missing her, one of us should go in while the other waits outside."

"Fine by me," said Patti. "I'll start there." She pointed at Sunkissed. Before Max could respond, she headed for the store's entrance.

"Sure," said Max under her breath. She sat down on a bench under the shade of a tree and settled in to watch the parade of shoppers hurrying from shop to shop. She knew that Patti would be a while because the shop was filled with the work of local artisans.

Now that she was alone, she could feel the day's tension spreading through her muscles. She needed to hear Jack's voice. Calculating the time difference, she pulled out her phone. *He should be home unless he's out running.*"

* * *

Ten minutes after Ken left, Jack swallowed the last of his beer and dropped the bottle into the recycling bin. It had been a little early for a beer, but considering what Ken had just told him, it was certainly appreciated.

"Well, Cat, wasn't that interesting?"

"Mrowh."

"I know. And you're right. We should be worrying about what Max and company will do."

Before Cat could answer, the phone rang.

"Jack, I'm so glad I caught you."

"Max, what's up? You're not calling for bail money, I hope."

She giggled. "No, nothing like that."

"So, what?"

"Well, we're in this really neat outdoor mall. Patti is in kind of an artsy shop, I'm sitting on a bench outside, under a tree, waiting for her, and Courtney is off looking for Jennifer, well, really, Patti is too, and I just needed to hear your voice."

It took a moment after she stopped for this rapid string of information to register with Jack. He got the parts about a mall and the shopping and Patti in an artsy shop. It was the parts about Courtney and Jennifer that he was having trouble understanding.

"Slow down, Max. Who's Jennifer? And why are Courtney and Patti looking for her?"

The line went silent. He could hear Max taking a deep breath, so he knew they hadn't lost the connection. "Max?"

"Yes."

"I'm not sure I got all of that. What did you say about Courtney and Patti?"

There was a moment of silence. Then she said, "They're looking for Jennifer."

"And who is Jennifer? Do I know her?"

"I don't think so. We actually haven't met her yet."

"You haven't met her, and Courtney and Patti are out looking for her."

"Ye . . . es." The way she strung out her answer, he knew she was hiding something.

"Max, start again, and this time tell me everything."

She did, and when she got to the part about Jennifer, a chill washed over him.

Silence fell, and then Max said, "Jack, what?"

"I assume you haven't found this Jennifer yet."

"No."

"I don't think you want to find her. In fact, I want you all to stop looking."

"Jack. Stop. You're scaring me. Why don't we want to find her? We only want to warn her about Edso."

"I understand that, and it's quite nice of you, but . . ."

"But what?"

"I just had a visit from Ken."

"Ken?" she paused, then repeated his name, obviously trying to understand why that name sounded familiar. "Ken! Courtney's rescue Ken?"

"The same."

"What's he doing there?"

"Sylvie sent him to see me."

"Sylvie! Jack, now who's not telling the whole story?"

"I'm sorry, Max. You don't know who this Jennifer is, do you?"

"She's part of the crew on that fancy yacht. We saw Edso talking to her."

"Max. Jennifer is Sylvie."

The phone went silent.

"Max . . . Max. Talk to me Max."

"What do you mean Jennifer is Sylvie?"

"When you sent me those pictures, I realized who she was. It took a bit, because I was so focused on him, and she's clearly using another disguise, but when I stopped looking at him and looked at her, I knew it was her. That's why Ken came to see me. He confirmed it in so many words."

"And when were you going to tell me all this?"

"I was about to call you when you called me. Ken just left."

"I've got to find Courtney."

"Max, listen to me. Don't hang up. You need to forget about finding Sylvie. Or Jennifer. Or whoever she's posing as these days. You also need to avoid Edso, if he is still around. I don't have all the details, but something bad is going on that you do not want to be anywhere near."

"I've got to go. I'll call you later. Bye, Jack."

The line went dead.

"Shit!" said Jack. He slammed his hand down on the counter. It startled Cat so badly, she went skittering off. A moment later, he saw her peeking from around the corner.

"I'm sorry, Cat. I didn't mean to frighten you. I just have a really bad feeling about what Max, Courtney, and Patti are up to."

CHAPTER 39

MAX'S HAND WAS SHAKING as she looked at her phone. She started to send a text to Courtney, but her fingers kept hitting the wrong keys so she had to keep starting over.

"She wasn't there, but look what I found." Patti was standing in front of Max. She was smiling and had a brightly wrapped package in one hand.

Max put her phone down, and Patti's smile froze.

"Max," Patti said, "you look awful. Is it the heat? Are you okay?"

"I just got off the phone with Jack."

"He's alright, isn't he? Wait, is it Dave?"

"No, no. They're fine."

"So, what's wrong?"

"We've got to find Court and get out of here."

"What do you mean?"

"This Jennifer we're looking for—her name's not Jennifer."

Patti sat down next to Max. "So what is it?"

"Sylvie."

"Your Sylvie? No—she can't be. We would have known. You would have known."

"Well, apparently we didn't. Plus, she was pretty far away. Jack figured it out based on those photos you took, and Ken just paid him a visit and confirmed it."

"Ken?"

"You know, that guy who helped rescue Courtney."

"Oh, yeah." She paused, then asked, "And why'd he visit Jack?"

Patti began looking through the cache of pictures in her camera.

"I'm not all that clear on it myself, but it has to do with Edso. According to Ken, he's tied in with a super-secret white supremacist group run by a guy named Giles Endroit."

"Who?" She looked up from her camera.

"Giles Endroit. He's a novelist. I've been rereading one of his books. Jack and I met him in Belize. Later, though, we found out that he was involved in those shady real estate deals in Rye Harbor a few years back. Remember that? June was in on it."

"Of course I remember that." She looked down at her camera again. "We thought Courtney might lose Ben's. So, what's this white supremacist stuff about?"

"I don't really know, but it doesn't really surprise me. Edso's grandfather was a Nazi. After we rescued Courtney, they both disappeared."

"That's right, I remember," said Patti, still looking at her camera.

"Come on," said Max, standing up. "We've got to find Court A-S-A-P."

"Wait. I found it."

"Found what?"

"That picture I sent to Jack. Look."

Max took the camera from her friend and looked at the image. "*How did I miss that?*" she thought. "Come on, we've got to find Court."

Quickly they searched in every shop—without success.

Reaching the end of the marketplace, Patti said, "Where'd she go?"

"I have no idea. Let's backtrack. You take that side and I'll take this one," said Max.

"See you at the end."

When Max came back out of the first shop, she paused for a moment. Then she heard a familiar voice behind her. "Max. We need to talk."

Max spun around and found herself facing her original quarry. She sucked in her breath while her heart began to pound in her chest. Yes, her hair was a different color and style, but it was Sylvie all right.

A thousand questions formed in Max's mind, but her voice remained frozen. Finally she choked out, "Where's Court?"

"She's fine."

"What have you done with her?"

"Shhh! Keep it down. Smile and look like we're old friends. Follow me."

"I'm not going anywhere with you. Where's Court?"

"Max. Please. We need to talk."

"Where's Court?" Max repeated her question. "I'm not moving until you tell me."

"Fine. She's in that spa. I had the girl at the desk tell Courtney that I'm getting a massage, and now she's waiting for me to come out."

Max looked over at the spa.

"Max. You'll have to trust me. She's in there. Now, will you please come with me?"

Max's resolve to find Court was weakening. After what Jack had told her, her curiosity about what Sylvie had to say was winning out.

"Come on, Max," Sylvie said softly.

Max relented as Sylvie took her elbow and guided her toward the Hotel Metropole.

After they stepped into the hotel, Sylvie led her past the reception desk. "This corner is relatively private. No one should bother us here."

Max quickly looked around, barely taking in the luxurious surroundings. "Okay. I'm here. What's going on? What's with this Jennifer character?"

Sylvie ignored the questions. "It's good to see you, Max. How's Jack?" Her tone was relaxed.

Max wasn't buying it. "You didn't answer my questions."

"There's no need to be unpleasant, Max."

Max simply glowered at her.

"Max, there's not a lot I can tell you, but here's what you need to know. Edso may be the key to bringing down some very unsavory characters. It has taken a long time to find him and create the right scenario that would draw him in."

"And that's why you're on that yacht, masquerading as Jennifer?"

"Yes. Now, can I ask you something?"

"Yes."

"How did you find out about me?"

"I just talked with Jack. Ken told him."

"I see. Men like Edso thrive on being able to exercise power over others. It's often subtle and may not even be noticed, it may come across as charm, but it is a form of dominance, none the less. The *Wonder* reminds him of his grandfather's yacht and his many conquests."

"Like Courtney."

"Yes. And others. My being on the crew of the *Wonder* is beginning to pay off. We—I'm exploiting his weakness."

"And to think we were trying to warn you about him."

"Aww, that's sweet. You're a good person, Max. However, one wrong move and you guys could blow our whole operation. You and your friends have to forget that you saw him—or me."

"I don't see how that's possible."

"I'm sure you'll figure something out."

"You know I'll have to tell Courtney and Patti."

"I'd have been surprised if you didn't. Look Max, we've known each other for quite a while now. I know that deep down, you do believe me."

"Here's what I do believe, Sylvie: whenever you show up, there's some kind of trouble."

Sylvie gave a slight shrug of her shoulder. "But, have I ever caused you harm?"

Max stared at her in silence for a moment. Then she also shrugged. "So, what do you want me to do?"

"I've already told you. Please. Get your friends away from here. Tell them whatever you need to, but get them away. The three of you must not get involved in any of this."

The intensity with which she said these words made them even more compelling.

Max paused for a moment to consider her response. Finally, she said, "I can't make any promises, but I'll try. We'll be going home in a few days. Then you can do your thing with no interference from us."

"I guess that's all I can ask. Thank you." Then Sylvie stood up. "It was good to see you, Max. Give me a minute before you leave. Say hi to Jack for me."

Max gritted her teeth and nodded. Sylvie had almost gained Max's sympathy—until she added that bit about Jack.

CHAPTER 40

MAX WATCHED SYLVIE WALK AWAY and then, in an instant, she was gone.

"Say hi to Jack for me," she repeated in her head. She could feel her anger rising. Under her breath, she said to herself, "She's gone. She doesn't want you around. Forget about her. Find Court and Patti, and get the hell out of here."

Max headed for the spa where Courtney supposedly believed that she waiting for Jennifer.

"Max!" A breathless Patti was rushing to catch up with her. "You okay? You look like you saw a ghost."

Max just shook her head.

"What happened?"

She grabbed Patti's hand and started walking to the spa. "Come on, we have to go."

"Max!"

"What?"

"What's wrong with you?"

"I just talked with her."

"You what?"

"I just saw her. Jennifer. We have to get Court and get away from here."

Patti hurried to keep up. "Max. What's going on?"

"I'll try to explain as soon as we get Court. She's in there," she said, pointing toward the spa.

As they walked into the spa, Courtney looked up from the magazine she was reading.

"Court, come on, we've got to go," said Max.

Courtney lowered the magazine into her lap. "She's in here getting a massage. We're not going anywhere until we talk to her."

"They lied to you. She's not in here. I just talked with her over in the hotel."

Courtney looked confused.

"Now come on. I'll explain as soon as we get away from here."

She looked at Patti. "Do you know what's going on?"

Patti just shrugged.

"Max, this had better be good," said Courtney.

As soon as she stood up, Max headed for the door. Her friends trailed behind as she quickly walked back toward the ferry.

Finally, Courtney caught up and grabbed her arm. "Okay Max, we're away. Now what?"

Max looked around nervously. "We get back on the ferry."

"But it doesn't leave for a few hours," protested Patti.

"Max, you're not making any sense. What's going on?" said Court. "What say we go find a place for lunch where we can talk?"

"How about there?" said Patti, pointing to the Bluewater Grill.

Max relented. Sylvie hadn't said anything about avoiding public places.

"Fine. Lunch it is."

* * *

Sylvie watched as Max left the hotel, collected Patti, and then headed to the spa to get Courtney. "Good job, Max," she whispered under her breath. She waited another five minutes after they were out of sight and then pulled out her phone.

"Edso?"

"I was wondering if you'd call."

"I had some things to take care of this morning. Are you up for some lunch?" The way she asked that last question left it open to several interpretations, and she was confident that he would take the bait.

"I am. What do you have in mind?"

"Meet me at the Hotel Metropole. How about in an hour, and we'll see?"

CHAPTER 41

"THIS IS NICE," said Patti, as they followed the hostess to a table near the railing overlooking the harbor. Patti's chair had the best view of the water. She pointed her camera in several directions, first toward the harbor, then back at her two friends, as she began to document their lunch.

At Courtney's request, the server brought them each a glass a wine and then wrote down their lunch orders. When he left, Courtney reached for her glass, took a sip, and said, "Okay, Max. What's going on?"

"I don't know exactly."

"What do you mean you don't know? You said you talked to Jennifer."

"I did, or rather, she talked to me."

"So?"

Max took a long swallow of wine. Putting the glass down, she looked at her two friends for a long moment. Then, slowly, she said, "Jennifer is Sylvie."

The silence at the table in that moment was profound. Seagulls still cried, a boat's engine roared to life, laughter and conversations continued at other tables, but Max was certain her friends never heard any of it.

"What!" said Courtney.

Patti pointed her camera at her. *Kchick, kchick* went the shutter on the camera.

"Patti! Stop," she said, before fixing her eyes on Max. "You're telling me that Jennifer and Sylvie are one and the same person."

Patti now trained her camera on Max. *Kchick, kchick.* As stunning as that news was, Patti seemed more interested in capturing their reactions to the news and each other.

Max took another sip of her wine. "Yes."

Putting the glass down, she looked at Courtney, and said, "So . . . she says she's been trying to make contact with Edso for quite some time. Apparently, he's tied in with some unsavory characters—her words—and she seems to think that Edso might be the key to bringing them down. She's afraid that if we hang around and he sees us, he'll get spooked."

At that moment, their server delivered their lunches and asked, "More wine?"

Court said tersely, "Yes, that would be nice."

Their server nodded, and as he turned, Courtney said, "Could you bring us a whole bottle this time?"

"Certainly. I'll be right back," he said, and quickly retreated from the table.

"Okay, Max, you have a lot to explain."

Max held up a hand to indicate that they should wait. They picked at their meals quietly until after the server returned with the bottle of wine.

As soon as it was served, Courtney broke the silence. "I'm listening."

While Max told her story, Patti continued to record her two friends' reactions.

Suddenly, the slow, measured *kchick, kchick* of Patti's camera became a rapid-fire stream of clicks and whirs.

"Patti! Stop!" Max said.

She didn't. She kept shooting and, slowly, began to pan away from her two friends.

When she finally stopped shooting, Max said, "What was so interesting out there?"

"I think I just saw Edso getting off a boat." She frowned. "But now I've lost him again."

Max quickly turned and stared out at the harbor. There were so many boats on the moorings, she wasn't sure where to look.

Courtney said, "Where did he go?"

Patti pointed again. "If it was really him, then he had someone pick him up and bring him to shore."

Max's thoughts turned back to Sylvie's warning to stay away. No matter how she felt about Sylvie, she knew her top priority was to keep Courtney safe.

"Well, not much we can do about it now," said Max. "Plus, we don't want to miss the ferry. Let's ask for the bill and get out of here."

When Courtney started to protest, Max kicked Patti's leg under the table.

To her relief, Patti seemed to get the message. "Max is right," she said. "There's really nothing else we can do."

Patti stood up, pushed back her chair, grabbed her backpack, and said, "Let's go."

"Okay, okay," said Courtney grudgingly. Then she stood and joined her friends for the walk back to the ferry terminal.

* * *

Edso looked out at the *Wonder* and gave a small prayer of thanks that she had called. After his meeting with Giles, he needed the distraction. Now all he had to do was wait for an hour. He placed a call for a Shore Boat to pick him up in forty-five minutes.

His stomach rumbled. The cup of coffee he had swigged down before his meeting with Giles had worn off long ago. He brewed another cup of coffee, grabbed one of the chocolate croissants, and stepped back outside.

Before he had time to take a sip, a helicopter swooped down over the harbor and passed low over his boat. Even though the sun blinded him, in his mind he was certain that Giles was in that helicopter heading back to the *Gendroit*. With a shiver, he recalled Giles' ominous words: "We have eyes everywhere, and we protect our assets."

This declaration reminded him of Otto. His grandfather had been so passionate in his steadfast belief that the Third Reich was alive and well and would rise again someday, Edso had always kept his doubts to himself. Now, with those words spoken by Giles, he found himself reassessing all that had happened in the previous few days, from the mysterious note from the law firm to the impressive technological capabilities he had witnessed on Giles' yacht. He thought back to the way he and his grandfather escaped from the East Coast and the help they had received to set up new lives.

His thoughts were interrupted by the sound of a motor from a passing Shore Boat. It wasn't the one he had ordered, but the reminder was enough. Time to leave these disturbing thoughts behind and get ready for lunch.

CHAPTER 42

WHEN EDSO WALKED INTO THE LOBBY of the Metropole, he didn't see Jennifer. He was about to ask for her at the desk when he sensed a presence behind him. He turned.

Where yesterday she was in brightly colored wide legged coulotte pants and a blouse, today she was wearing some skin-tight jeans that had been fashionably slashed, and a loose, white James Dean t-shirt that did not hide the fact that it was all she had on. She was wearing straw sandals and had slung a small pocketbook over her shoulder. Its long strap crossed over her chest, further emphasizing her form.

He sucked in his breath and remained silent for a moment as he tried to compose himself. "Jennifer, there you are. I was about to ask if they had seen you."

"Well, now you don't need to. Glad you were free. I have the rest of the day off. In fact, I don't have to be back on board the *Wonder* until we leave."

"And when is that?"

"Tomorrow," she said, with a sly smile.

He could feel his heart starting to beat faster. It was exactly what he had hoped to hear, and he smiled.

"Are you hungry?" he asked.

"Starved."

"Then let's start with lunch. I know the perfect place."

"Where?"

"Let me surprise you."

He gently touched her elbow. "Come on," he said, as he motioned toward the entrance to the marketplace.

Sylvie, concerned that Max may have been unsuccessful in getting her friends to leave, didn't want any surprises, so she walked slowly, stopping frequently in front of the different shops.

Finally, they stepped out onto the street, and she asked, "Where to?"

"Patience," he gently chided, his confidence growing. "This way."

Together they walked side by side down Crescent Street toward the Green Pleasure Pier.

"Are we going out to your boat again?" she asked.

He just smiled. "Maybe after lunch."

"In that case, where are we going?"

"I told you, patience," was his reply. He said that with a smile, but underneath she thought she detected a slight edge in his voice. *"Control issues?"* she thought.

After they walked a bit further, he finally announced, "Here we are."

They were standing outside the El Galleon. "Have you ever eaten here before?" he asked.

"No. You?"

"Yes. It's been here forever, and the food is terrific."

She readjusted the strap on her pocketbook, revealing the tantalizing shape of her breasts once again.

"Can't wait."

* * *

All the way to the El Galleon, Sylvie had been relieved that there was no sign of Max and company. *"Thank you, Max. I owe you one,"* she thought.

"You sit here so you can look out," said Edso, as he pulled out a chair for her.

"Thank you," said Sylvie. She took her seat, and Edso sat opposite her with his back to the street.

He smiled and she smiled back. "This is lovely," she said, careful not to give away her true motivation.

"I'm glad you approve."

The waitress chose that moment to introduce herself and welcome them to the restaurant. "May I bring you something to drink?"

She allowed Edso to take the lead, "Yes. Thank you. How about two of your margaritas, and a grilled jumbo artichoke."

As soon as he finished ordering, the waitress turned from the table and walked off.

"I know I didn't ask, but does that sound okay?"

"Yes, fine. I've just never had a grilled jumbo artichoke. How large do they grow?"

He chuckled. "It's a house specialty, trust me."

She gave him her best "I trust you" smile and said, "I had a wonderful time yesterday."

"I did, too."

"But you know, yesterday, we didn't really talk much."

He looked a little puzzled.

"I'm sorry, that came out wrong. We talked, almost nonstop. What I meant was, we mostly did what I call 'first date talk.' You know, 'Have you been there? Have you ever done this, or that?' That kind of stuff. So, as much as I kind of know you, I really have no idea who you are. Looking at you, I'd assume you are well off, but you said that you don't really have a job. How does that work?" She was probing, trying to see what would get a reaction.

He didn't answer her question. Instead he said, "It *was* a great first date, but really I saw it more as a second, or maybe a third. First we met in San Diego; then we met the other night in Newport Beach when I came out to the *Wonder* to see you."

"True enough, but those encounters don't count as dates. Still, they beg the question, what are you after?"

The bluntness of the question and the way she asked it clearly took him off guard. He sat back and looked hard at her. Then he smiled, leaned forward, and said, "Perfect."

"Perfect?"

"Yes, perfect. When I first saw you in San Diego and you told me not to loiter around the *Wonder*, you were so sure of yourself, so confident, and the way you totally dismissed me, I knew I had to see you again. So, the simple answer to your question is, I am after *you.*"

"And what makes you think that you'll be successful?"

"You called me."

She smiled. "Well, if you are so sure that you'll be successful, then you really must tell me more about yourself."

"I will," he said, "but let's enjoy our lunch first."

The grilled jumbo artichoke was served and devoured, and they washed it down with another round of drinks. Just as they finished ordering their main lunch, Sylvie saw Max, Courtney, and Patti passing by on the other side of the street. They were looking straight ahead and walking with purpose. Her eyes flicked down at her watch, and she realized that they must be on the way to the ferry. A wave of relief washed over her. She was grateful that Edso still had his back to the street.

"You okay?" Edso's question brought her back to the present.

"Yes, why?"

"For a second, it seemed like you were somewhere else."

"No, I'm fine. I think those margaritas are beginning to hit me."

CHAPTER 43

OVER DESSERT, Sylvie raised her line of questions again. "It must have been difficult growing up with only your grandfather for family," she began.

There was a long pause before he responded. In a low voice he said, "Yes and no."

She remained silent, allowing her silence to frame the question for more information.

"I'll try to explain. He lived on a yacht, not unlike the *Wonder*. I guess that's why I was standing on the dock looking at her when I first met you. She brought back many memories. He always sent me away to boarding schools. During my primary years, I rarely ever lived on the yacht. I don't think my grandfather really knew what to do with me. I saw more of the crew than I saw him."

"What was the name of the yacht?" she interrupted.

He paused. "*Vorspiel*. Why do you ask?"

She shrugged, and then added, "That's German, isn't it?"

"Yes."

Before he could say more, she added, "Does it mean what I think it means?"

Now it was his turn. "What do you think it means?"

She looked directly into his eyes and held them in her gaze. Then, at that moment when her gaze began to feel uncomfortable, she said slowly, in a low voice, "Foreplay."

Just as she had intended, it seemed to ignite his imagination. Based on his leering expression, it had produced the desired reaction.

"So, you know German," he said, neither confirming nor denying her answer.

"Some. But you were telling me about your childhood when I

interrupted."

It was as if she had dumped a bucket of cold water on his head. He frowned and said, "So I was. As I got older, he was more welcoming, and on school holidays, we traveled. During those trips, he taught me about the ways of the world—things that I didn't learn in school. Real-world stuff, not theoretical academic studies."

"I bet when you got older, you took full advantage of the yacht with women."

His face turned a soft pink, wordlessly answering her.

"When we first met, you told me that your grandfather had died and the yacht was lost in a fire. What happened?"

Before he could answer, the waitress returned to the table. She picked up their empty dessert plates and asked, "More coffee?"

Sylvie shook her head, and Edso said, "Thank you, no, just the check."

As soon as the waitress was away from the table, Sylvie asked, "Where do you live now?"

By his reaction, she could see that the question had taken him by surprise.

He didn't answer. Instead, he said, "What say we go out to my boat and watch the sunset? Mind you, she's not as grand as the *Wonder*."

She understood that her questions were hitting too close to home. He obviously needed to control each situation and felt that being on his boat would allow him to do this.

She nodded. "I'd like that," she said.

* * *

Less than thirty minutes later, they were standing in Edso's boat watching the Shore Boat motor away.

"*Verführer—Seducer. Why doesn't that surprise me?*" she thought. "*How did I miss that yesterday? This may prove easier than expected.*"

Edso turned, stepped up into the helm area, and unlocked the cabin door before disappearing below. Sylvie didn't follow him into the cabin, but rather climbed into the helmsman's seat. To starboard, it was more bench than single seat so two could sit side by side. A full suite of electronics complemented the two sets of instruments, one for each engine. To port, she saw another seat for guests. The helm was surrounded by clear plastic panels that were held in place by zippers. Above was a flying bridge from which the yacht could also be controlled.

She was still sitting there looking out when he emerged from below. "Jennifer."

She turned to see him standing in the companionway with two glasses of red wine in hand. He offered one to her. Sliding sideways, she patted the seat, indicating that he should sit next to her. Then she reached out and took a glass from him.

"Thank you," she said, with a smile.

He slid into the seat. It was close, making it impossible for them not to touch.

She said, "This is nice," deliberatly not indicating whether she was referring to the boat or their close proximity. She added, "On *Wonder*, I'm just a passenger. Sitting here, I can see how the captain would almost feel at one with the boat. It must be exhilarating to control that much power."

He pressed his thigh against hers and smiled.

"It is. I'd like to show you some time," he said.

She didn't reply. Instead, she slowly sipped her wine and looked straight ahead.

"What are you thinking about?" he asked.

"Nothing . . . well, actually, I was thinking how difficult it must have been for you to grow up without any family."

"I had family—my grandfather."

"Yes, but I meant real family, not someone who shipped you off to schools and camps until you were nearly an adult."

"There are many kinds of families."

"I'm sorry. I didn't mean to judge."

"You're forgiven."

She turned and looked into his eyes, thinking, *"You are so mine."*

"Show me the rest of the boat?" she asked.

"I thought you'd never ask." His expression reflected his antici-pated success.

He led the way down from the helm station, offering his hand to her as she descended the steps. Then, without letting go of her hand, he guided her into the cabin.

To port and aft was a day head. Forward of that was the galley, with stove, oven, microwave, refrigerator, and freezer. Straight ahead there was an open door, and inside she could see a large bed. To starboard and forward was another nav station with all the requisite electronics, but she noted that there was no way to drive the boat from there. It had to be done either from their earlier seated position or from the flying bridge above that. Aft of the nav station was a settee and table, with bookshelves and a wine rack behind.

"This is very nice," she said.

"Certainly nothing like the *Wonder*, but for my needs, she's per-fect."

Edso turned to her, lifted his glass, and said, "Well, here's to the rest of the day."

She returned the gesture, put her glass down, and said, "I'd like for you to do something for me."

"Oh? What?" To her amusement, he did not look prepared for what she said next.

"Stand over there. And don't move."

She motioned toward a spot in front of the bed. She kept her voice soft and silky smooth, but added a firmness to it that demanded com-pliance. His face reflected both surprise and curiosity at her request, but he complied. He put his wine down and then moved to the spot where she had directed him.

The sun was about to disappear behind the island, and as its final rays shone into the cabin, he lifted his hand against the blinding rays.

"I said *don't move*. Put your hand down."

He looked both puzzled and surprised, but he complied. Then she moved to the center of the doorway. She knew that by blocking the blinding sun she would become a silhouette, adding to the mystery.

CHAPTER 44

HE LOOKED MESMERIZED as he watched the silhouette of her arms rising up, pulling her shirt over her head, and then dropping it onto the floor. She heard him suck in his breath.

The sun's light was fading fast as it dipped below the island, and the cabin became increasingly bathed in shadow. She made slow, deliberate movements to make it obvious that she was slipping out of her jeans. She heard him release his held breath and start to move, so she cut her voice through the silence.

"Stop. I told you not to move." This time she removed the soft silkiness from her tone, making it very clear that this command was not to be disobeyed. She knew from his turbulent history that at some deep level, he was used to taking orders.

She reached behind and pulled the cabin door closed, further deepening the gloom in the cabin. "I want you to take your clothes off," she commanded.

He was now no more than a shadow, and she could hear his rapid breathing as he began to strip. When he started to say something, she broke the silence again. "Quiet. You are not to make a sound."

He obeyed, exactly as she had expected him to.

Slowly, she walked toward him. The closer she came to him, the more clearly she could hear his breathing. Stepping closer, she felt the warmth radiating off his body. Inhaling deeply, she caught the faintest hint of a scent she did not recognize, but she found it intoxicating. As she reveled in his scent she leaned in to whisper in his ear. Her breasts pressed lightly against his chest, and she felt him shiver. "Remain perfectly still."

She began to slowly circle him, her fingers tracing a path over his abdomen, around his side, and across his buttocks. She was certain that she could hear his heart pounding as his breathing alternated between shallow panting and held breath. She stopped and stood behind him. Slowly she slipped out of her panties, and even without touching him, she could feel him trembling.

Then, ever so slowly, she leaned into him, wrapped her arms around him, and pulled herself tight against him. As she gently kissed his shoulder, barely grazing the skin, her hands began to explore his body.

Then, without warning, she pulled away, walked around to face him, and pushed him down onto the bed, knowing full well that in that moment, all restraint and inhibitions would cease to exist.

* * *

Some time later, they were lying next to each other in the bed. Edso looked both spent and satisfied.

Sylvie said, "So. You were going to tell me more about your grandfather, how his yacht was destroyed, and where you live."

"What?"

"Your grandfather? His yacht?"

He remained silent.

"Come on, any man who would name his yacht *Vorspiel*—there has to be a good story there."

She turned on her side, her head resting on one arm. She looked him in the eyes and draped a leg over him as she began drawing small circles with her other hand on his stomach. He shivered, and she looked down and saw him stir.

She smiled and looked back into his eyes. "So, are you going to tell me?"

"There isn't much else to tell. My grandfather was a complicated man."

It was obvious that he didn't want to talk, so she increased the pressure.

"How so?"

Edso paused and turned his head toward her. "You're not going to let it go, are you?"

She smiled slightly and gave him a barely perceptible shake of the head. "No."

Edso caved. Turning his head back, he talked to the ceiling. "All right, I surrender, but under protest."

"Duly noted."

"Remember, I told you that my grandfather was a complicated man. During World War II, he served in the German army. He never talked much about it, but I always had a feeling that the war never ended for him. It was never clear to me exactly where he got his money from, and I learned at an early age that it was not a subject he would talk about. On *Vorspiel,* the crew was divided into two groups, and they rarely interacted with each other. The first group was the regular crew who made the yacht function. You know—chef, stewards, deck hands. Those were the people I mostly associated with, but they changed frequently. The people in the second group never changed. It was almost as if they were permanent passengers, because they rarely did anything to help with the running of the boat. In fact, I don't know what they did."

"What about the boat's name?"

"No idea. I never asked, but knowing my grandfather, it did have significance."

"How did *Vorspiel* get destroyed?" she said softly, tracing circles with her fingers on his stomach again.

Edso moaned and looked back at the ceiling. "We were on the East Coast, staying in a marina in New Hampshire. I was involved with a woman—"

She interrupted. "So I was right. You did use the yacht for getting women."

He ignored her comment and went on. "She turned out to be a bit of a nut, and I believe that she set the fire."

"Really," said Sylvie, knowing that this was pure bullshit. "And that's how you ended up out here?"

"Yeah. My grandfather was destroyed by the loss of his yacht. He wanted to get as far away as possible."

"Did she end up in jail?"

"I don't know. I'm not even sure she was ever arrested."

"But you said that she had set the fire."

"No, I didn't. I said I believe that she did. I'm not sure that the authorities believed it."

"That's crazy."

"It is."

"Can I ask you one more thing?" She knew that by now she was pressing her luck, but she still hoped he'd finally slip and reveal the truth.

"Go ahead," he said. She was pleased to detect a hint of resignation in his voice.

"When we first met in San Diego, what were you doing wandering around the docks?"

He turned his head toward her, and this time she saw the tension spread across his face. *"Have I gone too far?"* she wondered.

"I had just learned of my grandfather's passing, and seeing those yachts brought back many memories. I was just wandering around. No real reason."

She smiled as if satisfied with his answer, and she saw his face relax.

"He's good," thought Sylvie. *"Another lie. What else are you hiding, and who was on that gray yacht?"*

CHAPTER 45

"STAY THE NIGHT," he said, as she began to dress.

"I can't. I may be off duty until tomorrow, but I still have responsibilities."

The disappointment in his face was palpable.

"When can I see you again?"

"I'll call you. I'm not sure where we're going after leaving here."

"I hope you *will* call. I can meet you anywhere, anytime."

"You know, you never did tell me where you live. What if I want to surprise you?"

She already knew his address, but it was important that he tell her, and it was one piece of information she had not yet elicited from him. She caught a slight hesitation before he answered.

"Newport Beach, overlooking the entrance to the harbor. I'll write it down for you."

He got up from the bed, still naked, and brushed past her and into the salon. She watched him as he passed and smiled. Following him, she saw him at the nav station writing on a pad of paper.

"Here." He handed it to her.

"Thank you," she said with a smile, and she gave him a kiss on the cheek. "You should put some pants on before I have to ravage you again."

"That could be fun."

"Some other time; I do have to go." she said.

With her hand on the latch for the door, he said, "Give me a minute. I'll call for a Shore Boat and come out to say good-bye."

He turned and went below while she turned the latch and stepped out into the cockpit.

The sun had fully set. The harbor's inky surface now was a jumble of shadows and the reflected lights of Avalon. Some of the boats in the harbor had lights on inside and looked cozy and inviting. Others were dark shapes that bobbed in the gentle swell, and far out, at the outermost edge of the harbor, where it met the sea, sat the *Wonder* in all her lit glory.

"Oh," she said, as she turned and found him standing behind her. "You startled me. I didn't hear you come out."

"Sorry. A Shore Boat is on its way to come pick you up."

"Thank you."

There was an awkward moment of silence. Then he said, "Here comes your ride."

She glanced around, then turned back to face him and leaned in, her lips next to his ear. She whispered, "I had a *wonderful* time. I'll call."

She could feel him coming to life, but the Shore Boat's arrival interrupted the moment, and she gave him a quick kiss on the cheek as she pulled away and turned to board her ride. Just as the Shore Boat began to pull away, he called out, "When?"

She simply waved as the distance between them increased. It didn't take long for her to lose sight of him as the Shore Boat wove its way through the many anchored boats on the way out to the *Wonder.*

* * *

Edso retreated inside the cabin. He smiled, proud of the fact that his initial reaction to her had been correct. He didn't know when he'd see her again, but he was certain that he would. After all, she had said that she'd surprise him.

"Oh, Jennifer, what could you possibly do to top today?"

Then, just as he began to pull the cabin door shut, he thought he could hear a soft, whirring sound. He looked back, but he couldn't see anything, and the sound was gone. With a bit of a nervous giggle, he went inside and pulled the door shut. He said to himself, "Nah, it couldn't be Eva. No way."

Still, in the back of his mind, he remembered what Giles had said about having eyes everywhere. Then the memory of how his grandfather had filmed him and Courtney flashed through his head.

"No way," he said again. Then he flopped onto the bed and closed his eyes.

CHAPTER 46

THE CAPTAIN WAS WAITING for Sylvie as she stepped out of the Shore Boat and back onto the *Wonder*. "So, how'd it go?"

"Fine. Only one little hiccup, but I took care of it."

"What?"

"Turns out Max, Courtney, and Patti are out here on vacation. Quite by chance they saw Edso when he came out to the *Wonder* in Newport Beach Harbor. They came out here to warn me—well, to warn Jennifer—about him. Can you believe it? That's what Ken called me about: the fact that they know he's here. Fortunately, I got to Max first and convinced her that they should leave and forget about Edso., but she now knows that I'm Jennifer."

"And?"

"She seemed to take me seriously, and they did leave on the ferry this afternoon."

"You think they're gone?"

"I can only hope."

"You don't sound totally convinced."

Sylvie didn't answer his question. Instead, she said, "I asked Edso about his grandfather and the loss of his yacht. He's a good storyteller and an even better liar. He gave me a believable cock-and-bull story about what happened to the yacht. Had I not known what actually happened, I would have totally bought it."

"And Giles?"

"I asked Edso why he was on the docks in San Diego, but he said he was just aimlessly wandering about, reminiscing about his grandfather, who he had just found out had recently died. He said the *Wonder* reminded him of his grandfather's yacht."

"And, of course, then he couldn't resist you."

"Of course. I'll call him in a day or two, as soon as I'm sure that Max and her friends are back on the East Coast. Listen, I need to get some sleep. I'm tired."

As she started to turn to leave, he said, "I know you have his phone number. Did you find out where he lives?"

She pulled a piece of paper out of her pocket. "Right here."

"Excellent. Goodnight. We're leaving tonight and heading to Del Ray Landing in LA. See you in the morning."

"Goodnight."

CHAPTER 47

ON THE MAINLAND, Max, Patti, and Courtney were sitting around the fire pit, eating another delicious takeout meal from Taco Loco and discussing the woes of the world. The strings of small white lights that lined the perimeter of the deck and filled the trees were on, giving the entire yard a festive air.

So far, they had successfully managed to dance around the subject of Edso and Sylvie—and to work their way through most of the pitcher of margaritas. Suddenly, Max giggled.

"What?" said Courtney.

The question made Max giggle harder.

"Max!" she said. "It's been a rough day. What's so funny?"

Max took a deep breath and put down her taco. "I'm sorry. I just realized that Sylvie is like that whack-a-mole game in the arcades on Hampton Beach. Every time I hit the critter on the head and she disappears, she pops up again somewhere else."

Courtney's face began to brighten.

Max caught it. She tried to stifle her own smile, but failed miserably and the two friends began to laugh.

"Hey, what's so funny?" said Patti, having just returned from the bathroom.

"Nothing," said Max.

"You're laughing pretty hard for nothing," she said, sitting down across from her friends.

Courtney looked at her and said, "Max was just comparing Sylvie to a wack-a-mole game."

"I love that game!" Patti said. She belched, and all three laughed harder.

Then a shadow passed over Courtney's face again. "Max, tell me again what Sylvie said about using Edso to get at someone else."

"You mean the 'unsavory characters,' as she put it."

"Yeah, Who do you think she's after?"

"She didn't say any more than that. I don't know, and I really don't care. As long as she stays away from us—and Jack."

Max really wanted to steer the subject away from Sylvie again. At the same time, she hoped that Courtney's heightened curiosity meant that she was beginning to pull out of the funk she had been in ever since they had first spotted Edso.

"You're not curious?" Courtney asked.

Max shook her head.

"Not even a little bit?"

"No. I just don't want to have to deal with her—at all—in any way."

"Agreed," Patti said. "Did I show you what I bought today?"

Max looked over, "No. I'm sorry."

"That's okay. That first shop I went in, I found this cool mug from the Catalina Marathon. I bought it for Dave. Sit tight."

She disappeared, then returned moments later with the mug.

Courtney wasn't too impressed, and while Max looked at the mug, Patti said, "I thought it would be fun to go back there some time with the guys, and that marathon might just be the perfect excuse," said Patti.

"That's not a bad idea," said Max, handing the mug back to Patti.

Putting the mug down, she pulled out her camera. "Hey, look. I got some great shots of Avalon as we were leaving on the ferry today. Check this one out."

She offered her camera to Court and showed her the image. "See how the sun's angle is illuminating that yacht, the *Wonder*? It almost seems to have an otherworldly glow."

"It is a beautiful yacht," Courtney said. "Look, Max. I know you don't want to think about Sylvie, but it's almost too bad we didn't get on board. I bet it would have been really cool."

Max stared at the picture. "Can I?" she asked, reaching for the camera.

Courtney passed it to her, and Max stared at the small image. Then she used her fingers to make the image larger.

"What're you looking at?" asked Patti.

"I don't know. Look here," she said, holding the camera so Patti could see. "What do you suppose that is?"

Patti took the camera and looked at the image. Then she began going back and forth between the pictures taken before and after that shot.

"That's strange. It looks like the sun is reflecting off of something, but I don't see what it could be. What do you think, Court?" she said, passing the camera to her.

"What am I looking at?"

"There, in the sky above the yacht. There's a bright spot, almost like the sun glinting off of a windshield. It's only in this one picture. Hey, maybe I caught a UFO!"

Courtney rolled her eyes at Max and then handed Max the camera.

"I'm sure it's not a UFO," said Max, "but Patti's right. It does look like something unusual. Is there any way to zoom in on it?"

"I'll download it to my computer in the morning. These margaritas are getting to me."

CHAPTER 48

AFTER A SECOND PITCHER OF MARGARITAS, Courtney found that the new day came too soon. She was the first one up, so making coffee became the first item on her agenda. She brewed a large pot, and when it was ready she grabbed the largest mug that she could find in the kitchen, filled it, and walked out to the patio. The sun was already shining and reflecting off the placid ocean. Lifting her free hand to shield her eyes, she briefly returned inside to grab her sunglasses. Her head hurt, her body hurt, and were it not for the coffee, she would have gladly accepted death at that moment.

Courtney moaned, then put her mug on one of the tables by the fire pit. She began shuffling around, slowly picking up the detritus from the previous night and placing it all on the table. She didn't have the energy to lug it all the way to the kitchen. She took frequent stops for coffee, and with each sip she seemed to feel better. Still, experience had taught her that the feeling was illusory at best, and that time, rest, and fluids were what she needed.

As she cleaned, moments of the evening flashed in and out of her memory. Finally, she sat down in one of the chairs by the fire pit, pulled her legs in tight, tucked her robe tightly around her, and cradled the still-hot mug in her hands. Without thinking, she closed her eyes, and her head slumped forward and a little to the right. The sun's warmth felt good on her face, and almost immediately images began to fly in and out of her head: Edso, Brad, Sylvie, Max, Patti, Jack, the *Vorspiel*, Catalina, the Duffy Boat ride, and Brad. It was like a kaleidoscope of events and people. It made no sense at all and yet made perfect sense.

"Court." She could hear a voice calling to her.

"Court." She heard it again; this time it seemed closer.

The third time she heard her name called, she forced her eyes to open. The sun was still blindingly bright, and were it not for her sunglasses, she would have squeezed them closed again. Slowly she turned her head toward the voice.

"Court, you all right?" It was Max, and she looked equally miserable.

"I need more coffee," said Courtney. "Help me up."

She handed Max her mug, unfolded her legs, and stood up. Immediately, a wave of dizziness overcame her, and she had to grab onto Max. To her great relief, it only lasted a few seconds. She moaned, took her cup back, and moved toward the kitchen with Max walking beside her.

As soon as Courtney refilled her mug, Max started a new pot. Patti joined them in the kitchen, shuffling her feet and rubbing her head.

"Margaritas are evil," said Patti. She glanced at the pot brewing.

Max said, "It's almost done, Sweetie. Why don't you and Court go out onto the patio and I'll bring it to you as soon as it's ready."

* * *

As Courtney and Patti shuffled off, Max leaned on the counter, staring at the slim stream of coffee splashing into the pot. Knowing it would be a couple of minutes before the coffee would be ready, she went in search of her sunglasses.

With a wheeze and a gurgle, the stream turned to drips. As soon as Max removed the pot, those final drops of coffee hissed and turned to steam as they hit the burner, filling the room with the aroma of burnt coffee.

Max topped up her own mug, filled Patti's, and put her sunglasses on. As she pulled the door to the patio open, she saw that Courtney and Patti were sitting in the same chairs they had occupied last night. She stepped out into the sunlight, grateful that she had put her sunglasses on.

"Thank you. You're an angel," said Patti, looking up and shading her eyes with one hand as she took the mug from Max with the other.

"You're welcome."

Max settled into her seat, and for a few moments no one said anything.

"Well, it's been a while since we've done that," announced Max.

"Sure has," agreed Patti.

"What were we thinking?" added Courtney.

No one volunteered an answer. After a few more minutes of silence, Max turned toward Patti. "Did you have time to do anything with those pictures from yesterday?"

"What pictures?"

"The ones you took when we were leaving Catalina on the ferry. Remember? That one of the *Wonder* and the bright spot in the sky. You said it looked like a UFO."

Patti turned toward Max and shook her head.

"No, you didn't have time to do anything, or no, you don't remember those pictures?"

"Both."

"Do you want me to remind you?"

"No. My head hurts too much to think."

Max turned to Courtney. "Court?"

Courtney's head was tilted to one side, and because of her sunglasses, Max couldn't see her eyes.

"Is she asleep?" asked Patti.

"I think so."

"Poke her."

"No. That would be mean."

Patti laughed. Then she became really quiet as she started to slump down in her chair.

Max leaned back and closed her eyes. "You guys are such wimps," she said. Then her own head became too heavy to hold up another moment.

* * *

There was a loud bang, followed by a whirring sound and shouts. Max sat up with a start. Suddenly, she felt hot and realized that she was sweating. The sun was fully up in the cloudless sky, and even with sunglasses she had to squint. She could hear the sound of a large truck pulling away.

"Why do they have to make so much noise?" she thought to herself. *"Surely it must be too early for trash pickup. What time is it, anyway?"*

Looking left and right, she saw that Courtney and Patti were both still asleep.

"I have to pee," she announced to her unresponsive friends.

She eased herself up slowly, but she still had to pause when she was finally standing to let the pounding in her head subside.

Once inside the cottage, she dropped her sunglasses on the table and made her way to the bathroom, where she found relief. She had left her watch on the vanity next to the sink, and after she washed her hands, she reached for it. She stared at its face, her mind not fully comprehending what it said. Then, "Eleven o'clock!"

She hadn't pulled up her pajama bottoms properly, and her feet got tangled as she moved. As she swayed from side to side, she nearly blacked out, but she caught and steadied herself against the vanity. The face that stared back at her from the mirror reflected the effects of too many margaritas. She moaned and turned the water on in the sink. When it was running hot, she wet a washcloth, held it over her face, and breathed deeply, luxuriating in its warmth. When she finally lowered the cloth, she wasn't sure that it had improved her looks, but at least she felt better. Bending over slowly to pull up her pajama bottoms properly, she fought off another bout of the head spins.

As she left the bathroom, her eyes were not yet ready for bright sunlight, so she put her sunglasses back on. She headed back to the kitchen to brew another pot of coffee. Passing the doors to the patio, she glanced out at her friends. They hadn't moved.

CHAPTER 49

"IS THAT MORE COFFEE?"

Max turned toward the voice.

"Court. How're you feeling?"

"Awful."

"Me too. Can I say, you look like shit."

"Thanks, I love you too."

"Where's Patti?"

"Still out on the patio. She's really out."

"Did we do anything really awful last night?"

"Not that I can remember."

The door from the patio opened and closed. Courtney turned toward the sound.

"Patti, you're alive!"

"Shh. Don't talk so loud."

"Good morning Patti," said Max, from inside the kitchen. She tried to sound as cheerful as possible just to piss Patti off.

Patti looked in past Courtney. "What're you so cheerful about?"

"The sun is shining, and we're here on vacation. What's not to be happy about?"

"You're such an asshole," she mumbled.

"Here we go," said Max, as she handed cups of freshly brewed coffee to each of her friends. "Is anyone hungry?"

The glares she received over the rims of their coffee cups said no.

"Well, while you two work on becoming humans again, I'm going to take a shower and then work on some food."

* * *

When Max came out of her room, fluffing her hair with a towel, Patti was sitting on one of the stools by the kitchen island, still nursing her coffee. "Where's Court?"

"She's out on the patio. I know she perked up for a bit last night, but I think she's still really upset about Edso and Sylvie."

"I'm sure you're right. Why don't you go take a shower so we can grab some lunch in a while? I'll go talk with her."

"Thanks."

As Patti walked off, Max dropped her towel on one of the stools and headed for the patio.

Courtney was standing by the railing, staring out over the Pacific Ocean.

Max walked over and stood next to her.

"It's beautiful, isn't it?"

"It really is. It feels different from home."

Max had expected Courtney to sound upset, but there was simply a faraway feel to its tone.

"Court. You all right?" asked Max.

"I've made a decision."

"What're you talking about?"

"All that stuff yesterday out on Catalina . . ." Her voice drifted off.

Max hesitated, then asked, "What stuff?"

"You know. I just wanted to warn Jennifer about Edso. Then it all got so complicated. Jennifer turns out to be Sylvie. And she told us to butt out."

"I know."

"But I do have to sort things out with Edso. I need to add some closure to this."

Before she could continue, Patti's voice interrupted them. "Hey, guys."

Max and Court turned toward her voice at the same time. She was just walking out of the house, and all signs of her hangover had vanished. Her blonde curls shone in the sunlight, and between the curls, her shorts, and her white t-shirt, she looked every bit a Southern California girl. She raised her ever-present camera and said, "Smile!" Then the camera clicked.

As Courtney held a hand up to shield herself, Max caught Patti's eye and mouthed the word *stop.* By the time Patti reached them, Courtney was already staring back out over the ocean.

Patti walked over and stood next to Max. "What's going on?" she whispered.

Max turned toward her friend to answer, but before she could utter a word, Courtney said, "I've made a decision. I've decided to stay out here for a while longer."

Max felt her jaw drop. "Stay here? Why?"

At the same time, Patti said, "But, what about Ben's?"

"I'm sorry," Courtney said, rubbing her eyes, and Max realized just how exhausted she looked. "I didn't mean forever. I'm just going to stay a bit longer."

"Define 'a bit' longer," said Max.

"I don't know. A few days—maybe a week. I really don't know."

Patti said, "And may we ask why?"

"I need to finish this business with Edso. Then maybe I'll finally be free."

Patti said, "Are you nuts?"

"Maybe. But I can't just let him disappear again. I need to find him and confront him."

Max intervened. "Court. I can sort of understand what you're feeling, but are you forgetting that Sylvie is here and she's warned us to stay away? You could be in a lot of danger. And you don't even know where he lives!"

"I know, I know, and you're right, I don't know where he lives, but I feel like I have to try."

Max stared silently at her friend. Then she also turned and faced the ocean again.

For the second time, Patti asked, "But Ben's?"

Courtney turned her back to the ocean and said, "You two can take care of things until I return. It will be fine."

Then, before either could respond, she headed for the house. Over her shoulder, she called back, "I'm going to take a shower and get dressed."

*   *   *

"She's kidding, right?" said Patti, as soon as Courtney had disappeared into the cottage.

"I don't think she is."

"But, what she said is impossible. We can't get Ben's ready for summer."

"You're right. We can't. And you know what else? We can't leave her out here by herself, either."

CHAPTER 50

MAX WAS IN THE KITCHEN WITH PATTI, cooking a late breakfast, when Courtney reemerged, showered and dressed. The smell of bacon filled the air.

"That smells so good," said Courtney.

"Grab three coffees and go sit down," said Max. "We'll be eating outside."

"Got it."

Max continued to alternately scramble eggs in a large skillet and stir something in a saucepan. She had taken the mess from last night and piled it up by the sink. Beside her Patti was buttering a plate of English muffins.

"One more thing," Max said to Courtney. "OJ."

"Got that too," she said. "What are you cooking?"

"You'll see. I'll be right out."

Patti finished her task. "Muffins are all set. I'll take them out. We'll be outside."

"Perfect," said Max.

Moments later, Max walked out onto the patio with three large plates in her hands. "I hope you're hungry."

"Starving!" was the simultaneous response.

"What's for breakfast?" said Courtney.

"I made what I call Belizean eggs," said Max. She placed a plate in front of each of her friends.

"Looks interesting," said Court.

Max laughed. "You're always so hesitant to try something new. This is my version of a breakfast from one of our favorite places in Belize: Estelle's. Eggs topped with salsa, refried beans, and bacon. They would serve fry jack, which are Jack's favorite, but I subbed English muffins.

The jelly is guava. I found some when we were shopping before the Duffy Boat ride."

Patti took the first bite. "Oh, my god. This is sooo good. I've got to get my camera. Be right back." She got up as Max motioned for Courtney to dig in.

"Jack and I found this to be the perfect antidote for a hangover."

Just as Courtney took her first bite, Patti returned with her camera. "Scooch together and smile," she said, as the shutter went kchick several times.

"Patti, put the camera down, and eat your breakfast before it gets cold," said Max.

"Yes, Mom," said Patti.

Courtney said, "Max, you said that this would usually be served with fry jacks. What are they?"

"Basically, they're fried dough. We met this old guy who showed us how to make them. Instead of a rolling pin, he used an empty beer bottle. His procedure was to drink the beer first, then roll out the dough. I'll make them for you sometime when we get home."

Courtney didn't say anything; her mouth was full.

As they finished eating, Max said, "Okay Court, let's talk about this idea you have to stay out here."

She didn't respond.

"Your friend, the one who hooked us up with this cottage—I thought that we had to be gone by the time he returned—and that's in a few days. Besides, we have our airline tickets. We kind of have to leave."

Courtney simply stared at her, still silent.

Max pressed the point. "Okay then—Edso. Let's talk about him."

Patti picked up the dirty plates and as she disappeared into the cottage, Courtney said, "That was delicious."

Max said, "Thank you. . . . but, Edso? I'm not going to let this go."

Courtney sighed. "The truth is, I don't know what I'm going to do, but he really hurt me. I have to do something."

"Okay," said Max

"I would think that you, of all people, would understand my need for closure. I mean, come on. *Sylvie's* here, and she's after him. What's with that? Are we just supposed to walk away? You can't tell me that you're not the least bit curious."

"Of course I am. But Edso *kidnapped* you. He's dangerous. And hell, no matter what Sylvie says, I have a hard time trusting her. And we really do need to get back."

"You're free to go, Max. You should go."

"I'm not going without you."

"Where're you not going together?" Patti had returned in time for just the tail end of the discussion.

Max said, "We're discussing heading home."

"Oh. So, Court, you still planning on staying?" asked Patti.

"Yes."

"And Max, you won't leave without her?"

"Right."

"Well then, I'm in."

Max glared at Patti. "What do you mean, you're 'in'?"

"I'm in. If Court isn't leaving, and you're not leaving, then I'm not leaving. So, what's the plan?"

"There is no plan," said Max. She looked pointedly at Courtney and added, "And that is a big part of the problem."

"There's no problem," said Courtney.

"Yes, there is," said Max.

"I talked with my friend after my shower, and he said I could stay for as long as I need to. It's really nice to have someone who trusts you with no strings attached."

"Ouch. That hurt," said Max.

"I didn't mean it that way."

"Then, what did you mean?"

"I guess I meant that I don't want to drag you into another mess.

Edso isn't your problem; he's mine."

"I've got news for you—anyone who hurts you, hurts us. We're in this together whether you like it or not. Plus, I wouldn't mind a chance to keep an eye on Sylvie. So, what'll we do next?"

"I'd like to go back to the Duffy place and talk to Brad again. Maybe he can let me know if the *Wonder* comes back, or if he sees Edso's boat."

Despite the tension between them, Max smiled. "Are you sure this is about Edso? We saw how you were all over Brad."

Patti chimed in. "Perhaps a little unfinished business?"

"Max! Patti! How could you both think that? He's just a nice guy, and he's in the perfect place to help us."

Still, Max saw a hint of color come to Courtney's cheeks. "Right," she said, with a wink and a nod.

Patti giggled and said, "Busted."

Max turned to Patti. "To start with, why don't you go do whatever you need to do so we can get a better look at your photos."

Patti said, "Good idea. I'll leave you two to chat and take care of that right now."

She got up from the table and walked into the cottage, but not before snapping a few more pictures of her friends.

"So, I take it that you and Patti are staying?" said Courtney.

"We're not going anywhere," said Max. "I'll call Jack in a bit to break the news."

CHAPTER 51

"WELCOME BACK," said Jorge, when Edso returned to Newport Beach. "Your trip was a success?"

"Yes, it was. Thank you."

While Jorge secured the boat, Edso, sea bag in hand, walked up to the house. It was mid-day, and like just about every day in Southern California, it was sunny and perfect. Of all the places in the world that he had lived in or visited, this was by far his favorite.

As he cleared the final step onto the large deck that overlooked the entrance to Newport Beach Harbor, he turned and looked out past the breakwater to Catalina and smiled. His sojourn there had exceeded his wildest expectations. Jennifer was so much more than he had ever imagined, he was already feeling anxious about how soon he could see her again.

"Welcome home, Mr. Edso. You had a nice trip? You must be hungry!" Maria's voice brought him back to the present.

"Oh, Maria. Yes, I did, and yes, I am hungry. But I'd like to get cleaned up first. Say, in about forty-five minutes?"

"Forty-five minutes. Yes."

When she turned and walked off, he looked back at Catalina one last time before heading in to get cleaned up.

He adjusted the water in the shower to the point where it was almost too hot. He stood, back to the shower, with his eyes closed, head bowed, and let the spray massage the back of his neck. The rivulets of water running down his torso caressed him as her hands had. He marveled again at how hands as strong as hers could be, all at the same time, so soft and gentle. As he ran the bar of soap over his body, he imagined that it was her hand guiding it, and he sighed as his body responded.

* * *

Satisfied and refreshed, Edso emerged from the house and walked out onto the deck. A large umbrella shaded the table that Maria had set for lunch. He smiled. Her attention to detail would rival that of any five-star restaurant, right down to the small arrangement of fresh, bright red California poppies in the center of the table.

The table was set for two. He wasn't expecting anyone, and his heart rate quickly increased when he thought that Jennifer had planned a surprise. He didn't spot her anywhere, so he walked to the end of the deck to a point where he could see down the harbor. A large yacht was moored there, but to his great disappointment, he saw that it wasn't the *Wonder*. In the same instant he realized that it was Giles' mysterious gray yacht, he heard from behind, "So, was she everything you had imagined?"

He turned to face Giles. Trying to mask his surprise and concern, he answered "She was. You must be my mysterious lunch guest. Why didn't you tell me you were coming by?"

Before Giles could respond, Maria emerged from inside the house carrying a tray that had a bottle of wine and two glasses on it. Edso watched as she put the tray on the edge of the table and then placed a wine glass at each setting.

"Ah, good." Giles walked over to the table. He picked up the bottle from the tray and said, "Thank you, Maria. We'll have lunch in fifteen minutes."

She nodded and walked back into the house. Her deference to Giles was obvious, and Edso struggled to conceal his growing sense of alarm.

"Come. Come," Giles motioned him over and held out the bottle of wine for Edso to look at.

It was a rosé. The bottle was cold and bathed in condensation. Edso looked at the label. "Another one of yours?"

"Yes. Small production, but delightful." He motioned for Edso to hand it back.

With practiced ease, Giles deftly uncorked the bottle, poured two glasses, and then placed the bottle on the table. He handed one to Edso and raised his glass. "I offer this toast to your Jennifer."

If Edso had been confused by Giles' sudden appearance, he was now entirely perplexed by that toast. Lifting his glass, he nodded toward Giles. After taking a sip, he said, "That's nice. Very nice."

"Yes. It is," agreed Giles, with a self-congratulatory smile.

Edso realized that Giles was playing to perfection the part of host even though he was the guest, and with each passing second, Edso felt more and more uncomfortable. Finally, Edso said, "Are you going to tell me why you're here?"

Ignoring the question, Giles lifted his glass and looked at it closely as he swirled the wine around. After inhaling its bouquet, he took his first sip. His eyes closed, he swirled it in his mouth, swallowed, and then he smiled. Opening his eyes, he fixed his gaze on Edso and said, "Let's just enjoy the wine for the moment. And besides, lunch should be ready in a few minutes. We'll have plenty of time to talk."

Giles walked to the railing of the deck and looked up the harbor toward his yacht.

Edso said, "She's really unique."

Giles paused, then said, "Your Jennifer, or my yacht?"

Edso hadn't expected that question. "I suppose both."

Maria's voice broke in. "Excuse me, sirs. Lunch is served."

"Come," said Giles, touching Edso's elbow as if he were a date that required direction.

As they sat, Giles looked at his plate and said, "This looks wonderful."

"It's Asian Salmon over rice with grilled asparagus," said Maria.

"I didn't know there was such a thing as Asian Salmon," said Giles, with a twinkle in his eye.

"I'm sorry, sir." Maria was obviously embarrassed, and she stammered, "I meant that it's fresh Pacific salmon, baked and served with an Asian sauce."

"I'm sorry, Maria, I was just having fun with you. Please forgive me. This looks lovely."

She gave a hint of a bow and retreated into the house.

"That was mean," said Edso.

"I suppose it was," Giles said in an unrepentant tone. Then he motioned for Edso to begin eating.

Halfway through his piece of salmon, just after Edso had put another bite in his mouth, Giles looked at him and said, "Do you remember what I told you about the alert from Rye Harbor when we met out on Catalina?"

"I do."

"I think we've figured out the source of those photos." He paused for effect.

Edso swallowed his salmon and washed it down with a sip of wine. The look on Giles' face was chilling. "And?"

"It looks like that woman you were involved with back East is here—with her two friends."

Edso stared silently at Giles, trying to make sense of what he had just been told.

"Apparently, they are staying somewhere in Laguna Beach. We're working on exactly where, but regardless, they saw you here, in the harbor, and reported it."

"You're absolutely sure?"

Giles nodded and took a bite of his salmon. In that instant, his demeanor changed. "This salmon is delicious."

After hearing Giles' news, Edso found it hard to enjoy the rest of his lunch. Giles' attempts at further conversation were kept light, but they were punctuated with ever-increasing periods of awkward silence. When they had finished eating and Maria had disappeared into the house with the last of the dishes, Giles turned toward Edso and said, "I will be going now. Know this: your grandfather was a great man, and it is unfortunate that he will not see his years of service to the cause bear fruit. Toward that end, we will not tolerate anything or anyone who will put in jeopardy our ultimate success."

He paused to let that sink in. Then he added, "Not your new plaything Jennifer, not those women from back East." He stopped and stared hard at Edso, then added, "No one."

CHAPTER 52

"WHAT ARE YOU TALKING ABOUT?" Jack shouted into the phone.

"I'm sorry, Jack. We're going to be staying a few more days."

"Define 'a few more' days."

"I can't."

"Tell me again why you're staying."

"Courtney says she has unfinished business to take care of. She wants to find Edso and confront him."

"So you're staying to help her with this harebrained idea."

"Well, somebody has to protect her. He might be dangerous."

"Do you know how crazy this all sounds?"

Yes," she said, in a small voice. "Don't be mad."

"Max, I'm not mad. I'm worried. I can see this whole thing blowing up. Maybe I should come out."

"No, Jack. Please don't. We're fine. I bet Courtney won't even be able to find him, and we'll be home in a few days."

He didn't answer.

"Jack? You still there?"

"I'm here."

"Please. Trust me."

"You, I trust. The three of you together, I'm not so sure."

"It'll be all right. Miss you."

The phone went dead.

* * *

"Mrowh." Cat jumped up into his lap.

"Hey, Cat," he said, scratching her head.

"Mrowh."

"Yes, that was Max. It'll be a few more days before she gets home."

"Mrowh." She pushed her head under his hand, insisting that he keep rubbing her head and ears.

"Listen, I've got to go for a run," he said, as he stopped rubbing her ears. "I've got to think this through."

She sat back up and glared at him. "Mrowh."

* * *

Jack changed, checked his watch, and began a slow jog down the drive. He was thankful that the days were getting longer. Only a few months before, he'd have been running in the dark. Passing Ben's, he glanced at the parking lot. There were only a few cars, which was to be expected on a weekday before the busy season's arrival. Still, it was a good thing Courtney had assistant managers who could run the place. As he crested the bridge, he began to stretch out his stride and quicken his pace. At the Boulevard, he turned right and followed it as it wound around the harbor. He noted that empty mooring balls still outnumbered boats, but he knew that this would soon change.

By the time he reached Washington Road, he had decided what route he would take. He turned left and headed for the center of town. In the center, he'd bear left at the town hall, run down the hill, pass the cemetery, take a left on Locke Road, and then follow Harbor Road for the final half mile home. It was a good plan, just under five miles and long enough to clear his head.

As he approached the cemetery, he heard the *whoop whoop* of a police siren behind him. He turned to look and saw Tom waving at him. He waved back and continued on, but Tom sped up and pulled into the cemetery entrance, just before Jack got there.

"Jack, I need to talk to you," he said, as Jack slowed to a walk.

"What's up?"

"There's something that's been bothering me since you sent me those pictures of Edso, and I need to talk to you about it."

"Sounds serious. What did I do?"

"You didn't do anything. It's what I did. After you showed me those pictures that Patti took, I remembered something. After Edso and his grandfather disappeared, I questioned why it seemed that so little effort was being put into finding them. The higher-ups basically told me to 'fo-gedda-bou-dit,' but they said I should call a special number if I heard anything about Otto or Edso ever again. When you came in with those photos, I remembered what they had said to do, and I made that call."

Jack looked at him, puzzled. "Who'd you call?"

"I don't know. Whoever answered didn't say much. I told him about the photos, and he thanked me."

"And?"

"And then he hung up. That's all."

"Son of a bitch," Jack said, under his breath.

"What?"

"Max just called and told me they are staying out there for a bit longer. Something about Courtney wanting to take care of unfinished business with Edso."

"But that could be dangerous," said Tom.

"I agree," said Jack. "And there's more. Just after I showed you those pictures, Ken turned up at my place."

"Ken?"

"He's a friend of Sylvie's. He'd been up here doing surveillance on Edso and Otto, and he was instrumental in rescuing Courtney."

"And why didn't I ever hear any of this?"

Jack ignored his friend's question. "Like I said, Ken showed up and told me that Courtney, Max, and Patti should stay far away from Edso."

"Well, I agree with that."

"But there's more. Ken's a friend of Sylvie's, and she's in California, too. She caught up with Max this week and gave her the same warning about leaving Edso alone."

Tom's jaw dropped. Then he said, "Sylvie's out there?"

"Apparently."

"That can't be good."

"Ya think?"

Tom got real quiet. Then he said, "Jack, remember that security bulletin I received that included Giles Endroit?"

Jack nodded.

"Well, if Edso and Otto were white nationalists, and Giles is a white nationalist, maybe they're all involved in something dubious together. The slimy pool that those people reside in must be pretty small."

A knot formed in Jack's stomach as he listened to what Tom was saying. Hearing the words aloud made his earlier doubts and fears seem so much more real.

"Tom, I've got to get going. I've got to speak with Max again."

"You want a ride home?"

"No. I need the run. Talk to you later."

"Well, be careful, Jack. You be sure to tell those girls not to do anything stupid. And keep in touch."

CHAPTER 53

"OKAY, MAX. CHECK THESE OUT," said Patti.

Max was sitting in the living room looking at *The Weekly World News*, a guilty pleasure she'd picked up one day from a checkout line—ten items or less.

Patti walked in and sat down next to Max.

"What're you looking at?" she asked, leaning over to see.

"Nothing," said Max, closing the magazine and shoving it under a pillow that was on the couch next to her.

"Whatever. I finally downloaded the pictures I took."

She turned her laptop so that Max could see the screen.

"Check this out. Here's Edso's boat. He had just gotten off, and I caught its name. Maybe that'll help us find him."

"*Verführer*? German? I wonder what it means? Remember his grandfather's yacht was named *Foreplay*."

"Never could understand that."

While Patti kept scrolling through the photos—their lunch and the sunset pictures as they were leaving Avalon—Max grabbed her phone to look up *Verführer*.

"I've got it. It means seducer," said Max, just as Patti said, "There." She turned her computer toward Max and pointed at the bright spot in the sky. "Now watch." Patti kept increasing its size until it nearly took up the entire screen.

"What the hell *is that?*" said Max.

"I told you last night. It's a UFO! It practically matches the one on your magazine cover."

Patti leaned over Max in an attempt to reach the magazine.

"Patti, stop. It does not," said Max, trying to keep it out of Patti's grasp.

Patti won and held it up. "Look." She held it up next to the image on her laptop. "It is!" she said triumphantly.

Max looked at the laptop and then the magazine.

"Patti. You know the magazine picture is photoshopped. It's probably someone's football."

"But, is it?" Patti giggled, and for a moment, Max had to join in.

"Stop. You know it is." Recovering, she asked, "So, what is it then? Balloon?"

"I don't think so."

"Could you send these to Jack?"

"Sure, no problem."

Patti picked up her laptop and began walking away.

"Hey, send him the shots of Edso's boat, too."

"Sure. I'll do it right now."

As Patti exited the room, Courtney walked in.

"What's she doing?" asked Court.

"Where've you been?" asked Max, at the same time.

"I just called Brad. Then I made the mistake of lying down on my bed. I must have been abducted by aliens, because I have no idea where the last hour went."

"That's interesting," said Max. "Patti and I were just discussing aliens."

"What?"

"Not really. We were looking at the photos that she took on our way back from Avalon. When she blew up the one with that shiny spot in the sky, it looked like a UFO. She's sending it to Jack."

Courtney didn't say anything.

Max prodded, "So, you got hold of Brad?"

"I did. He's taking some people out this afternoon, but he'll be around later, so I'm going over to see him then."

"Patti also got a good picture of Edso's boat. You can clearly see the name. She's sending it to Jack as well."

"Really? What's it called?"

"*Verführer*. It means seducer."

"Figures. I'll be right back."

Courtney hurried out of the room. A few minutes later, she and Patti returned together. Max noticed that Courtney was looking at her phone while she walked.

"Thanks, Patti," said Courtney.

"What'd you do?" asked Max.

"Just sent the pics to Court too."

* * *

Jack couldn't get home fast enough. Accepting the ride from Tom would have been the quickest solution, but he needed the physical release, so he pushed the pace hard, and by the time he reached home, he was spent. It wasn't until he was standing in the shower, head bowed with the spray pounding on the back of his neck, that he was able to think more clearly about the conversation he had with Tom.

His unconscious self had already decided that he would fly out to California, but his conscious mind was just beginning to grapple with the idea.

Edso was out there. Giles Endroit was out there. Sylvie was out there. Courtney, Max, and Patti were out there—and they were going in search of Edso. It was a recipe for disaster. On the phone earlier, Max had insisted that he stay put, but now he knew he would not.

Showered, dressed, and with his mind made up, he felt calmer. He headed to the kitchen, where he cracked a beer and warmed some leftover pizza in the microwave.

As soon as he opened the microwave oven door, Cat suddenly appeared, rubbing against his leg. "Mrowh."

"Sorry, Cat, this is my pizza."

"Mrowh."

"I know. You'd like some, but I'm not giving you any. Pizza is not good for kiddens."

"Mrowh." She head-butted his leg and mrowhed again. Jack looked down at her, sure that she was saying, "Hey, I eat raw mice. I can handle pizza."

He bent down and scratched her head. Then, standing, he picked up his pizza and his beer, walked over to the window, and looked out. Courtney's cottage was dark. It had been dark ever since the girls had left on their trip, but this was the first time he really felt its emptiness.

"Cat, I've got some bad news. I need to go out to California."

She rubbed against his leg, purring loudly.

"I'll see if Dave'll come by to feed you and let you in and out."

"Mrowh."

"I know, but it'll be all right. He's really an okay guy."

Cat looked up at him silently,

"I wouldn't do this if it weren't important. It'll only be for a few days. It'll be okay, you'll see."

* * *

Jack swallowed the last bite of pizza, washed it down with the last of the beer, checked his watch, and decided to wait a bit before making the call to California. However, his phone rang a second later, and it was Max.

"Jack. I'm so glad I caught you. I have something to tell you."

"Perfect. I have something to tell you too."

"What?"

"You first."

"Okay. When we were on the way home from Catalina, Patti took some pictures. In one of the photos, there is a shiny thing in the sky. We just enlarged it up on her computer, and it looks like a flying saucer."

"Have you been drinking?"

"That was last night. Seriously, it is really weird. Patti just sent it to you."

He heard his computer ding, announcing the arrival of an email.

"I just heard my email ding. Let me check."

"She sent a picture of Edso's boat as well, and you can clearly see its name."

Instead of replying, he walked across the room and opened his laptop. "Okay, I'm in. Let's see."

He scrolled up and down for a moment and then said, "Got 'em . . . Wow, it really does look like a UFO. I'll show it to Tom to see what he thinks."

"You see the picture of his boat?"

"Yep, nice boat . . . That's an interesting name."

"So, what were you going to tell me?"

"I'm going to come out."

"No, Jack. You don't need to."

"I think I do."

The line went silent for what seemed an eternity. Finally, she said, "When?"

"Not sure yet. I'll let you know as soon as I book flights."

"I wish you wouldn't."

"Leaving you girls on your own isn't an option anymore."

CHAPTER 54

"I'M LEAVING TO GO TALK TO BRAD," announced Courtney, several hours later.

Max looked up from the book she was reading. "Look at you," she said.

Courtney was wearing skinny jeans, a cream-colored tank top with a navy blazer, and sandals.

"Talk—right," Max added, sarcastically.

"Yes. Talk."

"Well, if that's the case, I'm coming with you."

"No, you're not."

"Yes, I am. Patti!" she called out. "We're going on a road trip to see Brad."

"I'll be right there."

Courtney flashed Max a look that said, "*No, you're not.*"

Max shrugged, grinned, and mouthed the words, "Yes we are."

"Fine," said Court. "But I'm talking to Brad ALONE."

"'Talking'? Of course you are."

A few minutes later, Courtney was behind the wheel, Max was riding shotgun, and Patti had resumed her position in the back seat, where her already curly blonde hair was blowing about wildly.

"Can you imagine riding around this time of year at home with the top down?" shouted Patti. "I love it!"

Max turned and smiled at her friend, then looked over at Courtney. She was looking straight ahead, totally ignoring her two friends.

"Come on, Court, We're only here to help."

Court turned toward Max and stuck out her tongue. Max could tell that try as she might, she couldn't hold back the beginnings of a grin.

Max returned the gesture, and they both began to laugh.

Traffic on the Pacific Coast Highway was light and the drive was pleasant and quick, only slowing as they drove into Newport Beach.

"Before we go home, we need to have lunch there one more time," said Patti, as they drove past the Sherman Library and Gardens.

The closer to Balboa Island they came, the slower the traffic moved. "There's the turn," said Max. "I think we should grab the first parking spot we come to and then walk the rest of the way."

"There's one," said Patti, but Courtney just kept on driving.

Court said, "Brad told me to drive all the way down to the office. He said he'd have a place for me to park."

"You sure?" asked Max.

"That's what he said."

By the time they reached their destination, the sun was setting, and the sky was turning shades of orange, rose, and gold. Patti had her camera out and ready before Courtney even stopped the car. While Courtney walked into the office, Patti and Max walked around to the dock. Max could see the white lights outlining the Pavilion and the Ferris wheel at the Fun Zone on the other side of the harbor. Reflections of their lights, as well as other lights all around the harbor, were beginning to dance on the water's surface.

Max gave Courtney a few minutes to speak with Brad alone, but when she and Patti joined them in the office, Brad was actually on the phone. Based on Courtney's frown, and the impatient tapping of her foot, Max realized that she must not have had a chance to speak with him yet.

Andrea walked in and joined them just as Brad was hanging up the phone. He looked up and smiled, but Max could tell from his confused expression that he had been expecting only Courtney.

Andrea spoke first. "Brad told me you were coming by, but he didn't tell me why. May I ask?"

"Of course you may," said Court. "But first, did I ever tell you how much we enjoyed our harbor cruise?"

"Not in so many words, but Brad filled me in."

"Good. Now we're looking for help in finding a particular boat. We thought that maybe you two could help."

A puzzled look washed across Andrea's face. "A boat?"

"Yes. It's a long story, but we are looking for the owner of this boat." She held out her phone to Andrea and showed her the photo.

Andrea shrugged and shook her head. "*Verführer*? Doesn't sound familiar to me, but then, if anyone knows it, Brad will."

In response, Brad gave Andrea a pointed look, and she suddenly said, "Hey, I'm running out for a coffee. Anyone want to join me? Patti? Max?"

Courtney quickly chimed in. "Could you ladies bring one back for me?"

"Uh, sure," said Max. She looked at Patti and said, "Let's go."

"Great," said Andrea, and she led the way out the door.

* * *

Brad looked at her, "Tell me again what you need."

She stepped up to the counter. "Like I said, I need some help finding this boat. She held out her phone so he could see the picture.

"And why this boat?"

She hesitated a moment. Then, pulling her phone back, she began waving her fingers frantically over it's screen before saying, "It belongs to a man who . . ." She took a deep breath and shuddered slightly.

He moved from behind the counter, came around to the front, and stood beside her. Gently, he touched her shoulder. "What's wrong?"

"I'm sorry." She inhaled deeply again, turned, and faced him, clutching her phone in her hand. "A while ago, a man, this man," she held up her phone for him to see, "held me hostage on his boat. A different boat. He was never charged with a crime; in fact, he escaped from the area right after that. But we saw him here when we were on the boat ride with you. He was talking to a woman on that beautiful yacht, the

Wonder. I know it sounds a bit crazy, but we decided to find the woman and warn her. We tracked her down on Catalina Island, but she . . . well, it's complicated. She's with law enforcement or something. Max actually knows her. She warned us to leave, but we can't. I can't. I have to get some answers from him so I can finally move on."

"Woah, slow down. That's an awful lot to digest."

"I'm sorry."

"Can I see the picture of the boat again?"

Her fingers swiped at the screen, and when she stopped, she held her phone out to him. He took it and looked at the screen.

"Tell me you recognize it."

"I do."

"You do?"

"Yes. I don't know him, but I know the boat, and I know where it's kept."

Courtney launched herself onto him, her arms pulling him close into a tight hug, and she kissed him. "Thank you. Thank you. Thank you," she said, between kisses.

Courtney heard the door open just then, and her friends and Andrea walked in.

"Courtney!" said Max. "Ten minutes! You couldn't even wait."

"It's not what it looks like," stammered Brad, as he pulled back.

"No?" said Andrea, as Courtney quickly adjusted her clothes. She was relieved to hear that it sounded like Andrea was trying not to laugh. "Then you tell me what it looks like."

"Brad recognized the boat. He knows where it is," said Courtney.

Brad's face was still a little pink. Courtney looked at him and made a small motion with her finger, pointing at the corner of her mouth. He quickly wiped at the lipstick smudge on his mouth.

"I'm sorry." She mouthed the words, while looking at him.

"So, what about the boat?" said Max.

"He was just going to tell me," Court answered.

CHAPTER 55

BRAD LOOKED AT MAX. "Like I was telling Courtney, I've seen that boat. Kind of hard to miss with a name like *Verführer.*"

Max motioned for him to continue.

"It's kept on a dock just south of the harbormaster's office near the place where the channel makes the final turn into the harbor."

Then, looking at Andrea, he said, "You know the house. It's that huge one up on the bluff with all the windows. Any time we go out of the harbor, you comment on it."

"Oh, right. I just never noticed the boat."

"Any idea who owns it?" asked Courtney.

"No. But, I know someone who might. We met at a club."

"What's her name?" asked Andrea.

"I never said it was woman."

"Really, Brad. I know you."

He got real quiet.

"Brad! So what's her name?"

"Maggie."

"Can you call her?" Andrea was not cutting him any slack.

"Let me see if I have her number," he said pulling out his phone.

"And why do you think she might know it?" pressed Andrea, her tone getting a bit snarky.

"Hey, give me a break. We had a lot to drink that night. I haven't seen her since, but I remember we were talking about those homes up on the bluff and she said she knew who the guy was who owned that one."

Again, Max interjected herself, asking a bit more gently, "When was this?"

"Not sure. Maybe a month ago."

"Did she say who it was?"

"I don't think so. Hold on, here it is." He began pressing numbers and then sat with the phone pressed to his ear for what seemed to Max like forever, and then he put it down on the counter. "No longer in service."

"Thanks for trying," said Max. "Maybe we should get going." Then she began moving toward the door.

Patti and Andrea followed her out.

* * *

As soon as they were alone, Court turned and faced Brad. "Thank you. I'm sorry for the way they ganged up on you."

"That's okay. I could take you over and show you the boat."

"Really? You would do that?"

He stepped close in front of her. "I would. How about tomorrow?"

"What time?"

"How about noon?"

"I'll be here."

"Alone?"

"You bet."

With that answer, he put his arms around her, pulled her close, leaned down, and kissed her. Their lips met, tongues touched, and she felt the electricity.

* * *

"I thought I told you I was going to talk to him alone," Courtney said to her two friends as they drove off the island.

Max spoke up first. "You did. But after we got the coffee, Andrea dragged us back in. Come on, Court, lighten up."

Patti said, "He is kind of cute though."

"But so young," added Max.

"You guys are such shit heads," said Courtney, as they left Balboa

Island behind.

"Seriously, though," said Max. "You might want to keep it on the light side. Andrea told us he tends to fall for every attractive woman he meets."

"Why should she care?"

"Just sayin'."

Courtney shrugged and said, "I'll take that as a compliment then."

They were halfway home when Max's phone beeped to indicate that she had a text.

She looked and then announced, "Jack's bought his plane ticket."

"What!" Courtney and Patti said in unison.

"He's flying out."

"What's that all about?" said Patti.

Max didn't say anything for a moment, as her fingers were busy responding.

"He's worried we'll do something stupid. I mean, Edso's out here, Sylvie's out here, and I sent him those pictures of the UFO."

"Good point," Patti said. "Still, so much for just us girls."

"I couldn't stop him," said Max.

"Anyone getting hungry?" said Courtney.

"I'm starving," said Patti.

"Me too," said Max.

"Brad recommended a place. What do you say to Italian? It's close enough to the cottage for us to walk."

Patti grinned, and Max answered for both of them, "Sounds great."

"Then it's home, then dinner."

CHAPTER 56

"OH, COURT, THIS IS TOO COOL," said Max. "You always hear about the best places."

The restaurant had a small patio right on the street. Those tables were full, so they were seated just inside. Even if Max had not been hungry already, the tantalizing aromas would have made her so.

"Good evening, and welcome to Alesso. My name is Marco." Their waiter spoke with a thick Italian accent, and he was obviously in his glory waiting on the three women.

Patti leaned over to Max and whispered in her ear, "Polo." Stifled giggles followed, and Courtney gave them a stern look before asking Marco to recommend a bottle of red wine.

Marco smiled and said, "I know the perfect wine."

"You two behave yourselves," Courtney hissed, after the waiter left the table.

"Marco?" whispered Max.

"Polo," Patti replied under her breath. This time their giggles were even louder.

When the waiter returned to the table, he held three glasses by their bases in one hand, and a bottle in the other. Setting the bottle on the table, he placed a glass in front of each of the three friends, before picking up the bottle and presenting it to Courtney. He had chosen a Chianti.

She studied the label and nodded her acceptance. With practiced ease, he drew the cork out with a flick of his wrist. He poured a sip for Courtney and stepped back while she tasted the wine.

"Ooo, that's delicious," she said, looking up at him.

Glasses poured, he excused himself from the table.

"Here's to Courtney's new boy toy," said Max with a smile.

Courtney ignored her comment. Instead, she joined her two friends as they lifted their glasses, touched rims, and drank.

"What do you think?" asked Courtney.

"About what?" Patti asked. "The wine, Brad, or Marco?"

"Polo," Max said under her breath, eliciting another stern look from Courtney. Then, recovering, she said, "I'm sorry. I couldn't help it. Court, this is really good."

"Thank you." She put her glass down, looked at Max, and said, "Now, what's this about Jack coming out?"

"I don't know any more than what I told you in the car. He texted that he's planning on coming out tomorrow. I texted him back, but he hasn't replied."

Patti finished a second sip of her wine and started to look at the menu. "Everything looks so good."

"I think we should each order something and then share," said Max.

"Great idea," said Patti. "I'm going for the pizza bella. Fontal and homemade mozzarella, organic cherry tomato bruschetta, and Italian oregano." Looking up, she said, "Sounds kind of like a white pizza."

"That sounds good," said Max, as she continued to study the menu.

"I'm going with the scampi ravioli," said Courtney. The table went silent as Max and Patti read the description on the menu.

"Yum," said Patti. She reached for her glass and took another sip.

Max looked up and saw that her two friends were now looking at her. "I'm still thinking."

Marco suddenly materialized tableside. "May I answer any questions you might have?"

Courtney looked up at him and smiled. "We'll have one pizza bella and the scampi ravioli."

Without writing anything down, he asked, "Will that be all?"

Court shook her head and looked at Max.

"Miss?" asked Marco, as he followed her gaze.

Max looked up and said, "I'll have the veal Marsala."

"Very good." Then, before stepping away from the table, Marco asked if they would require another bottle of wine.

"Perhaps with our meals," said Courtney.

He had only taken a few steps from the table when a busboy brought them some bread and butter.

Max turned toward her friends. "Miss? Am I a miss?"

"At least you weren't a ma'am," Patti said.

Courtney swallowed her last sip of wine and was reaching for the bottle to refill her glass when Marco reappeared. He picked up the bottle, filled her glass, and then did the same for Max and Patti.

"Thank you," said Court.

"Your dinners are about ready. Shall I bring another bottle of wine?"

"That would be nice."

When he left, Courtney turned back to her friends. "Brad offered to show me where Edso keeps his boat."

Max said, "When?"

"Tomorrow."

Before Courtney could say anything else about the proposed trip with Brad, Marco and another server brought their dinners and the new bottle of wine.

"Oh, my god," said Patti. "This pizza is amazing. Take some."

Courtney spooned a ravioli onto each of her friends' plates, while Max served them each some veal Marsala. The wine was disappearing as quickly as their meals when Max's phone beeped again to announce a new text. Several heads in the restaurant turned to stare at her reproachfully. Embarrassed, she quickly silenced her phone and mouthed the word *sorry* to the people around them.

"Jack?" asked Patti, as Max looked at her phone.

"Yes. His plane arrives tomorrow at noon."

"Noon?" said Court.

"Thereabouts."

"I'm meeting Brad at noon," said Courtney.

"So, how about Patti and I drop you off at Brad's and then we go to the airport to meet Jack. We can pick you up again at Voyagers on our way back home."

At that moment, Marco reappeared. "You enjoyed your dinners, yes?"

"Yes. Thank you. It was delicious," said Courtney.

Deftly he cleared the entire table save for their wine glasses and the bottle.

"So?" asked Max.

"So, what?"

"We drop you off, pick up Jack, and come back for you. Okay?"

"That could work," said Court.

"And that way it'll only be Court and Brad," Max thought.

They declined dessert and coffee but continued to nurse the remaining wine. Their conversation became more animated as they discussed Edso and Sylvie, and why Jack was coming out.

CHAPTER 57

IT WAS FORTUNATE that the restaurant was within walking distance to the cottage, because the two bottles of wine had definitely slowed their progress. The walk home was quiet in stark contrast to their lively conversation at the restaurant.

"That dinner was amazing," said Max, as they finally walked into the cottage.

"It was," agreed Patti. "Thank you, Court. I'm done in. Goodnight."

As she walked off, Courtney said to Max, "Can I talk to you for a minute?"

"Sure."

She moved toward the patio door. "Let's go outside."

"You go ahead. I'll be right out," said Max.

Minutes later as Max stepped out onto the patio, she saw that Courtney had lit the gas fire pit and was sitting in the same chair she had occupied the previous evening. As she pulled the door shut behind, she couldn't tell if her friend was awake or asleep.

"Court?" she said, as she approached.

"Come sit."

"What's up?" Max dropped into the chair next to her. "The fire feels good."

The evening had cooled, and the fire provided just enough warmth.

"It does."

"You ever just sit and watch a fire burn?"

"Yeah."

"I mean, really watch it."

"What are you talking about?"

"Fire. Think about it. It's real. You can see it, you can feel it, you can experience the result of it, but you can't hold it like you would a ball or a wine glass."

"Court, where's this going?"

"I don't know. I was just thinking about Jack coming out here."

"And?"

"And it's sweet. He really loves you, you know."

Max didn't respond. "Court, you've had too much to drink. You're not making much sense."

"No, I am. Listen. Jack's feelings for you are like that fire. You can feel it, you can see it, but it's not something that you can physically touch."

Courtney's head began to nod. "Max, don't be angry with him. He just loves you." Her words tailed off as her breathing deepened.

Max looked at her friend and said softly, "I know." She wiped a tear from her eye.

"Court," she said. "Time for bed."

There was no response, so she pried herself out of her chair, went inside, got a blanket, turned off the fire, and tucked the blanket around her friend. Then she whispered, "Goodnight."

* * *

There was a loud knocking on her door. Max rolled over and squinted at the clock. The hands read 10:03 a.m.

"Max. Time to get up. Rise and shine." Courtney's voice gave definition to what Max's eyes had just seen. In that instant she was wide-awake and scrambling to disentangle herself from the covers, nearly falling as she jumped out of the bed.

The door opened a crack, and Courtney said, "Hey, sleepyhead, time to rally."

"I'm up. Be right out," she mumbled, as she fought off a vicious head rush.

Max retreated into the bathroom and turned on the shower. As she waited for the water to get hot, she slid out of her clothes and faced the mirror. Because she had slept in what she had worn the day before, her skin was marred with lines and creases from the previous day's clothing. Still, despite those imperfections she liked what she saw, and she knew that Jack would like it too.

The water was hot and rejuvenating, and by the time she emerged, those sleep-induced lines and creases were gone, leaving nothing but pink, smooth skin. She pulled on a pair of tan shorts that she knew Jack loved. She topped them with a white, spaghetti strap tank with built-in support that left little to the imagination and eliminated unsightly underlines. A pair of flirty sandals and a dangling necklace that couldn't help but draw attention to where it fell, completed her outfit. She smiled at what she saw in the mirror, knowing what Jack's reaction would be.

Max walked into the kitchen, her curly red hair still damp. "Is there any coffee?"

"Your cup's on the counter; the pot's only a few minutes old," said Courtney, without looking up.

"Where's Patti?" asked Max, while she fixed her coffee.

"She's outside. She was the first up." Then Courtney looked over at her friend and paused a moment. "Look at you. If I didn't know better, I'd say you were excited to see Jack. And by the way, thanks for leaving me out on the patio."

Max couldn't tell if Courtney's comment was genuine or snide. She replied, "You're welcome. You're looking pretty hot as well."

Courtney was wearing a pair of loose boyfriend jeans that were rolled up at the ankles, sneakers, and a dark-gray, cotton, off-the-shoulder, long-sleeved shirt. She had pulled the sleeves up past her elbows, creating a casual but sexy look.

Courtney then asked, "Last night, did I say anything?"

"What do you mean?" asked Max.

"I don't know. I have a feeling that we had a long conversation about fire and Jack and love, but I'm not sure if it really happened or if I was dreaming."

"You must have been dreaming," said Max. She didn't want to get into a discussion about 'drunk-speech.'

"So you and Patti'll drive me to Brad's?"

"Yes. I checked, and Jack's plane will be in just after noon."

"Perfect. I told Brad I'd be there between eleven-thirty and twelve."

"Then we should get going."

CHAPTER 58

WITHOUT A RESERVED PARKING PLACE, Max dropped Courtney off a block away from the office.

"We'll see you in a few hours," said Max, as Patti climbed into the front seat.

"Text me."

"Bye. Have fun, stay safe."

"Yes, Mom," said Courtney.

Five minutes later, Courtney was walking into the office. Andrea was at the counter. "Hi, Court. He's down on the dock."

"Thanks."

As she began to open the door, Andrea stopped her. "Listen, I'm sorry about last night. I said some things to your friends about Brad—"

Courtney cut her off. "There's nothing to be sorry about."

"It's just that I feel I have to watch out for Brad. He can get a bit impulsive sometimes, and on occasion, things haven't turned out very well."

Courtney smiled. "I know all about impulsive things going south. He's lucky to have someone watching over him."

"Thanks. Have fun today."

"I expect to."

"Hey, sailor," said Courtney a few minutes later, when she walked up behind Brad. He must not have heard her coming from behind, and as he spun around he nearly knocked her into the water.

"I'm so sorry," he said, catching her.

"No harm, no foul. So, is this our boat?"

He smiled and shook his head. "Not this afternoon. That is." His grin widened as he pointed at a center console boat with a T-top and a huge outboard on the stern. She had seen boats like this back home many times, but she had never been in one. They were used mostly by fishermen in Rye Harbor and this one appeared to be no different since there was an assortment of rods bristling from rod holders.

"Wow! Yours?"

"I wish. It belongs to a friend, but it's better for our purposes today. Hop aboard."

Courtney climbed over the gunwale, and he followed. While she walked around the center console to the bow, Brad started the engine. As soon as it was running smoothly, he moved aft, reached over, and freed the stern line from the dock. Then, he moved forward to release the bow line. When he pulled on it, the bow swung into the dock while the stern swung out. As soon as he was able to reach where it was tied to the dock cleat, he untied it and handed it to Courtney.

"Here, could you coil this up? Then we'll get out of here."

He moved back to the controls, shifted into reverse, and backed away from the dock. With coiled line in hand she moved to join Brad behind the console.

"Where do you want this, Captain?"

"It goes in there," he said, pointing to a closed box that also served as a seat. "Could you grab the fenders as well?"

"Aye, aye," she said, giving him a smile and a salute.

By the time they were well away from the dock and into the channel heading toward the harbor entrance, the dock lines and fenders were stowed. Courtney moved to stand next to him.

"The entire harbor, all the way to the entrance, is a No Wake Zone," said Brad. "That means it will be a slow ride until we get out of the harbor."

"So, where's his boat?"

"It's on a dock up there," he said, pointing to the left and ahead. "It's just past the Coast Guard station and the Harbor Patrol headquarters. We've got a few more minutes until we get there."

"I couldn't help but notice that Andrea seems a bit protective of you. What's with that?"

He went silent, obviously trying to ignore the question by focusing on driving the boat. However, she had no intention of letting him off the hook.

"Did I tell you how great you look today?" he said.

"You didn't, but thank you. . . . Now, what about Andrea?"

"We're just friends." Then he quickly added, "And business partners."

"And?"

"That's all—just friends and partners."

She looked at him for a moment before saying, "Fair enough."

He had given her no reason not to believe him, but she remained certain that there was more to the story than he was telling. She didn't challenge him, but rather allowed her silence to be her answer.

"There," he said, pointing. "You see the Coast Guard station? Just past it is the Harbor Patrol's headquarters."

"Yes."

"Now look just past, high on that bluff, and you'll see a large glass house. I'm pretty sure that's where he lives, since there's a ramp leading down from that house to the dock where the boat is."

They motored on in silence until he said, "Look, there it is."

"Can we get closer?"

"Of course." He altered course until they were heading right toward the dock.

"That's it, right?" he asked.

"That's the boat," said Courtney. She couldn't stop staring at it. It was tied next to the dock, stern to the channel, its transom proclaiming *Verführer*. On the end of the dock was a sign that said *Private Property* and had the red circle with the slash through it over a picture of a boat.

"Keep moving. Stay clear of the dock!" A man exited the cabin of the boat and waved and shouted at them.

She forced herself to smile and wave back, all the while wishing that she had something heavy she could throw at the boat. They were that close.

"That him?" asked Brad.

"No."

"Not very friendly, is he?"

"Apparently not."

"I think it's safe to say that most of the people who have these docks don't like uninvited guests. Look, at the other end of the dock."

Courtney followed his gaze and saw a locked gate with another sign that said *Private Property*. And if that wasn't enough, there were wings on either side of the gate that would prohibit anyone from getting around it. From that gate, a long aluminum ramp led up to a landing at the base of the deck. From the landing, there was a door set into the wall supporting the deck as well as a set of outside stairs leading up to the deck that overlooked the water.

The man in the *Verführer* continued to glower at them, hands on his hips, as they pulled away.

Brad steered for the center of the entrance channel and continued toward the ocean. As they reached the end of the breakwaters, he pressed the throttles forward. The boat lifted up, and they flew along parallel to the coast.

"Where're we going?" asked Courtney, shouting over the sound of the motor, the rushing wind, and the hull slapping on the water.

Brad's answer was lost in the wind.

CHAPTER 59

"ARE YOU EXCITED TO SEE JACK?" asked Patti.

Max just looked at her and smiled.

"Sorry, dumb question. I just can't believe he came all this way. Dave must have had to work."

Max looked over at her friend thinking that she heard a hint of sadness in her voice.

"I couldn't talk Jack out of it. It will be good to have another person to keep an eye on Courtney, though. I was really hoping we could keep her away from Edso. And now she's gone to look for his boat . . ."

"I know," said Patti. "I wish I hadn't taken those photos now. And—"

"And what?"

Patti didn't answer.

"Come on, Patti. What?"

"I'm worried about you."

"Me?"

"You. Come on. Sylvie's here, and Jack's about to arrive. You don't see a problem with that?"

"Awkward, maybe, but I'm sure that's about it. We're all here because of Courtney and Edso, aren't we? That's the real issue to worry about."

"I suppose." She shrugged. "I just want you to know that while Jack is helping you keep an eye on Courtney, I'll help you keep an eye on Jack."

"Thanks, Patti. You're a good friend."

* * *

Hugs, kisses, and tears met Jack at the airport.

"Where's Court?" he asked, as he put his bag in the trunk of the car.

"She's out with Brad, looking for Edso's boat."

"She's what?"

"Get in, we can talk as we drive," said Max.

Max started the car and headed for the parking lot exit.

"You hungry?" she asked, looking over at Jack.

"Starving."

"Good. I thought you might be. There's an In-N-Out Burger that's kind of on the way home. We went there when we arrived."

"Sounds good," said Jack. "Anything like Lexie's Joint?"

"How's Dave?" asked Patti from the back seat before Max could answer Jack.

"He's good. He won't admit it, but he really misses you. He had to work and is taking care of Cat."

"And you're good with that?"

"Sure. I know he calls himself a dog person, but he'll be just fine. Cat'll whip him into shape."

"Somebody has to," she said.

* * *

The burgers met every expectation, and while they ate, their small talk turned serious.

Jack said, "So, tell me about Court and this Brad and why they're looking for Edso's boat."

Max gave him a quick summary.

"She's always been stubborn as a mule. Why can't she just let this go?"

"She's obsessed with Edso. I agree that she should just walk away, but we haven't been able to dissuade her."

Lunch finished, they headed for Balboa Island to pick up Courtney. This time, they got lucky and found a place to park a short walk from Voyagers.

"This is amazing," said Jack, when he got his first glimpse of the harbor. "A bit different from the harbor at home."

CHAPTER 60

"HI, ANDREA," SAID MAX. "THEY BACK YET?"

"Hey, Max, Patti. No, not yet." The expression on her face asked, "*Who's this?*"

"This is Jack," said Max. "Jack, this is Andrea."

She extended her hand to him and said, "Nice to meet you. Welcome to sunny Southern California." She looked at Jack then added, "You're Max's significant other, right?"

Max thought that she saw Jack's face flush a bit. "Yes," he mumbled.

"I thought they'd be back by now," Andrea said. "You're welcome to wait down on the dock if you like." Then she added, "Max, you said that Jack is a sailor, right?"

"He is."

"Better yet, then, Max, one of our boats is on the dock. It's free today, so if you'd like to take it out for a short ride around the harbor, you're welcome to it."

* * *

Andrea walked them down to the dock. The Duffy that was tied up was the same one that Brad had taken them out on. After a quick orientation for Jack, she helped cast them off. Then she watched and waved as Jack drove the boat away from the dock.

"Isn't this cool?" said Max.

"It's different," said Jack.

As they got to the main channel, Max pointed toward the mouth of the harbor. "Patti, didn't Brad say that Edso's boat was over there?"

"I think so, but he also said that these boats are restricted to the harbor proper."

"I know, but I'm curious. Maybe if we see it for ourselves, we can think of a way to stop Courtney from doing anything rash. Jack, what do you say?"

He pointed the boat toward the area where Max was pointing. "What the hell. I'm only going to be here a few days. I can be a dumb tourist if someone calls us out."

Ahead, Max could see the entrance channel, with its nonstop parade of boats going in and out of the harbor. She opened a door in the helm console, reached in, and pulled out Brad's binoculars.

They were nearly at the beginning of the jetties that defined the limits of where they could roam when Max shouted, "I see it!"

"What?" said Jack.

"His boat."

"You're sure?"

"I can see the name. It's his."

Patti changed the lens on her camera, sighted through it, and began depressing the shutter release.

"Holy shit," said Max, as she raised her glasses to look up at the house. "Look at that house. Patti, there's someone up on the deck. Get a picture."

Patti's camera clicked away.

Jack began to turn the boat back.

"Where're you going?" said Max. She turned to keep the binoculars trained on the boat and the house.

"Back. The Harbor Patrol is coming this way. Dumb tourist or not, we don't want to cause any problems for Andrea."

Max sighed but said, "Fair enough."

The Harbor Patrol didn't stop them, and they exchanged friendly waves as they passed.

* * *

Edso was standing at the deck's railing. He looked down at his boat. He looked to the north at all the activity in the harbor. He looked west, out to Catalina Island, standing proud on the horizon. Returning his gaze down onto the entrance channel into the harbor, he studied the steady stream of boats moving in and out of Newport Beach Harbor. Everything appeared to be as it should be.

Then, out of the corner of his eye, he saw one of those pesky Duffy Boats moving closer than it should to the beginning of the entrance channel. He looked down on it as three faces peeked from underneath its surrey top, gazing up. He saw a camera point in his direction, and then the boat abruptly turned back toward the harbor.

"Tourists," he thought with disdain. He was used to seeing people looking up at his house, taking pictures and gawking, so he didn't pay too much attention to it.

He smiled as he saw the Harbor Patrol boat moving in its direction on the way back to its base. Those Duffy boats were restricted to the harbor proper, and that one had strayed a bit too close to the entrance channel. The Harbor Patrol didn't stop them, but their presence had the desired effect.

CHAPTER 61

EDSO'S THOUGHTS WERE INTERRUPTED by the sound of Jorge's voice. "Sir, Maria and I are going out for a few hours. Is there anything you need us to do for you before we leave?"

Instead of answering immediately, he continued to stare straight ahead.

"Sir?"

"I'm sorry. No. I'm all set. You two go on." He waved a hand in Jorge's direction as if to brush the man away.

"I have my phone if you think of anything."

Edso nodded and turned back to looking out over the water.

It had been twenty-four hours since Giles' visit, and Edso was worried. Giles' words kept echoing in his head, and the more he thought about them, the more sinister they seemed. Giles knew all about Courtney. What had his grandfather told him? The filming? And Jennifer—had they been filmed?

"Son of a bitch," he hissed. "I bet he did."

* * *

Edso jumped up and rushed down to the dock, happy that Jorge and Maria had gone out. While the house was Maria's territory, the boat was Jorge's, and the man was meticulous in his attention to detail. As Edso stood next to the boat, his breathing heavy, he studied it. The lines that tied it to the dock were perfectly coiled, ready to cast off at a moment's notice. The topsides gleamed in the sunlight. The windscreen that surrounded the helm station was perfectly clear, no water spots, no streaks. Nothing was out of place. Everything was perfect. At least, that's how it appeared.

He swung his leg over the gunwale, boarding the boat. Moving quickly to the cabin door, he put the key in the lock and turned it. There was a reassuring click as the lock released its hold. He took a breath and slowly turned the knob. As he pulled the door open, cool air rushed out. The air conditioning was on. Puzzled, Edso considered the implications, his imagination beginning to run wild. After all, Jorge had cleaned the boat the day before. Maybe he had forgotten to turn it off. But it wasn't like him to be sloppy.

Without turning, Edso pulled the cabin door shut and leaned back against it. His heart was pounding. He felt like a little kid doing something he shouldn't. He let out a nervous laugh at how ridiculous that was; this was his boat.

As his eyes adjusted to the low light inside, he began to look around the cabin. Everything was in its place. Nothing seemed unusual. Switching on the lights, he began to methodically search the cabin—pillows, cushions, books, the galley, everything. He touched and inspected the walls and fixtures. He saw nothing suspicious, although he wasn't entirely sure that he'd know it even if he saw it.

Satisfied, he moved into the forward cabin where the bed was located. As before, he stood and looked around first, then began a more careful inspection. This time, his fears were confirmed. He found not one, but two, small lenses, each pointing at the bed from different directions. Had he not been looking, he never would have noticed them, but he had no doubt what they were.

Before further investigation, he left the cabin, closing the door behind him, and searched out the tool box he knew was on board. With a screwdriver, a knife, and some electrical tape, he returned to the cabin. First, he put a small piece of tape over each lens, telling himself that if anyone was watching, at least now they wouldn't be able to see exactly what he was doing.

Next, with a wavering sense of security, he began to disassemble the cabin, looking for any place where recording or transmitting equipment could be hidden. The bed was on a built-in island with storage underneath, accessed by drawers set in its face. There were also air-conditioning vents on the face.

When he pulled out the first drawer, it stopped as soon as its interior space was fully exposed, but it did not tilt the way a drawer would if it was close to the end of its slides, nor did it come out any further. He didn't see or feel any kind of a releasing mechanism that would allow the complete removal of the drawer. He concluded that the drawers had been designed like that to ensure that they remained stationary as the boat moved. Each drawer was constructed the same.

He then removed the mattress, which exposed the top of the island. The island was made up of several panels, each held in place by screws. When he removed the screws on one of the panels and lifted it, he felt a noticeable rush of cold air from underneath. His first thought was that one of the air conditioning ducts must have a leak, but almost immediately he saw that this diagnosis was wrong. Each of the drawers was actually built like a double drawer, the back of one becoming the front of the other. Only the front section of each drawer was exposed when it was pulled open. The hidden side did not have sides or a back; it was more like a shelf. Mounted on each one was a piece of electronic equipment with a small red light, which was on.

Edso could see that air-conditioning ducts ran into the space the drawers occupied, leaving that space to serve as a plenum for cooling the equipment. There was no ductwork running directly to the vents in the cabinet's face. He wasn't an electronics expert, but he was certain that he was looking at several hard drives, and a router or transmitter.

"Giles, you son of a bitch," he said. A wave of nausea washed over him as he realized that it was just like on *Vorspiel*, only this time he wasn't dealing with family. Suddenly, that meeting with Giles on Catalina and the surprise lunch on his deck made so much more sense, and he knew he was in serious trouble.

Then, once again, he added, "Grandfather, what have you gotten me into?"

CHAPTER 62

IT DIDN'T TAKE EDSO AS LONG to put his boat back together as had taken him to search it. The last thing he did before locking up the boat and walking back up to the house was remove the tape off of the lenses that he had found.

Walking in, he was relieved to see that Jorge and Maria had not yet returned. He needed time to compose himself before facing either of them. His heart was pounding in his ears, and it felt as if his whole body was vibrating. He needed to settle his nerves. His first inclination was to pour himself a strong drink, but before he removed the cap on the bottle of single malt, he paused and looked at it.

"No. They'll know something's wrong."

He replaced the bottle of scotch into the rack. They'd find out soon enough that he knew, and he wanted to delay that inevitability, if only for a few hours, but he still needed a drink.

A glass of wine wouldn't draw too much attention, since he often had a glass in the afternoon. Something light, like a rosé, or a sauvignon blanc, would be perfectly normal for him to have on a beautiful Southern California afternoon, but he needed something more substantial. Looking over the wine rack, he chose a full-bodied Bordeaux. They might notice, but it was less of a risk than having a scotch.

He found the pop of the cork and the glug, glug, glug as he filled the glass soothing. He took a sip and savored it, as he swirled it in his mouth before swallowing. Edso then walked out onto the deck and returned to the railing where he had been when Jorge had said good-bye.

"*Jorge, how could you?*" he thought. The more he thought about it, he realized that he shouldn't have been surprised. He knew that Jorge and Maria were part of the Network, but he had assumed that Jorge was only there to provide security for him. He had never suspected that Maria was anything more than a talented housekeeper. Now, having found the surveillance equipment on the boat, he began to wonder what other roles they might be playing.

Fear began to grip Edso as he recalled Maria's deference to Giles at lunch the day before. To prepare such a lunch, she must have known he was coming, yet she hadn't said anything about it to him.

* * *

Edso heard the door from the house open. As he turned, he saw Maria stepping onto the deck.

"Hello, sir. Did you have a nice afternoon?" asked Maria.

"Yes. Yes, I did," he replied.

As he spoke, Jorge joined her on the deck. He said nothing.

Edso tried to discern whether there was anything about them that might indicate that they already knew he had found the equipment on the boat. He couldn't tell.

"How was the traffic? Based on the harbor, it seems like a busy summer's day," he said.

It was Jorge who answered. "It's always busy, but you're right. I did see many more people who just had that *tourista* look. They always seem to cause such trouble. As a matter of fact, this morning when I was checking on the boat, I had to wave off a boat that was way too close to the dock."

"No kidding? Any idea who it was?"

"No. But I'm guessing that they had either rented the boat, or the owner was playing tour guide."

"Why do you say that?"

"The boat had a California registration."

"Did you get the name of the boat?"

"I did. *Dream Weaver.*"

"Doesn't sound familiar. You think you could find out who it belongs to?"

"I'm sure I can." In Jorge's answer, Edso heard the implied question: "Why?"

"Giles strongly suggested some extra vigilance when he came to lunch," Edso added.

Jorge nodded in silent agreement. He didn't move as Maria asked, "What would you like for dinner tonight?"

"I think I'm going to eat out tonight. Why don't you both take the night off?" He forced himself to smile and added a wink.

"Thank you, sir."

"I'll see you *tomorrow*," he said, with extra emphasis to show his intentions. Edso watched as they turned and walked back into the house.

CHAPTER 63

"I LIKE BRAD AND ANDREA. They seem really nice," said Jack, as they drove home on the PCH.

"They are," agreed Courtney.

Jack was riding shotgun. Max, leaning forward with her head next to his, was pointing out all the landmarks and places they had visited during their trip.

"I'm going to make a quick detour for some food," said Court, as she drove past the turn for the cottage.

"Where to?" asked Max.

"I thought Loco Taco. Jack needs some good Mexican."

"Yum," said Patti.

"We have enough beer?" asked Max.

"Plenty," said Court.

* * *

Jack could only stare as Courtney turned into the drive.

"This is your cottage?" he said, as they walked through the door. "I assumed that it was some kind of a small, rustic place."

"Courtney has some really good friends," said Max. Jack noticed that her pointed tone seemed to add air quotes around the word *good*. "She won't tell us anything about him. He also set up our Duffy ride, which is how we met Brad and Andrea."

"Must be an international man of mystery," said Jack, looking at Courtney.

She just smiled. "How about lighting the fire pit and helping get stuff out so we can eat?"

"I'll get the beers," said Patti.

"Here, bring these," said Max to Jack. She handed him a stack of plates while grabbing napkins and silverware. "Come on, Jack," she said, leading the way to the patio.

"You've got to be kidding," said Jack. He put the plates on the table and walked to the railing. The sun was nearly touching the horizon, and the clouds were awash in color.

Max came up behind him, wrapped her arms around his waist, and squeezed. "I'm so glad you're here," she said, her voice muffled as she pressed her head against his back.

He wriggled around and put his arms around her. Pulling her tight, he looked into her eyes. "Cat has really missed you," he said, trying to hide a smile.

She pulled away and gave him a playful slap. "You are such a jerk."

All he could do was smile.

"Food's ready," said Court.

Max turned and, grabbing his hand, gave a tug, "Let's eat. Jerk."

The fire pit was burning, and four chairs, each with a small table next to it, were arranged around it. A beer was already on each small table. Patti and Courtney weren't waiting; they were already filling their plates.

"Oh, man, you're right. There's nothing like this at home," said Jack, as he wiped chunky guacamole off his chin.

Conversation was sparse until each finished eating. Eventually, Courtney said, "Okay, Jack. Why are you here?"

He said nothing as he swallowed the last of his beer. Then he said, "I think that you're in more danger than you know."

"Explain."

"Tom and I are worried about Edso's possible connection to a guy called Giles Endroit. Max and I met Endroit in Belize, and at the time, we thought he was just a cheesy novelist. But then he tried to buy up all that land in Rye Harbor. Now, according to Tom, he might actually be something else entirely."

Three pairs of eyes stared at him. "Based on Tom's security bulletins, it seems he is involved with a white supremacist group and may be involved in some kind of a larger operation that is causing concern. When you sent me that picture Patti took of Edso, I shared it with Tom. He sent it to his higher-ups, and shortly after that, Ken showed up in our apartment."

"Ken?" said Court. "The one who helped rescue me and killed that guy from Otto's yacht?"

"The same. And Ken confirmed that the woman in the photo is Sylvie. He made me promise to try to keep you three away from them. But we all know how that's turned out. The safest move would be to pack our bags in the morning and take the first flight East. Tom and Dave agree with me. This looks like a really lovely place, but you need to come home."

Before Courtney could reply, Max broke in.

"Jack, it's already been a long day. How about everyone sleeps on it, and we talk again in the morning? You must be exhausted with the jet lag and all."

Patti immediately grabbed some dirty dishes and handed a tray to Courtney. "I'll wash if you wipe," she said, pulling her toward the kitchen. "Let's let these two get to bed."

CHAPTER 64

"COURT, CAN I ASK YOU SOMETHING?"

"Sure."

Patti and Courtney had just finished cleaning up the evening's meal.

"What's going on?"

"What do you mean?"

"You know. With Edso."

"Honestly, Patti, I haven't made up my mind. Part of me wants to confront Edso, but another part knows it's a bad idea. I thought that staying out here a few more days would help me decide. And then you and Max decided to stay. And now Jack's here."

"If you want my opinion, I think you should forget about Edso and have a fling with Brad."

"Patti!" said Courtney, feigning shock.

"Come on, face it. He's hot. He's interested in you, and you could use a good lay."

"Patti! Stop."

"Sorry, I couldn't help it. But, face it, it's not a bad idea."

Courtney gave Patti a look that said, "This conversation is over." She walked out of the kitchen and back out onto the patio. Patti followed.

The night air had cooled. The fire pit was still burning. Silently, they sat down next to each other by the fire.

"Have I told you how incredible this vacation has been?" said Patti.

"Every day."

"Why did you do this?"

Courtney looked over at her. "I don't have a lot of really close friends, even though I know so many people because of Ben's. Tom,

Jack, Max, you, and Dave are my true friends, and after what happened, I just wanted to give us all a break."

* * *

"Jack, how worried should we be?" Max asked in a whisper.

They were lying next to each other. Jack was on his back, left arm under his head and right extended out to the side. Max was pressed up against him, on her side, lying on top of his extended arm with her head propped up by her left hand, which allowed him to caress her shoulder. With her right hand, she was drawing lazy circles on his naked midsection while her leg was draped over his. She felt him stir.

"I think if Courtney could just decide to stay away from Edso and enjoy her time here, then there wouldn't be anything to worry about. But making contact with him could be a real problem. We really need to convince her of this in the morning."

"I'm so happy you're here."

"I'm happy to be here."

Gently, he put a bit of pressure on her shoulder. She leaned in and kissed him, then slowly slid on top of him, and they became one again.

CHAPTER 65

AFTER LEAVING CATALINA ISLAND, the *M/V Wonder* sailed north to Los Angeles to a reserved berth in Del Ray Landing. Located in Marina Del Ray, the marina provided easy access to all that Los Angeles had to offer, and it was close to LAX if a flight was needed.

"Got a minute?" Sylvie said to the captain. Several days had passed since their arrival, and Sylvie had just walked onto the bridge of the *Wonder*.

He turned and looked at her. He was getting ready to go down to the marina's office.

"I think it's time I go visit Edso," said Sylvie.

"Oh?" he replied.

"Yeah. He's not expecting me, so the surprise should be enough that he'll be easy to manipulate."

"When?"

"I was thinking a bit later today. I've got to arrange for a car, and I'd like to try to avoid the worst of the traffic."

"Take your time; we can stay here as long as necessary. Oh, and there's something else. I just heard from our sources back East."

She froze and stared at him.

"Those women from Rye have apparently extended their stay here."

"What!"

He repeated what he had just said, then added, "And if that weren't enough, some guy is coming out to join them."

She continued to stare at him, then in a low, halting voice asked, "What guy?"

The captain looked down at a piece of paper in front of him. "Ja—"

"Jack Beale," she said, cutting him off.

"Yes. How did you know?"

"That's a long story."

"I don't have to tell you that for us to get this close, these sorts of complications could jeopardize everything."

"I know."

"It won't be a problem—will it?"

Her voice trailed off as she started to turn away. "It won't be."

"Sylvie." He rarely spoke her real name aloud, and this stopped her in her tracks. She turned to face him.

"It *won't* be a problem—*will* it." This time his words did not pose a question.

"It won't," she repeated. "Excuse me. I have to arrange for a car."

* * *

One of the benefits of renting a car in LA was the wide range of choices, from high-end exotics to dented wrecks that still started right up. After a short search, she found the perfect car: a BMW M4 Competition Coupe in mineral grey.

The sun was well into setting by the time she had secured the car, and it was dark by the time she entered the traffic flow south on the 405. As she was unable to think of anything other than the news that Max and company were staying and Jack was here, the car became an extension of her arms and feet as her subconscious guided her toward her destination.

"What are you doing here, Jack?" she thought.

It wasn't until she saw a sign for her exit appear that she returned to the present. As she exited the highway, the Captain's last words echoed in her head: "It *won't* be a problem—*will* it."

She had agreed, but now as she drove into Newport Beach, she wasn't so sure.

"Focus," she said out loud. "Edso is the target. Find him, get the answers, and . . . and what?"

She didn't know what, but after their interlude on his boat in

Avalon, he was clearly the key.

* * *

She checked the address Edso had written down for her. She was close. As much fun as surprising him might be, she decided to call first. She pulled out her phone and dialed his number. After the fourth ring, she heard his voice. "Hello." He sounded stressed.

"Edso, it's me, Jennifer. You up for some company?"

She could tell from his voice that she had surprised him.

"Where are you?" he said, recovering quickly.

"Does it matter?" She wanted to keep him a bit off balance.

"No, no. Of course not."

"Good answer. Are you hungry?"

"I am. I was just about to go out for a bite."

"How about I pick something up and bring it to your place?"

She could hear him smiling. "That would be great."

"What do you feel like eating?" she asked.

"Surprise me." The stress she had heard in his voice was now gone.

"See you in a bit," she said, and ended the call.

CHAPTER 66

"I BROUGHT THAI," said Jennifer. She marched in, brushing past Edso as soon as he opened the door. No hello. No "It's so good to see you." No "Nice house." Only, "I brought Thai."

Edso noticed that she was clutching a large, brown paper bag with handles. Mouth-watering aromas emanated from within. Her entrance was so abrupt that he didn't get a good look at her appearance, but what he saw was enough to ignite memories of their last encounter. He smiled broadly.

"Well, hello to you too," he mumbled under his breath. Then he pressed the door closed and watched from behind as she walked through the house toward the kitchen.

She was wearing a knee-length, white, short-sleeved dress. "Yes," he mumbled. The rhythm created by the clacking sound of her footfalls on the tile floor was neither hurried, nor slow and seductive. Yet the way she moved was all the more irresistible because of the manner in which her dress swayed with each step.

"You have any wine?" she asked, as she disappeared from sight.

"I do. What do you have in mind?"

"I think a Riesling would do very nicely with Thai."

"Anything else I can do?"

"No, just get the wine."

The wine refrigerator was built into the bar, which was out of sight of the kitchen, so other than his brief glimpse of her as she walked past him, he really hadn't been able to get a good look at her, and her mysterious behavior was definitely piquing his curiosity.

"I've got the wine and glasses. What say we eat out on the deck?" he called out.

"Perfect. Go on out; I'll be right out."

He had just uncorked the wine, sampled it, and filled two glasses when she walked out onto the deck carrying a tray with everything needed for dinner: plates, utensils, and several bowls of food.

Edso looked up and froze.

She stopped and giggled.

"What's so funny?" he asked.

"Nothing," she said, as she placed the tray on the table.

"Nothing? No—that wasn't the laugh of nothing."

"I'm sorry, but the look on your face . . ." She picked up one of the glasses of wine and took a sip in an apparent effort to hide her smile.

"What look?"

"Ooo, this wine is perfect," she cooed.

"Forget the wine. What look?"

"Come on, let's eat before it gets cold."

"No. You need to explain. What look?" he insisted.

She took another sip. "All right. You looked like you had never seen a girl before."

He could feel the blood rushing into his face. "I'm sorry. I didn't mean to stare."

"You're staring right now."

He couldn't help himself. Before, when he had only seen the dress from behind, his curiosity had been piqued, but now, seeing it from the front, memories from that night on the boat overwhelmed him. He wanted her. The dress was what could best be described as a shirt, only longer. He couldn't tell if it was cotton or linen, but that didn't matter. Its cut was neither form-fitting tight, nor loose and shapeless, and it accentuated her body in the best possible way. A row of buttons from top to bottom held it together, and a belt around its waist gave definition to its shape. Unbuttoned down to the belt, it gaped open enough to reveal that it was all that she was wearing.

She smiled. "You're still staring."

* * *

"That was delicious," said Edso.

"And the wine was perfect," she added, picking up the empty bottle. "Is there more?"

"Of course. I'll be right back." He excused himself and went inside for the wine, leaving her alone on the deck. She got up from the table and walked to the railing of the deck overlooking Newport Beach Harbor.

A few moments later, she heard his steps and turned. "It's beautiful," she said, making sure that her dress gaped open just enough to tease. His eyes betrayed his interest as he handed her a full glass of wine.

"I'm assuming that you mean the harbor," he said.

"Yes." Then she added, "And your house."

"Thank you."

She turned away, deliberately focusing her attention on the view once again.

"So, you live here alone."

"Mostly. There's a couple of caretakers, Maria and Jorge. They came with the house."

"Define, 'came with the house.'"

"Well, when I moved in, they were already employed here as caretakers, and there's never been a reason for them to leave. She cooks and cleans; he takes care of the grounds and the boat."

This was news to her. She looked at him. "Do they live here?"

"No. They have a place of their own, but they might as well live here. I never really thought much about it until you asked."

"Must be nice."

"It has its advantages." He paused.

"And . . .?"

"No matter how I say this, I'm going to sound like some kind of an elitist."

"Try me."

"In some ways, they're like furniture. You know they're always here, but you just don't notice them. Yet at the same time, you couldn't do without them."

"Who are they? Innocents or players?" she wondered. Aloud she said, "I didn't see anyone. Are they here?"

"No." He frowned for a second, as if distracted by a memory, then quickly added, "Tonight it's just us."

Still leaning on the railing, she turned toward him and smiled. "So we're alone?"

He nodded and took a sip of his wine, his anticipation unmistakable.

"Time to push some buttons," she thought.

"Can I ask you something?" she said.

"Sure."

"Remember the last time we were together on your boat? You told me about your grandfather and what it was like for you growing up."

"I do," he said, indifferently.

"I'm curious about something you said about the time we met on the dock in San Diego."

He suddenly looked more alert, and she could see that she had caught his full attention now.

"You told me you had just found out that your grandfather had died, and you were reminiscing about his yacht."

"Ye-es."

Despite the wariness in his voice, she pressed on.

"I was pretty curt with you that day."

"You were."

"Here's what I'm curious about: when we were tied up there, on several occasions I thought I heard a soft whining sound. At the time, I convinced myself that it was my imagination, but now I'm sure I heard it again when we were in Catalina. Did you ever hear anything like that when you were wandering around?"

"Not that I can remember," he said.

She looked at him, uncertain whether he had paused or not before answering with a lie.

"One more thing I thought was strange. There was a really odd-looking yacht in San Diego. It was all gray and mysterious, kind of creepy. I guessed that it was either military or some kind of a research vessel, but something about it gave me the chills. Did you see it while you were there?"

She stopped and looked deeply at him.

"I didn't."

This time she was certain: his answer was a little too quick, reinforcing her earlier impression that he was a world-class liar.

"Okay," she said, as lightly as possible. She had found out what she needed. He was clearly connected with Giles. Then, leaning in to him, she gently brushed her lips against his cheek and whispered, "Let's go inside."

CHAPTER 67

UNLIKE THE NIGHT ON HIS BOAT, she made no attempt at domination, although he clearly had enjoyed that scenario. This time she let him take the lead. It would be his reward for what his lying had confirmed.

"Thank you," exhaled Edso, as they lay spent on the bed. She was resting on top of him, head raised, chin perched in her hands, looking in his eyes.

"Can I ask you a question?" she said.

"What?"

"Something you told me has been bugging me. Maybe I misunderstood."

"What are you talking about?"

"When you moved out here from back East, after your grandfather's boat burned and sank. I'm assuming that you left together. How did you lose track of each other?"

For a split second, she saw a shadow pass through the expression on his face. But his recovery was almost instantaneous, and he smiled.

"It's complicated. We did leave New England together, but shortly after, before we got out here, my grandfather insisted that we travel separately. I don't know why, but after the loss of his beloved *Vorspiel*, he changed. I saw it, or rather, I more felt it. In any event, there was no arguing with him—he was always a very determined man—so we parted and agreed to meet in California, but I never heard from him again. That is, until I was notified of his passing."

"That is so sad," she said, not letting on that she already knew most of what he had said. "But you tried to find him?"

"Of course I did, but California is a big place."

Again, she thought she detected a hint of wariness in his voice.

"I'm sorry. That came out wrong." She gently shifted her hips, pressing them into him, confident that the distraction would be enough to allay any suspicions he might be feeling.

She felt his response and smiled at him. His hands moved to her hips, applying gentle pressure, guiding her movements. For her part, she lay her head on his chest and reached for his hands, interlocking her fingers with his. With hands locked together, she pulled his arms up until they were extended above his head. Then she lifted her shoulders and arched her back, which increased the pressure of her hips on his. Slowly, she looked down at him and lowered her head to kiss him, adjusting her hips until, once again, she felt him inside her.

Edso released a long-held breath and moaned softly. "You're forgiven."

* * *

Finally, spent and satisfied, they separated and rested beside each other in the dark quiet of the room.

Sometime later, she awoke with a start. Disoriented at first, she looked around. The room was dark. Edso, betrayed by his deep, regular breathing, was sleeping soundly.

"What time is it?" She didn't see a clock anywhere in the room, but as her eyes adjusted to the darkness, she could make out the windows by the faint light coming from around the edges of the curtains.

Being careful not to make any large movements that might wake him, she slowly slid off the bed and tiptoed naked across the room to the windows. Pulling the curtain back just enough to get a glimpse outside, she confirmed that it was late but still couldn't pinpoint the time. Quickly and quietly she moved to the door, and with a practiced hand she opened it silently and slipped out of the room. The house was cool and dark. The darkness wasn't complete but rather complicated shades of gray and black, and as her eyes adjusted, she was able to move about with ease. *"Everything must be on timers,"* she thought, remembering that when they had disappeared into the bedroom, lights had still been on throughout the house. She moved to the kitchen, drawn by the faint light of the clock on the stove. Two a.m.

Leaving the kitchen, she walked slowly around the room. Unwilling to risk turning on a light, her search for hard evidence would have to wait. Until then, she would have to be satisfied with her feelings. Sliding open one of the doors to the deck, she silently stepped outside. The night air was warm, with a hint of moisture, and it felt good against her bare skin. She walked across to the railing and looked out over the harbor. Much of the shoreline was dark, save for street lights and an occasional business. Most of the boats in the harbor were just dark shadows against the inky water, although a few still had some lights on. Far out over the sea, she could see the dark shape of Catalina Island.

She pretended not to hear Edso coming up behind her. He wrapped his arms around her, and she had to admit to herself that the warmth of his body felt good as he pressed against her. He whispered in her ear, "Hey, you okay?"

She wriggled around to face him, "Yes. I couldn't sleep and you were sleeping and I didn't want to wake you, so I came out here."

The warm night air suddenly felt cool, especially compared to the heat from their tightly pressed bodies.

"You feel so good," he whispered. He looked down and kissed her.

It was obvious what he had in mind, but she needed to get more information before giving him what he wanted.

"Can I ask you something else?"

He pulled back slightly. "What?"

She could tell, both by his tone and his rapidly diminishing reaction to her, that he didn't want to talk, which gave her a great deal of leverage.

"After your grandfather passed, how did the person who gave you the news know where to find you?"

"I never really thought about how they found me."

"Who's 'they'?"

"Some attorneys. I just assumed they were my grandfather's lawyers."

"Oh. Go on."

"Not much else to say. They found me, they gave me the news, and that's about it."

"And how did you find this gorgeous house?"

"When I first arrived, I stayed in a hotel, looking around at my options and calling some realtors to ask about places for rent. One day I got a call saying that this place was available. The rent was cheap, relatively speaking, and I couldn't pass it up."

He pulled her close again and bent to kiss her. She dodged his kiss and said, "How lucky for you that Maria and Jorge came with the place. It can be so hard to find good help."

"True. The day I moved in, they just showed up and as they say, 'the rest is history'."

"You have to be the luckiest guy in the world."

"I might be," he said, as he gently pulled her closer again and leaned in for a kiss.

This time, she kissed him back, and when she began to feel his reaction, she pressed her hips into him and whispered, "Let's go back inside."

"No," he moaned, and gently lifted her up.

She wrapped her arms around his neck and her legs around his waist, and they became one once again.

CHAPTER 68

"GOOD MORNING," said Edso softly.

Jennifer shielded her eyes from the bright light shining in on her. She could see that he was freshly showered and dressed.

"What time is it?"

"Time to start the day."

"Is that coffee I smell?"

"I brought you a cup. Here."

Jennifer sat up, making no effort to cover herself, having decided that he deserved another look.

As he handed her the steaming cup, he took that look, smiled, and said, "Maria is making us breakfast."

Holding the cup in one hand, trying not to spill, she quickly attempted to pull the sheets up with her free hand.

"Relax. It's okay. She's in the kitchen. We're quite alone. Did I ever tell you how gorgeous you are?"

"You did. Multiple times."

"Well, you are. Now, I'm going to leave you alone so you can get showered and dressed, and I'll see you out on the deck for breakfast."

The hot shower felt good, and she used this time alone to reflect on the past twenty-four hours. She had learned as much from what he hadn't told her, as she had learned from what he had said.

* * *

As she emerged from the bedroom and started to walk toward the deck, the wonderful smells coming from the kitchen drew her to the doorway. Looking in she saw a short, unsmiling Mexican woman, who was shuffling from stove to counter preparing breakfast.

Without looking up, the woman said, with a thick accent, "Good morning, Señora,"

She stopped, surprised, and smiled and said, "Good morning. You must be Maria."

Still without looking up she said curtly, "Mr. Edso is outside on the deck,"

"Thank you."

She turned from the kitchen and walked quickly to the deck. The perfect Southern California morning promised blue sky, perfect temperatures, and an afternoon breeze. She saw Edso standing at the railing, looking up into the sky. She looked up and didn't see anything, but she was pretty sure she heard a low humming sound. *The drone? Why?*

"Hey, stranger, what're you looking at?" she said.

"Nothing," he replied quickly, turning to face her.

Jennifer thought she detected something off in the way he reacted to her question, but she couldn't be sure.

"Hungry?"

"Starving."

"Then let's eat."

"I assume that the woman inside is Maria?"

"Yes. You met?"

"Sort of. She seems a bit grumpy."

"Don't let her vivacious personality put you off," he said with a wink and a grin. "She's an amazing cook and housekeeper."

As soon as they were seated at the table, Maria appeared with a pot of fresh coffee, a plate with two chocolate croissants, and a dark stare at Jennifer.

"Thank you, Maria. This is my friend Jennifer," he said.

It was obvious that Maria's smile was forced. It only lasted a second as she said, "Señora." Then she quickly retreated from the table into the house.

"She doesn't say much, but she has an uncanny ability to know exactly what you want when you want it."

Sylvie took a sip of her coffee after inhaling its aromas. "This is really good."

"I don't know where she gets it, but it is hands down the best. Try your croissant."

He watched as she slowly chewed her bite.

"Ooo, you're right. This is delicious." She took another bite.

He continued to watch her, nodding in agreement. Then he went strangely silent, still staring at her. After a few long, awkward moments, she looked into his eyes and after swallowing said, "What?"

"My grandfather always said, 'Those who truly have power set the rules. Those who don't, well, they're just out of luck.' And you have it."

"Have what?"

"Power. Over me."

His words surprised her. "What? Where did that come from?" she asked.

"I'm sorry. That's not exactly what my grandfather meant, but I'm using it as an analogy for how I'm feeling."

"What exactly did your grandfather mean?"

"He was talking about the new world order, and how now, it's becoming a reality sooner than anticipated and we must be ready."

"A new world order?" she said.

As soon as she said that, from the way he looked at her, she felt that she may have gone too far. "I'm sorry, I shouldn't have asked. Listen, it's a beautiful day, Maria's croissants are to die for, and last night was truly special. Maybe another time you could explain your grandfather's ideas to me."

Edso forced a smile and she reached over and put her hand on his arm. She could feel him relax. Hoping that she hadn't pushed things too far, she said, "I do need to get back to the *Wonder.*"

She saw the shadow lift off him, and he instantly resumed his role as the charming playboy. "Can I see you again?"

"I'd like that."

"When?"

"I'll call—maybe tonight."

*   *   *

Breakfast finished, he walked with her to the door. As they passed the kitchen, out of the corner of her eye, she saw Maria watching them.

"Hold on a minute. I'd like to say thank you to Maria."

As soon as she turned toward the kitchen, Maria turned away in a failed attempt to mask the fact that she had been watching them.

"Breakfast was delicious. Thank you," she said, from the doorway into the kitchen.

Maria nodded. Then, just as Jennifer was turning away, she said, "Will you be coming back?"

That question took her by surprise. She turned back to Maria and said, "I don't see why not."

"When?"

"I don't really know. Maybe tonight."

CHAPTER 69

"GOOD MORNING, MAX."

Max was blinking her eyes against the bright sunlight as she stepped out onto their deck. "What time is it?"

"Nearly eleven. Where's Jack? Is he okay?"

"Ha ha. He's fine, just a little jet-lagged."

"Right," said Courtney.

Max heard the sarcasm dripping from her voice and noticed that she had added a broad smirk on her face to match.

Max gave her a dirty look. "Is there any coffee?"

"In the kitchen."

As Max walked into the house, Jack emerged from the bedroom. "Where is everyone?"

"Court's outside. Not sure where Patti is. You want some coffee?"

"Love some."

He followed her into the kitchen, and as she put two mugs on the counter and began to fill them, Jack slid up behind her and wrapped his arms around her, managing to caress one of her breasts.

"Jack, stop it. You'll make me spill."

He stopped and stepped back. "No, we wouldn't want that, would we?"

She turned and handed him a cup. "Jerk."

He grinned sheepishly and shrugged. "So, what's up for today?"

"Don't know. Let's see what Courtney has in mind."

They headed out to the deck.

"Good morning, Jack," said Court. She looked up from the magazine she was reading.

"Mornin', Court. Nice place. Now, how exactly did you score this place?"

"She has a secret friend. Won't tell us," said Max.

Jack nodded, and with a wink he said, "I see. So, any plans for today?"

"Patti's out doing her thing with her camera. I think she went down to the beach. She'll probably be back before too long. Then we can make some plans."

Before he could reply, her phone rang. She glanced at the screen and immediately got up from her chair. "I've got to take this," she said. Then she walked over to the railing.

Jack looked at Max and raised his eyebrows.

She shrugged and said, "I don't know, but if I had to guess, I'd say it's Brad. You hungry? Let's go in and give her some privacy. We can harass her later."

They left her at the railing and went inside in search of food.

Just as Max was heating a pan to cook some eggs, Courtney walked in.

"Hey guys, before you ask, that was Brad, and he invited me out for the day. We're going kayaking. He's picking me up shortly. You can have the car, and I'll see you tonight. Max, I'll leave you the keys."

Stunned to silence and before they could say anything, she turned and walked off.

"Well, I guess that answers my question," said Jack.

Max finished cooking the eggs, and they ate them at the table with a pile of toast that Jack had made.

"Patti will be back soon, and then we can decide what to do," said Max. "In the meantime, I'm going to change into my suit and head out to the deck to get some sun."

"When do you think Patti will be back?" he asked. He was staring at her bathing suit. It was the one-piece suit with the tropical leaf pattern in greens and blues.

She smiled as she remembered the last time he had seen her in that suit. "Forget about it, Jack Beale."

"Forget about what?" he said plaintively.

"You know what."

Then she softened her tone and said, "Would you rub some lotion on my back?"

"Bye guys," Courtney called out from inside the doorway. "Behave yourselves. Keys are on the counter."

Max looked up. Courtney was wearing a pair of khaki cargo shorts, a coral-colored t-shirt, sneakers, and a navy sweatshirt tied around her waist completed her outfit.

"When will you be back?" called out Max.

Courtney just gave a silent wave as she turned and disappeared from sight.

Jack winked at Max. "She was carrying a small backpack. Bet we don't hear from her until tomorrow. At least it will take her mind off Edso."

Max turned and gave him a playful slap on the shoulder. "Pig."

"I'm just saying. You wanna' bet?"

"No. Finish my back, and don't get any ideas."

Lotion rubbed in, he said, "Maybe I'll go for a short run."

* * *

Jack was gone less than an hour. When he returned, Max said, "How was your run?"

"It was good. A little warmer than I'm ready for, but nice. Patti back?"

"She is. She's downloading pictures. Now that we're all here, how about going out for lunch?"

"Sounds good to me."

"Good. We're going to take you to the Sherman Library and Gardens."

"Library? Gardens?"

"You'll see. Go get cleaned up and I'll let Patti know. Then I'll grab a quick shower to wash off this lotion, and we'll go."

CHAPTER 70

"WE'RE HERE," SAID MAX, as she turned off the PCH and onto the narrow street leading to the entrance to the gardens.

"Just so I understand, this is both a library and a botanical garden, right?" said Jack.

"Yes."

"But it's not a library like where you need to have a card and you can check out books."

"Correct. It's a historical research library."

"Kind of like the Hotel California. You can check in, but the books can never leave."

Jack chuckled at his cleverness, but Max cut him off.

"Close, but not really."

"Let's go in."

"Hey, you two, go stand over there," directed Patti. "I want to get a picture of you."

Jack and Max sighed simultaneously. Still, they gave in and posed for Patti.

"Come on, you guys, stop messing around," she said, after a few shots. "Jack, if you look good, Max is making a face. Max, if you look good, Jack is squinting. Pull it together for once!"

Suddenly, Max noticed that Patti's demeanor had changed. She was still snapping pictures, but she seemed so much more serious—even distracted. It was as if something else had caught her attention.

"You okay, Patti?"

"Yes. I'm sorry. I think I have enough pictures. Let's sit and have lunch."

Max could tell that Jack had missed the subtleties of what had just transpired. He said, "Great!" and began walking toward the restaurant.

Max reached for Patti's arm. "Patti, what's wrong?"

"Nothing."

"Don't give me that. Something just happened, and I want to know what it is."

"Fine. I think I just saw Edso."

"What? Where?" Max whipped her head around, looking for him.

"He's gone. And I'm not 100 percent sure it was him."

"Tell me you got a photo."

Patti quickly scrolled through the pictures, then shook her head. "I didn't. And like I said, I'm not even sure that it was him."

"Well, nothing we can do about it now. Let's assume it wasn't Edso and go have a nice lunch. Jack's waiting."

Lunch was as good as they had experienced on previous visits, and then they spent an hour roaming the gardens.

"This place is really cool," said Jack. "We have anything like this at home?"

"We must," said Patti.

"That'll be something to look into when we get home," said Max.

"So where are we now?" asked Jack.

"Corona del Mar," answered Max. "It's just south of Newport Beach. We're near the harbor where Andrea loaned us the Duffy boat."

"And where Brad is," chimed in Patti. "Anyone else curious about what's going on there right now?"

"Patti! Stop it. He seems like a nice guy, a little young, but, hey, we're talking about Court. She's allowed."

Patti looked surprised. "Hey, I didn't mean anything bad. He seems really nice. Don't you think so, Jack?"

"Hey, leave me out of this," said Jack. "I just got here."

"Come on, let's get going," said Max. "Anyone interested in going up to the Top of the World?"

"What's that?" said Jack.

"It's a park up in the hills overlooking Laguna Beach. I read about it in one of the tourist brochures that was in the cottage. There's a look-out point up there that's supposed to have spectacular views. Sounds kind of cool."

"I'm game," said Jack.

Patti said, "If I can snap pics of the sunset, it sounds like a great idea to me."

CHAPTER 71

"IS HE GONE?" Jorge asked Maria as he walked into the house.

"He left shortly after his lady friend. Said he was going out for the day. Is everything all right?"

"I think he knows," said Jorge.

Maria looked stunned. "What?"

"I went down to check on the boat. The birds were kind today, so I didn't have to do much cleaning. But, inside, something didn't feel right. The bed was not made the way that you make it. I looked closer and the mattress had been moved. When I checked the equipment I could tell that the recording equipment had turned on, but there was nothing recorded. He must have taped over the cameras. Normally I wouldn't have checked them until after his next trip out."

"I don't trust her," said Maria.

"What?"

"That woman he was with last night. I don't trust her."

"You know, we'll have to report this."

"Yes. Have you checked the other recordings?"

"Not yet. I wanted to wait for you."

"Did Edso say when he'd return?"

"No, just that he was going out for the day."

"Come."

* * *

"Ay, dios mio," exhaled Maria, as they watched the recording of Edso and Jennifer in bed.

"She is very talented," whispered Jorge, putting his arm around his wife's shoulder and pulling her close.

She didn't pull away, and they watched in breathless silence.

"We'll have to report this," he said under his breath.

Her hand was beginning to wander. He sucked in his breath, let out a soft moan, and whispered, "What if he comes back?"

"We have time, and then we will report."

Inspired by the video, Jorge discovered that time both flew by and stood still all at the same time. They took advantage of that time to more fully study the video and enjoy an encore.

* * *

"Si. Yes, I understand," said Jorge. After he closed his special phone and took initial steps to destroy it, he shared the instructions he'd just been given.

"Both of them?" asked Maria.

"Yes. I'm going down to the water to get rid of this," he said, holding out the pieces of phone in his hand. "You know what to do."

"When?"

"The next time she comes over."

"What about her car?"

"The Network can take care of that."

CHAPTER 72

"AND HOW WAS YOUR VISIT to our friend?" the captain asked Sylvie, when she arrived back at the *Wonder*. It was nearly midday.

"Interesting."

"Interesting?"

"Yes. I drove down last night and surprised him with dinner."

"What did you bring?"

"Does it matter?"

"Not really. I'm just curious."

"Thai. He was alone, and I got lucky and caught him as he was about to go out. The caretakers had the night off, so it was just the two of us."

"What kind of car did you rent?"

She stopped and gave him a look. "Does it matter?"

"Not really, but again, just curious."

"A BMW M4." Then, without giving him a chance to ask, she added, "It was a coupe, and it was mineral gray."

"Thank you."

"May I continue?"

"By all means."

She took a deep breath. "We had dinner, we talked, and we had sex—in case you're curious about that too. He's very good and has remarkable recuperative powers."

"That was more than I needed to know, but thank you again. So, did you learn anything?"

"Well, he's definitely involved. This morning at breakfast, quite out of the blue, he began talking about how his grandfather believed that those who are true believers will wield the true power. It was kind of strange. When I asked him about what that meant, he said that it was about the coming new world order, and how now, it's becoming a reality sooner than anticipated, and we must be ready. When I questioned him, he abruptly stopped and went back to being a happy-go-lucky innocent."

"That's interesting. Do you think he was sounding you out?"

"Maybe, but not aggressively. The caretakers had returned by the time we got up this morning. I met her—name's Maria, Hispanic, kind of grumpy, but she does make a really good cup of coffee. I got a strange vibe from her. I don't think she's just a housekeeper."

"Why not?"

"There was something about the way she watched us that was more than simple curiosity. I didn't meet her husband. Edso said they came with the house. We should look into them."

"Are you going to see him again?"

"I am. I may even push it a bit harder and visit again tonight."

"Good. One more thing. That Jack Beale is in town."

She paused and then simply said, "Is he?"

"We've been keeping an eye on all of them."

She said, "Might have been nice if you'd told me."

"I'm telling you now. Mostly they're just doing touristy stuff, but Courtney went out on a boat with the owner of Voyagers, and they got pretty close to Edso's dock."

"So much for my warning," said Sylvie.

"I'll let you know if I find out anything else."

"Okay, thanks. And one more thing, remember how I heard that strange humming sound in San Diego? I'm sure I heard it again as I left his house. I think someone is watching with that drone. But Edso denied hearing anything at all."

"Interesting. Listen, I've got some work to do, and you must need some rest, especially if you're going back there tonight."

That last part he added with a smile, which she ignored.

* * *

Sylvie opened her eyes. Her cabin was mostly dark. She heard the clock chiming. She counted—two times followed by another pair and then a single bell. Five bells—6:30 p.m. She sat up sharply. She hadn't intended to sleep so long. Shaking the sleep from her head, she got up and looked out the porthole. Outside, it was dark save for the countless lights around the harbor, each doubled by its reflection off the water.

Without turning on any lights in her cabin, she picked up her phone. Its screen was almost blinding as she dialed Edso's number.

"Harding residence," Maria answered. Her voice was unmistakable to Sylvie—dry, flat, and emotionless—leaving no chance that it could be anyone else.

"Is Edso available?" She tried to sound cheerful and open in stark contrast to the cold words that had greeted her.

"Uno momento." The line went silent as the phone was put down.

It seemed a long time before she heard footsteps and a more cheerful, "Hello?"

"Edso? You around tonight?"

"Jennifer. Yes. All night." She could hear the lust in his voice.

"Will Maria be there?"

"Doesn't have to be."

"Good. See you in a bit."

"Define a bit."

"How's two, two and a half hours sound?"

"Perfect."

She ended the call.

The rejuvenating power of a long, hot shower met her needs, and by the time she got out, she was relaxed and ready for whatever the night would bring. She was determined that tonight she would make sure that Edso gave her the information she was seeking. The dangers that his grandfather and his ilk posed were real, and the fact that they existed out in the open as respectable members of society made them all that much more dangerous. They stoked fears and hatred, real and perceived, simplified and amplified with rhetoric designed to sound truthful, but based in half-thruthes and lies.

Most of their followers were cowards, sheep who simply followed. While these sheep often allowed themselves to be goaded into committing senseless acts of violence that frequently sowed fear, it was that small, influential group of leaders, bent on the disruption of the world order, who were the real problem.

To Sylvie, it seemed so preposterous that their ideas could gain traction, and yet, it was no joke. She knew that the mistakes of the past were being repeated as these scumbags gained influence in the United States, Germany, Poland, Brazil, Italy and elsewhere. She'd seen how France was being tested, and how the Russians and Chinese were exerting ever greater influence while taking advantage of the chaos. All indications were that Giles Endroit was one of those leaders, maybe even the most influential, and Edso may be the key to taking him down.

Setting these thoughts aside for the moment, she turned and studied herself in the mirror. She smiled as she imagined Edso's reaction. She was wearing tight, black, skinny jeans, with a loose-fitting, low-cut, silvery gray, short sleeved shirt. She decided that there was no need to wear anything under that shirt, but over it, she pulled on a lightweight denim jacket. To complete the outfit, she added a pair of black leather ankle boots. After one more long look in the mirror, she added a thin, gold chain necklace, several hoop bracelets on her right wrist, and a hybrid sport watch above her left wrist. The result was sufficiently casual and more than sexy enough to help her accomplish her goals.

CHAPTER 73

"MARIA," CALLED OUT EDSO.

As he had anticipated, she appeared silently.

"Yes."

"Maria, I need to ask you a favor. I will be having company again tonight, and I'd like to have the house to myself."

"I understand. I will find Jorge and we will go. Shall I return to cook breakfast?"

"Yes, that would be nice, if you would. I can't imagine starting the day without a cup of that coffee you make."

"Did she just start to smile?" he thought to himself. It was a rare day that her expression ever changed, but she had turned away before he could be sure.

As Edso waited for Maria and Jorge to leave, he found it easy to remain calm, but once they were gone, his anxiety, brought on by anticipation, skyrocketed. Since finding the recording equipment on the boat, there had been no opportunity to thoroughly search the house. He then began to walk slowly around the house looking for evidence of cameras.

His seach was cursory at best, and when he went into his bedroom, images of the previous night with Jennifer filled his head. He saw no obvious evidence of cameras and after having looked at his watch for the umpteenth time, he said out loud, "Stop it. Looking at your watch will not get her here any faster."

"I know," he answered himself. He closed his eyes and took a deep breath before continuing on. His last stop was out on the deck. He lit the fire pit and then moved to the railing, where he stood looking out over the harbor, remembering every moment he had spent with her.

* * *

"Edso." The sound of her voice startled him, and he turned. She was standing in the doorway, and for the briefest of moments he must have looked confused. *"Hadn't the door been locked?"*

"I knocked, but there was no answer and the door was open, so I came in. I hope you don't mind."

Recovering, he moved toward her and said, "You look amazing."

"Thank you. You look pretty good yourself."

She stepped out onto the deck just as he reached her, and they exchanged a cordial hug and a welcome kiss.

"Would you like some wine? Have you eaten? How was the traffic?"

"Edso, slow down." She smiled at him, then added, "A glass of wine would be nice."

"I'm sorry. Yes, of course." He moved past her into the house.

"Stop saying you're sorry. You have nothing to be sorry about, *yet.*" she said, with a hint of the tone she had used on his boat.

"Red?"

She had followed him in. "You don't have to shout. I'm right here."

It was impossible for her not to notice how flustered he was, and she hoped that with some wine he would settle down.

He handed her a glass, looked at her, and said, "Can I start over?"

She smiled and said nothing.

"Here's to us and tonight."

She touched the rim of her glass to his and took a sip, her smile her only response.

"Did I tell you how great you look?" he asked.

"You did, but thank you, again. Shall we go outside?" She led the way.

He followed her out and stood nearby as she settled into one of the chairs that ringed the fire pit. He sat opposite and said, "You look mesmerizing by the firelight. I think—"

She immediately held her finger to her lips and cut him off. "Shhh. Do you hear it?"

"Hear what?" he said, in a whisper.

"That low humming sound."

He cocked his head, listened, and then shook his head. "No. I don't."

Something in his tone left her unconvinced, so all she said was, "I must be hearing things again."

Edso pointed at her empty glass. "More wine?"

She smiled and nodded. "Please. It's delicious."

He retrieved the bottle, and as he bent to fill her glass, she reached up and gently pulled his face to hers and kissed him. It was a slow, sensuous kiss, which she let linger longer than necessary. When she finally let him go so he could fill her glass, she saw that the kiss had had the desired effect.

After he refilled his own glass, he sat down in the chair next to hers. He pulled one leg up under the other and turned sideways so he could look at her.

"Edso, do you remember when I told you about the creepy yacht I saw in San Diego?"

Before he could reply, she added, "I saw it just before I was leaving the *Wonder* today." It was her turn to lie. "I feel like it's following me."

"I'm sure it's nothing," he said quickly.

"You think it might be some kind of a naval vessel? I mean, San Diego is a major base, and Long Beach has military there as well."

"No idea, but I wouldn't worry about it."

Despite his words, she could see a trace of panic forming in his eyes.

"I'm probably just being silly." She put her hand on his knee.

Slowly, without taking his eyes off of hers, he lifted his glass to his lips and took the last sip.

"This wine is making me sleepy. Come. Let's go inside." He put his glass down, untwisted his legs and stood up.

She looked up at him, smiled, and held out her hand. Gently he helped her stand, and then he pulled her close and kissed her. She pressed into him and could feel him respond.

CHAPTER 74

OTHER THAN SEVERAL RECUPERATIVE CAT NAPS, they got very little sleep. Shortly after sunrise, Edso was the first to awaken. The smell of the coffee brewing told him that Maria had returned. He slipped out of the room to find a cup of coffee. Maria was in the kitchen and as soon as he walked in, she handed him one. *"How does she do that?"* he thought. "Thank you."

Edso took his coffee and walked out onto the deck. Maria had already set the table for breakfast. As before, she had placed on the table a vase filled with bright red California poppies. He smiled in anticipation of breakfast and the day ahead. After drinking half of his cup, he returned to the kitchen to top it up and get a cup for Jennifer. Maria had Jennifer's cup ready and waiting.

"Come on, sleepyhead!" he said. "Time to join the world of the living!"

When she mumbled a reply, he handed her the cup of coffee. "I think you could use this."

Then, as she cradled it in her hands, he lifted a sheet and draped it over her shoulders.

"Thank you," she said demurely.

"I'll check with Maria to see about breakfast while you wake up."

"You're such a gentleman."

He just smiled as he pulled the bedroom door closed.

Maria seemed busy with breakfast when he looked into the kitchen. She didn't look up, so he said, "Maria, I'm going to be outside. When Jennifer gets up, will you please tell her that's where I am?"

She nodded and then turned away from him.

"What the hell has gotten into her?" he thought. *"I'll have to talk with her after Jennifer leaves."*

After fifteen minutes on the deck alone, he began to wonder what was taking her so long. He got up and walked back into the house. Maria was standing by the entrance to the kitchen, talking with Jorge. As he approached, Maria turned away without so much as a glance and disappeared into the kitchen. Jorge stood in the doorway and just stared at him. "Everything okay?" he asked Jorge.

His attitude didn't seem much friendlier, but at least he replied. "Si. Everything is okay. The birds made a mess on the boat."

"Listen, after we have breakfast, I'd like to take my friend out on the boat. I don't know if she'll agree, but could you have it ready just in case?"

When Jorge nodded, Edso turned and walked toward the bedroom door.

"Knock, knock," he said, leaning into the closed door to listen for an answer. Hearing nothing, he turned the knob and went in, quickly shutting the door. The curtains were still drawn, her clothes were on the bed, and he could hear the shower running. He smiled and began to unbutton his shirt. Then he decided to leave on his pants. If she *wasn't* waiting for him, it would be less awkward; if she was receptive, she could help him take them off.

Slowly, as quietly as possible, he turned the knob. "Jennifer," he said softly, as he gently pushed the door open. The room was filled with steam, making it hard to see, and he was immediately hit with a rush of hot, moist air flooding out.

"Jennifer," he said again, as he slipped into the room. The bathroom had a tub, large enough for two, built into the far wall. Its surround was wide and flat, affording space for magazines, shampoos, or wine glasses, depending on how it was being used. The curtain was pulled closed and steam billowed over the top.

Again, there was no answer, only the sound of the continuous flow of water. Curious, he moved to pull the curtain aside.

"Jennifer," he said for a third time, with increasing concern. A thousand and one thoughts flashed through his head, none good, as he began to pull the curtain back.

The first thing he saw was her coffee cup, tipped on its side, its dark, rich liquid spilled onto the surround and running into the tub. As he ripped the curtain open, he was not prepared for what he saw next. Panic and confusion washed over him, and it took a moment for him to understand what his eyes were seeing.

Jennifer was crumpled in the bottom of the tub, her position anything but natural. Her skin was pink from the continuous stream of hot water still flowing over her, and a small rivulet of blood from her head tinted the water that flowed down the drain red.

He lunged forward toward her lifeless body. He reached for her neck to check for a pulse. She was warm to the touch, and there was a pulse. It was faint, but it was there.

He shut the water off and shouted for help. Realizing that Maria and Jorge probably couldn't hear him, he ran out of the bathroom, raced through the bedroom, ripped the door open, and shouted into the house for help before returning to Jennifer.

All the adrenaline in the world wasn't going to allow him to pick her wet, limp body out of the tub without causing her yet more injury, so he covered her with a towel and left again to call for help. This time, Maria appeared in the hall outside the bedroom.

"Call 911. Jennifer has slipped and fallen in the shower," he shouted at her. "And get Jorge. I need his help."

As soon as Edso shouted those instructions he turned and ran back. Time seemed to stand still as he sat by the tub looking down at Jennifer. He held a cloth to her head where she was bleeding. It wasn't a large cut, and he was able to stop most of the bleeding after a few moments.

It seemed an inordinately long time before he heard a knock on the doorframe. Turning, he saw Jorge standing there, looking in at him.

"Maria called me and said you needed some help."

With panic in his voice, Edso said, "Yes. I need your help getting her out of this tub and into the bedroom."

"Do you think that is a good idea?" said Jorge. His voice was very calm.

Edso slumped, realizing that Jorge was right. Moving her could cause more harm, especially since he didn't know just how badly hurt she was, save for the cut on her head.

"You're right. Has Maria called 911?"

"I saw her on the phone."

Relieved, he said, "Could you hand me another towel?"

Without saying a thing, Jorge picked up a towel, took several steps toward Edso, and handed it to him.

"Thanks."

As Edso was leaning over the tub to tuck the towel around her, he felt a sudden sting in his neck. He turned and saw Jorge looking at him.

"I'm sorry." These were the last words Edso heard as he slumped over the edge of the tub.

CHAPTER 75

"MARIA, QUICK! COME HERE!" Jorge called out after he dragged Edso from the bathroom to the bedroom floor.

She arrived in seconds, and he asked, "Did you make the call?"

"I did."

"And?"

"And, we are to take care of the situation and then disappear."

Jorge saw her glance at Edso. She asked, "Is he . . . ?"

"Yes. Go check on the woman."

Maria was gone less than a minute. "She's still alive. Her pulse is very weak."

"Okay. We'll come back for her. First, we have to get him down to the boat."

"How're we going to do that? He can't walk. We can't drag him or carry him. That would draw too much attention."

"Maria. Stop. Anyone watching will simply see that we are going to install a new air conditioner in the boat. Get that big box from the one we just replaced here in the house. It should be big enough."

She nodded and hurried out of the room.

While Maria hurried off to get the box, Jorge went to get some zip ties and duct tape. By the time he returned, she was waiting in the bedroom with the box.

"Is this the one you meant?"

He looked at the box, then at Edso's limp body, then back at the box. Made of extra heavy cardboard, it looked strong enough, and since it was in the room, he knew it would fit through the doorway.

"Yes."

Maria said nothing as she watched Jorge wrestle Edso onto his knees and then folded him down as if he were in some kind of a yoga pose.

"Help me," said Jorge, nodding toward the tape and ties. As he worked to hold the body in position, Maria used the tape and zip ties to keep it that way.

"Good," said Jorge standing up and admiring their handiwork. "Now, we get him into the box."

It was not easy wrestling him into the box, and when they finally closed and taped it shut, Maria said, "You know, maybe after we leave, we should become yoga instructors. I think we left him in a perfect child's pose."

Jorge stopped and looked at her. "What are you talking about?"

"The other day I saw on television a show about yoga, and he looks like he's doing one of the poses."

"Sometimes, Maria, I do not understand you."

"I bet his friend could do yoga. Remember how flexible she was?"

He knew she was baiting him.

"Enough. Help me. We have to get him down to the boat."

With great effort, they wrestled the box containing Edso down into the cellar and then out the door by the head of the ramp, where they loaded it into a large cart and wheeled it down to the boat. Jorge was sure that to anyone watching, it would appear quite innocent. People were always putting things on their boats.

"Are we going to do the same with the woman?"

"Yes."

"Is there another box? I didn't notice one, Maria said as they climbed off the boat.

"I believe so. Then, as soon as we package her up and get her onto the boat, we'll head far off shore and drop them both overboard before disappearing."

"When I called, I was given a number to call for further instructions as soon as it's done."

"Good." He was grateful to hear that, since he had not yet figured out what they would do after completing the disposal.

They headed back up to the house. She led the way while he pulled the cart.

Reaching the top of the ramp, Jorge said, "I'll go find that other large box while you go check on the woman."

He could hear the tap of her shoes as she climbed the stairs to the deck, while he went in the same door to the cellar they had used to bring him out of the house.

Inside, all was silent, and he realized that after today, he and Maria would never return to this house again.

CHAPTER 76

AFTER SPENDING THE NIGHT WITH BRAD, Courtney finally convinced him to take her to Edso's house.

"Thank you, Brad," she said, as they prepared to head out. She was buckled into the passenger seat of his bright red Honda Civic Type R. As soon as he turned the key, the engine roared to life.

"You're welcome. You ready?" he asked.

She nodded, and he shifted into drive.

"Then let's go."

"Jesus!" she exclaimed, as the car leapt forward and turned into the street.

He grinned at her and said, "She has a racing suspension, pretty stiff. Makes it fun to drive."

They careened though his neighborhood, onto Irvine Boulevard, and then onto Dover Drive. The traffic wasn't overly heavy, but he wove from lane to lane on the way to the Pacific Coast Highway.

Courtney glanced over at him each time he changed direction.

"Hey, Court, do you really think this is a good idea?" he asked.

"What, the way you're driving?"

His grin returned. "Not that. Do you think it's a good idea to go to Edso's?"

"Probably not, but it's something I feel I have to do."

To her relief, both conversation and speed ceased as they turned off the PCH and onto Bayside Drive. After passing the Harbor Patrol Office and the Coast Guard, they continued further on until they reached a gated side street off of Bayside.

"His house is down there," said Brad, motioning toward the closed gate. He turned off the car and looked over at her. "We'll have to do some walking."

He opened his door and climbed out, but she didn't move until he came around and took her hand. Then he led her toward a drive next to the gated street. At the end of the drive, she could see Edso's deck and the dock where his boat was tied up.

A man and a woman were guiding a cart down the ramp. Courtney dropped Brad's hand and said, "Look!"

From appearances, whatever was in the cart was heavy. When the couple reached the boat, she saw that it took both of them, with great effort, to get a large box out of the cart and into the boat.

"What do you suppose that is?" asked Courtney.

"No idea."

"Come on," she said, tugging him along.

"Where're we going?"

"Back to the car. We're going to wait for the gate to open for somebody else, and then we'll slip in."

"Court, that only works in the movies."

"Maybe, but do you have a better idea?"

"Sorry, I don't."

"Okay. So, we'll wait."

* * *

"I can't believe it," said Brad. They had just climbed into his car when a delivery truck showed up at the gate. He had to hurry to start the car and followed the truck through the gate. It turned into the second drive down the road, but they kept going until they reached the end. Edso's house was the final drive, and Courtney saw a gray BMW M4 parked in the drive.

"Nice car," said Brad, parking next to it and getting out.

Courtney joined him. "What do you think? He's home?"

He felt the hood of the car. "That's my guess. The engine's cold, and I'd bet that this car doesn't belong to those folks on the dock. They must be his staff or something. He's probably here."

She took a deep breath and said, "Only one way to find out."

To her relief, he walked closely beside her all the way to the door. She knocked three times and waited.

There was no answer, so she knocked again.

Again, there was no answer.

"Nobody home," said Brad. He began to turn away.

She grabbed his arm. "Wait, I'm not giving up that easily."

She knocked again with the same result.

"Let's go around back. Maybe he's out on the deck," she said.

"Court, you're acting a bit crazy."

"Whatever. You coming?" She began to walk toward the corner of the house, and he followed.

CHAPTER 77

AS THEY NEARED THE BACK OF THE HOUSE, she heard the clanging of feet on the aluminum ramp that led from the boat to the house, followed by silence, then voices.

"Shhh," said Courtney. She pulled Brad back against the side of the house and whispered, "Did you hear that? What woman?"

He nodded. "I did. We should get out of here."

"No. I didn't come this far to not see Edso. I'm going to try the door again."

"Suit yourself."

They retreated back to the front of the house, where she went straight to the door and, this time, knocked on it much harder.

As before, there was no response. She knocked again and called out. This time, the door was unlatched. It opened just enough for her to see a short, Hispanic woman.

"Hello. I'm sorry to disturb you, but is Edso Harding in?"

The woman shook her head and began pushing the door shut, saying, "No, Señora. Yo no hablo inglés."

Warning bells went off in Courtney's head. She had just heard the woman speaking English moments before. Without thinking, she put her foot in the door, preventing it from closing.

"Court, what are you doing?" hissed Brad.

"Something is going on in there."

"But it doesn't concern you."

"Ow!" she yelped, as the Hispanic woman opened the door a little and then slammed it hard on Courtney's foot. Courtney lost her balance and toppled backward. Immediately the door slammed shut, followed by the loud click of a deadbolt being engaged.

"Brad!"

He steadied her and said, "You okay?"

"I'm fine. We've got to get in there."

"No. No, we don't."

"Yes, we do."

She quickly moved around the corner of the house, relieved again to hear Brad's footsteps right behind her, even though he continued to protest. As they reached the back of the house, she saw the couple running down the ramp toward the boat. They stopped and watched as the man jumped on board and started the engine while she untied the boat.

"They're stealing Edso's boat!" Courtney yelled, starting to run toward the ramp.

Brad grabbed her, "Court. Stop. They're gone."

She stopped and turned toward him, panic in her eyes. "Didn't she say something about getting the woman? What woman? I only saw the two of them taking the boat."

Before Brad could reply, she ran up the stairs that led to the deck.

"Court, wait!" he called out as she disappeared onto the deck without answering.

In her panic, she had run right past the open door that was near the top of the ramp. Brad walked over, assuming that it led into the cellar of the house. Looking inside he saw, near the door, a collapsed cardboard box.

She leaned over the deck railing and hissed at him, "Brad."

He looked up and saw her looking over the railing down at him.

"They left the door open. Come on."

"Court, no! Let's just call the police and get out of here. Better yet, let's just get out of here."

She ignored him and disappeared from sight.

"Shit," he muttered, and moved up the stairs. When he reached the top of the stairs, he could see that the entire wall of the house facing the deck was made up of a series of French doors, and the center one was open. And she was peering in the open door. As he stepped onto the deck she turned and rushed over to him, grabbed his hand and tugged him toward the door.

"Come on."

They stepped inside, and she stopped and looked around the room, which seemed to serve as the hub for all of the others. Opposite was the door that the Hispanic woman had slammed on her foot. No one else seemed to be around, so she followed the aroma of coffee through a doorway to the right. It led to the kitchen. She found a pot on the stove, simmering away, so she took it off the fire and turned the burner off.

Behind her, Brad opened the door next to the kitchen.

"What's in there?" she asked.

"Looks like the way into the cellar."

"Let's finish checking out the house first. Then we can go down there."

"Nice place," said Brad, as they returned to the main room.

The room was large and made for entertaining. The furniture looked comfortable—and expensive. It was perfectly matched. Wall space was either filled with paintings or bookshelves, with the exception of a giant state-of-the-art television.

"It looks like these books are just for show. I don't think any of them have ever been opened," said Courtney, as she walked around the room.

"Is this him?" asked Brad. He held up a picture that he had taken off of one of the bookshelves.

"Let me see." Courtney took it from him and studied the picture. "Yes. And that's his grandfather. I'm not sure who the other man is."

As she replaced the picture on the shelf, she saw that there was also a picture of *Vorspiel*. Pointing at it, she said, "That was his grandfather's yacht, where he lived growing up, and where . . ." Her voice trailed off.

To her relief, Brad didn't ask her to finish the sentence. "Let's see what's down there," he said, gently taking her hand and pointing toward a hallway lined with three closed doors.

The first two doors revealed unused guestrooms. Before opening the third door, Brad stopped. "Last one. You know what they say— third time's the lucky charm." He turned the knob and slowly pushed the door open.

CHAPTER 78

THE ROOM WAS DARK, but not middle-of-the-night dark. With just enough light coming in from around the drawn curtains, it was possible for Courtney to see around the room without turning on a light. The bed had not yet been made, but the covers had been loosely pulled back into position, and someone had laid out a set of women's clothes, which looked ready to be pulled on. There was a closet to the left of the bed. To the right was another door, pulled shut.

As Courtney moved around the bed, her foot kicked something on the floor, but when she looked down, she didn't see anything. She dropped to her knees. Just under the bed, she discovered a roll of industrial packaging tape, some zip ties, and a man's shirt.

"Brad," she said, "look!" She held them up.

"Where'd you find those?"

"Under the bed."

"Weird place for them."

"I know," said Courtney. She dropped them on the bed and walked toward the shut door. "Bathroom?"

He turned the knob and poked his head in. "Looks like it."

He moved back, and Courtney stepped into the room first. The lights were on, and a damp towel was on the floor. The air in the room was warm and moist, and there was still steam on the mirror.

She took a few more steps and stopped. Ahead, she could see a closed shower curtain at the far end of the room.

"Hello," she called softly. The only sound was that of an occasional drip of water.

"This can't be good," whispered Brad.

Cautiously, she moved toward the drawn curtain.

As she began to pull it aside, she said, "Brad, there's some blood here."

He joined her, and for a moment they both stared at the red stain on the edge of the tub. As she took a deep breath, he slowly reached up, grabbed hold of the shower curtain, and pulled it the rest of the way open.

He had only pulled it open a few inches when Courtney saw a woman slumped inside the tub. She had blood across her face and appeared to be unconscious. Then, Brad ripped the curtain all the way open.

Courtney was so surprised, at first she struggled to speak. "Sylvie!" She was covered in soaking-wet towels. One of those towels was also stained with blood from a cut on her head.

"You know her?"

Courtney reached in and checked for a pulse. "Yes. And she's still alive."

"I'll go call 911," said Brad, turning from the tub.

"No. Don't. Here, take my phone and call Jack."

"Jack?"

"Just do it. Then find some dry towels."

Her tone must have convinced him that discussion was not an option.

He dialed the number.

* * *

Jack put his phone back into his pocket and shook his head before mumbling under his breath, "Son of a bitch."

"Who was that?" asked Max.

"Get your stuff. We've got to go." He hurried toward the door.

"What? Who was that?"

"Courtney."

"What's going on? Is she all right?"

He stopped and faced her. "Yes. She's fine. She and Brad went to go see Edso."

"They what?"

"They went to see Edso. He wasn't there, but they went into his house anyway. Court thinks some people just stole his boat. She said they've found Sylvie in his bathtub, just barely alive."

"What!"

As soon as Max cried out, Patti walked in. "What's going on?"

"We have to get over to Edso's," said Jack.

"Where to?" said Max, grabbing the car keys.

"She gave me the address. She said it's somewhere over by the Sherman Gardens. Patti, if you're coming with us, let's go."

She rushed off. "Meet you at the car. I have to grab my camera."

Jack turned to Max. "You're driving. And don't be bashful."

Once they were in the car, he handed Patti the address. "Find the directions in your phone and tell Max where to go."

To Jack's relief, Max wasn't bashful, and as they headed north on the Pacific Coast Highway, Patti began guiding her.

Trusting that they were on the right route, Jack began looking through his phone for Ken's number.

"Ken."

"Jack? What's wrong?"

"It's Sylvie." Jack shared what little information he had and gave Ken the address.

"I'm in the area. I'll meet you there."

* * *

"Give me a towel," said Courtney, when Brad returned with an armful. He stepped toward her and reached out, handing one to her.

"Thanks."

"Brad. Back it up," she said, as she saw him staring into the tub.

"Sorry." He stepped back.

Slowly and carefully, Courtney lifted the wet towels off of Sylvie and wrapped her in the dry one.

"Come over here now and help me get her out of the tub."

"Should we be moving her?" asked Brad.

"Probably not, but we are. If we call for help, we'll probably be arrested. We're lucky no one has noticed us yet. Now, are you going to help me?"

With some effort, they managed to get Sylvie out of the tub and onto the bed.

"How about you go outside and wait to open the gate for Jack. I'll do what I can for her here."

"Got it."

Sylvie's breathing and pulse were getting stronger. Courtney added a blanket to the towel and turned her attention to the cut on Sylvie's head. Returning to the bathroom, she found a clean washcloth, wet it, and went back into the bedroom to clean the wound.

"Did that son of a bitch do this to you?" she whispered, as she cleaned the drying blood off of Sylvie's head.

She stayed by Sylvie's side for what felt like ages until she finally heard Brad's voice saying, "She's in there."

She could hear a rustling on the other side of the door. Slowly it swung open, and she saw Max's face appear in the doorway. "Court?"

"Max. Thank God! Come in," she said, as she stood up from the bed.

Max walked in. She glanced over at the bed but stepped toward Courtney and held out her arms. Courtney fell into them and burst into tears.

CHAPTER 79

WHILE MAX CONSOLED Courtney and Patti started taking photos, Jack checked on Sylvie. Her condition seemed stable, so he signaled to Brad to meet him back in the hallway.

"So, what happened?" asked Jack.

Brad proceeded to tell Jack the story, and as he reached the part where they opened the bathroom door, there was a loud knocking on the front door.

"You expecting anyone?" asked Jack.

"No, you're the only call we made."

"Good," said Jack as the knocking continued.

He hurried toward the door but before he got there, Ken's voice rang out. "Jack?"

"That was fast," said Jack, as Ken pushed the door shut.

"Where is she?"

"Down the hall, last door." The words were barely out of his mouth before Ken was heading down the hallway.

"Who's that?" said Brad, the surprise evident on his face.

"Ken. He's a friend of Sylvie's. I called him."

Brad still looked perplexed.

"Not so long ago, he helped rescue Courtney from Edso. It's complicated. Let's just say they're on the same team."

"How'd he get here so fast?"

"I have no idea. But based on past events, I'm not surprised."

* * *

As soon as Ken walked into the room, Courtney turned from Max, her surprise evident, and said, "Ken! You're here."

"How is she?"

"Better. When Brad and I got here she was barely breathing, and her heartbeat was pretty faint. Both seem stronger now."

Ken went to the bed and sat on the edge. He gently stroked Sylvie's forehead. Then he leaned down and whispered in her ear. "I'm here now. Those bastards won't get away with this."

As he sat up, still staring at her, he thought he saw an eyelid move. He touched her forehead again and then stood up.

"Courtney, thank you. Jack told me you found her."

She nodded. "I convinced Brad to bring me here this morning. I intended to confront Edso."

"In other words, you didn't listen to Jack."

She looked down at the floor. "I suppose not, but you have to understand—"

He cut her off. "I do understand, and if you had followed my warnings to Jack and kept away, she'd probably be dead. Thank you. Now, I need you to tell me everything."

He saw Courtney exchange a look with Max.

Max reached over and squeezed Courtney's hand. "It's okay. Go find Brad so you can talk with Ken together. Tell him everything. Patti and I will stay here so she's not alone."

* * *

Ken returned to the main room with Courtney.

"You must be Brad," he said, as he extended his hand to Brad.

"Yes."

"Let's sit. I need you both to tell me everything."

Over the next thirty minutes, Brad and Courtney told their story. When they had finished, she looked at Ken and said, "Any idea what could have happened to Edso?"

Ken said, "I don't know, but based on what you've told me, my guess is that Edso was in that box you saw them loading into the boat. I think they probably killed him, and your arrival is what saved Sylvie."

Max walked into the room and approached him. "Ken, she's conscious. I told her that you were here. She wants to talk to you."

"Thank you."

* * *

Max watched Ken hurry back toward the bedroom. Then she went to stand next to Jack.

"You all right?" he said.

"I'm good. But what the hell is going on?"

"Your guess is as good as mine."

Brad stood up from the couch. "Hey, Jack, what say we go look around?"

Jack turned to Max. "You mind?"

"No, go ahead. I want to talk to Courtney anyway. Take Patti with you."

Jack called Patti, and when she came into the room, they both followed Brad outside.

Max sat down next to Courtney.

"Quite the morning," said Max.

Courtney forced a smile. "It has been. Thank you for coming."

"Can I ask you something?"

"Of course."

Max looked at Courtney. Working to suppress a smile she said, "So, how was Brad?"

"What do you mean by that?"

"Come on, Court. You know exactly what I mean."

"No. I don't."

"Yes. You do."

She looked at Max with a blank expression, obviously forced.

"Okay then, you want to be like that. Did you really go kayaking?"

"We did."

"You went kayaking," said Max, both making a statement and asking a question all at the same time.

"His house backs down to what he called the Back Bay."

Max's look demanded more information.

"Technically it's the Upper Newport Bay Nature Preserve and the view from his house is amazing. After kayaking, he made dinner."

"And he cooks! He made you dinner?"

"Oh yeah, did he ever."

"What did you have?"

"Dinner last night, we had a bottle of Cabernet with a T-bone steak. He swore that using mesquite for the fire was the secret for proper grilling. According to him, it burns hotter, and he wrapped potatoes and vegetables in foil and cooked them on the grill too."

"And dessert?" asked Max, grinning.

Courtney just smiled.

"Ah, ha!" said Max with a big grin.

"All I'll say is that he's got great hands. After kayaking all day my shoulders and back were killing me. He gives the most amazing back rubs."

"I bet he does," said Max, still grinning. "How did you convince him to bring you over here?"

"I just asked."

Max nodded knowingly.

"So, tell me exactly what happened when you got here."

Courtney repeated the story again.

"Oh my god. I can't imagine."

CHAPTER 80

KEN SAT ON THE EDGE OF THE BED and reached for Sylvie's hand.

"Syl, what happened?"

She tried to sit up. "Oh, my god, Ken. I am so happy to see you. But, how did you get here?"

Gently, he pressed on her shoulder, and with a moan she lay back down.

"Shhh. All that's important is that I'm here."

"Edso?" Her voice was weak, but her eyes maintained an intensity that reflected her toughness.

"I'm sorry. He's gone."

"Gone?"

"As best I can piece together, the caretakers packaged him into a large box and took him down to his boat. I think they were coming back up for you when Courtney and Brad showed up. They bolted and took off on the boat."

"Brad? Who's that?"

"Some guy from the Duffy boat company. Seems to be Courtney's date. She said she talked him into bringing her here."

"How did you get here?"

"Jack called me."

"Jack. Is he here? I only saw Max and Patti."

Her eyes began to water, and she used the edge of the sheet to wipe them dry.

Ken said, "Can you tell me what happened?"

She closed her eyes for a long moment. When she finally opened them again, she said, "There must have been drugs in the coffee. He brought a cup in for me, and then he left the room so I could get showered. I don't remember much else, but I still feel awful."

"If I had to guess, I'd say you didn't drink quite enough to kill you. But from what Courtney said, it must have been certainly close."

She motioned for Ken to move closer. "I was so close to getting the information we need," she whispered, then her eyes closed and she was asleep.

* * *

Ken sat watching her for a few minutes, but she was out. Satisfied that she wasn't in any immediate danger, he slipped out of the room.

"How is she?" said Max.

"She's dozed off, but we can't stay here too much longer. For one thing, all of the cars are lined up out there make it look like we're having a party. We don't want anyone in the neighborhood to call the cops. Do you think you could get her dressed so we can get out of here?"

"Sure," Max said.

Then he said, "That's Patti with the camera, right?"

"Yes."

"She good?"

"Very."

"I'm going to need her to take photos of the whole place so I can study everything later. Is she thorough?"

Max said, "Very. And I think she has done a lot of that already."

Then Courtney added, "We'll ask her as soon as she comes back in."

Ken went into the kitchen. The first thing he checked was the coffee pot. He raised it to his nose and sniffed it. Even though it was mostly cold, its aroma was amazing. He found a package of beans in a cupboard and began looking for something he could use as an evidence bag to put them in. He found some plastic wrap and covered the coffee pot so he could have it analyzed later.

"Hey, Ken." At the sound of Jack's voice, he turned. The two men were standing in the doorway watching him.

Jack added, "Courtney just talked to Patti, and she's gone into the bedroom to take more photos. Find anything here?"

"Don't know. I think whatever they gave Sylvie was in the coffee. Where've you been?"

Jack answered. "We went down to the dock and then checked out the cellar. Not much down there, actually, other than a large, collapsed box on the floor. It was empty."

"Probably intended for Sylvie," said Brad.

"Hey, guys," It was Patti. "I need you to come see something."

"What?" asked Ken.

"In the bedroom. I think there might be some hidden cameras."

Conversation ceased as they hurried after her. However, just as Patti reached the bedroom door, Max poked her head out and said, "Sylvie's dressed. Can you help us get her out of here?"

Ken looked at Brad and Jack and said, "You guys go ahead and help her to the main room. I'll take a quick look at what Patti's discovered, and we'll meet you there."

After they slowly led Sylvie away, he turned to Patti.

"So, Patti?"

She pointed toward the wall opposite the bed. Then she mouthed the words: "There, nearly at the ceiling."

He looked where she was pointing. Well hidden within the pattern of the wallpaper was a tiny, almost impossible to see, lens.

"How did you ever see that?"

"I was panning around the room, and as I swept by, there was a tiny glint of light. Maybe it was a reflection. I don't know, but it caught my eye."

"Good eye. Can you leave the room for a minute?"

"I'm not quite finished with the photos."

"That's okay."

* * *

As soon as Ken was alone, he took a small knife out of his pocket and began to carve away at the wall. It took very little time for him to expose the lens and the cable it was attached to. He tugged on the cable, and a couple of feet pulled out of the wall.

"Fiber-optic," he whispered to himself. *"That means there has to be some equipment somewhere,"* he thought.

He gave it another tug, but any preexisting slack was now gone.

He stuck his head out of the room and called for Jack and Brad.

Coming to the door, Jack asked, "Find anything?"

"How's she doing?"

"Better by the minute."

"Good. Patti found a camera lens. Looks like it's on a fiber-optic cable, which means that somewhere there is equipment. You want to help me search? I'll do the room next door. How about you and Brad do the other one?"

"Sure."

CHAPTER 81

"HEY, KEN, WE'VE GOT IT!" Jack called out.

When Ken joined them, he saw that Brad was inside the closet, looking into one of the ends.

Ken asked, "What've we got?"

In a sheepish tone, Brad said, "Sorry. I was a bit eager and kind of ripped it open. There's some electronic equipment in here."

"No worries." Switching places with Brad, Ken looked at what had been exposed. He muttered to himself, "Well, what have we here?"

Then he turned and called out to Brad. "How'd you find it?"

"The dimensions of the closet didn't look right."

"Good eye."

"So, what've we got?" asked Jack.

Ken stepped out of the closet. "Looks like a couple of hard drives, a router." He turned back, disconnected equipment, and handed the various components out to Jack and Brad.

"Could you find a bag or something for all this stuff and then put it in the BMW outside? Ask Sylvie where she put the keys."

In short order, everyone gathered in the living room. Ken looked at the group and said, "We better get out of here. I want to get Sylvie back to the *Wonder*. I'll take her in her car."

Sylvie, who had been resting on the couch, suddenly stirred. "What about your car?" she said.

"I got dropped off. No worries."

Then he turned to Courtney and Max. "Ladies, can you help her out? Patti, a word."

"Sure," said Courtney. "Come on, Max."

"Yes," said Patti.

Ken pointed at her camera. "Can you send them to me?"

"Sure."

He handed her a card. "Send them here; it's a secure email."

She put the card in her pocket, then turned and followed Max and Courtney as they helped Sylvie walk out to the car.

Then he turned to Jack. "If you and Brad could make sure the house is secure and locked up, that would be great. I'll meet you out by the cars."

Ken got out to the car as Courtney and Max were gently easing Sylvie into the passenger seat of the BMW. The moment the seatbelt clicked together, her eyes closed and her head fell to the side. She was asleep.

As Jack and Brad joined them, Jack said, "Everything's closed up."

Ken said, "Thanks. Now, we should all leave at the same time so the gate only opens once. Jack, it was good seeing you again. Please thank Courtney again for ignoring my advice. I think Sylvie got really lucky."

"She gonna' be all right?"

"I'm not a doctor, but I'd say yes. She's one tough lady."

"Tell me about it."

"Say bye to everyone else for me."

Before Jack could say anything more than "I will," Ken climbed into the BMW, hit the gas, and headed down the drive, leaving the others no choice but to hurry into their cars and follow.

CHAPTER 82

"SO WHAT'RE WE GONNA' DO NOW?" Max said, when they reached the main road. Ken had sped away so quickly, Jack had already lost sight of the BMW.

"Pull over and wait for Court and Brad and see what they want to do."

It wasn't long before Jack heard the distinct sound of Brad's car pulling over behind them. He watched in the mirror as Brad got out and walked over to them. When he reached Jack's side, he said, "How about you follow us to my house? I can invite Andrea, too. Steak sound good?"

"Sounds great," said Jack. "Can we stop on the way to get some wine?"

"Not necessary. I have plenty. Just follow us."

* * *

Jack opened one of the bottles of wine that Brad had placed on the table. It took all of the first bottle to fill their glasses. He called Max over and said, "Hand these around, will you?"

As soon as they each had a glass in hand, Brad cleared his throat and said, "I'd like to propose a toast to all of you, and especially you, Courtney. I have never met such a caring group of friends who trust each other and have each other's backs the way you four do."

Rims clinked, and Courtney said, "Thank you. Max, Patti, Jack—and especially you, Brad—I don't know what to say."

Jack wasn't sure what to say either, so he was relieved when Patti broke in.

"Okay, before things get any more sappy, I need all of you outside for a group picture."

She herded them outside, and as she directed them into position, she kept looking up at the sky, which was turning shades of pink and purple. Behind them, the sky was reflected in the bay, which added to the drama of the shot. She fiddled with the camera, then sat it on top of the cover of the unlit grill.

"Ready?" She pushed the button and hurried to join her subjects.

"Smile!" she said, a moment before Jack heard the camera click.

"Who's hungry?" asked Brad, as they dispersed.

Everyone answered at the same time. While Brad explained to Jack the merits of mesquite, Courtney, Max, and Patti moved back inside for more wine. Foil-wrapped potatoes and vegetables were first on the grill. Then, just as Brad was about to throw the steaks on, Andrea arrived.

"Andrea, you made it," said Brad. "Wine's inside."

"I've brought one out for her," said Max, handing her a glass. "I'm so glad you're here. Things probably would have been very different had you and Brad not helped us."

"Uh, you're welcome," said Andrea. "But what happened today?"

"Oh, my god. You aren't going to believe it."

Jack helped Brad tend to the steaks, as Max, Court, and Patti filled Andrea in.

* * *

A third bottle of wine carried them past dinner and through moonrise. When the sky began to brighten in the east, they finally said their goodbyes. Then, as Jack drove back to the cottage, Max and Patti proceeded to interrogate Courtney about Brad. To Jack's amusement, Courtney's lips remained sealed, so the discussion moved on to include Brad's house and Andrea.

As they pulled into the drive at the cottage, Courtney said, "I think it's time to go home."

They all agreed.

CHAPTER 83

ALL THE WAY to the *Wonder*, Ken spoke softly to Sylvie, even though she remained asleep until they stopped in the marina's parking lot.

"Huh, where are we?" she said, as he shut the engine off.

"We're home."

"Ken. What're you doing here? Where's Edso?"

"You don't remember? We can talk when we get on board."

He walked around to her side of the car and opened her door. She slumped toward him slightly but remained buckled in.

He unclipped her seatbelt and reached in to try to get her out of the seat.

"I don't feel so good."

With catlike reflexes he jumped back a split second before she leaned out the door and emptied her stomach on the parking lot pavement.

"Come on, Syl. Let's get you on board."

She wouldn't let him carry her, but by supporting most of her weight, he was able to walk her onto the *Wonder*.

"How is she?" asked the captain, after Ken settled her into her room.

"She'll be fine. She was lucky. If that woman, Courtney, had not been hell bent on seeing Edso, she might have disappeared and we never would have known."

"We were all lucky."

"So, any word on his boat?"

"Nothing definitive. But we did pick up some radio chatter. It was garbled, but it sounded like maybe a boat was sinking."

"Tell me more," said Ken.

"Another boat called in that they had responded and were pretty sure it was a prank call because there was nothing in the water to indicate that a boat may have sunk."

"Where did it happen?"

"Best guess, about half way to San Diego and maybe twenty miles off shore. Again, the transmissions were pretty garbled."

"Do you suppose it could have been Edso's?"

"I suppose. Anything's possible."

"At Edso's house, we found some secret recording equipment in his bedroom. It's out in the car. Let me go get it. Maybe it'll give us something on what happened today."

* * *

"Holy crap!" said Ken.

"That's disturbing," the captain agreed.

There were two hard drives, and they had just watched the first one. The footage clearly showed the couple stuffing Edso into a box.

The captain said, "Now we know what happened to Edso, and we can pretty well guess what happened to our girl. Do you think this is it, or was the recording transmitted somewhere else?"

"My guess would be that it was transmitted. As soon as our people get that equipment, we'll know for sure. I'll bet you that Giles is behind all of this."

"Wouldn't surprise me, but even with what's on this hard drive, there is no direct proof that any of it is linked to him."

"Shall we look at the other hard drive?"

They did, but upon seeing the content, they immediately turned it off. They agreed that since Sylvie was their friend and colleague, it wouldn't be right to watch those private moments without her consent. When she recovered, they would let her watch first and she could decide what to do.

* * *

Shortly after sunrise, Sylvie arose and went up on deck. Ken was already up and sipping a cup of steaming coffee.

"Good morning, Sunshine," he said when he saw her walk out.

"Mornin'."

"Coffee?"

"I think not. How about a cup of tea?"

"Let me get you one."

He returned with a cup, and they went inside and sat down in the main salon and watched the birth of another perfect Southern California day.

"Did I thank you?"

"You did. Many times. But it was really Courtney and Brad who saved you. They saw a man and woman load a very large box onto his boat. We found video recordings that prove it contained Edso's body."

"Were they Hispanic?"

"Yes."

"Had to be Maria and Jorge—his caretakers. The way she looked at me never felt right. I never really saw him."

Ken continued. "So, Courtney and this Brad arrived, and they must have spooked the caretakers, because they took off in the boat. Then Courtney and Brad went in the house and found you nearly dead in the tub."

"The coffee. It had to have been in the coffee. The last thing I remember was having a cup of this incredibly delicious coffee that Maria made. I had had some before, but obviously it hadn't been doctored the other time."

"Courtney had the presence of mind not to call 911. Instead, she called Jack. And it was Jack who called me."

"Where is he?"

"I don't now. We all left the house pretty much together. I don't know where they went after."

Sylvie almost smiled, "I guess neither of us did a very good job of warning them off, did we?"

"I guess not. Good thing. Saved your life."

"I suppose," she said, her voice fading away as she thought about what he had just said before asking, "So what do we know?"

"Well, we know for sure that Maria and Jorge killed him, and we have videos of them taking care of Edso's body. And his boat is missing. We can only presume it was sunk somewhere with him on board."

"Any sign of Maria and Jorge?"

"None."

"Wouldn't surprise me in the least if they were eliminated along with the boat. Face it, Giles isn't known for leaving loose ends around.

"You're probably right." He paused, then said, "Syl, I have something else to tell you."

"What?"

"There are other videos. Of you."

"Me?"

"And Edso. Private moments. I saw only the very beginning before turning it off. We're going to let you watch them first, and you can decide what to do with them."

"Shit."

"Yeah, I know. But there's more. There's a high probability they were transmitted."

"To where?"

"We don't know yet. However, if I had to guess, my bet would be to Giles. But we may never know."

"I'm going to get that s.o.b. Do you suppose that he thinks I'm dead?"

"Maybe we should get that out into the media."

Sylvie put her empty tea cup on the table and stood up. "I'm hungry, and we should get out of here."

CHAPTER 84

"LADIES AND GENTLEMEN, we will be landing soon. Please stow any of your belongings under the seat in front of you or place them in the overhead bins. Make sure that your seatbelts are fastened and that your tray tables are closed and your seats are in the upright position."

Max was in the center seat, Jack was on the aisle, and Patti had the window, where she was busy photographing what she could given the limited size of the window. Dave had promised to pick them up at the airport, and he and Jack had already scheduled a run for the upcoming weekend. Courtney was across the aisle from Jack. Her eyes were closed, and there was the smallest hint of a smile on her face.

Max rested her head on Jack's shoulder, and he looked down at her and smiled.

Had anyone asked, it would have been hard to tell who was happiest to be home.

Just one more reunion to go—no doubt the happiest of them all: seeing Cat.

In 2009 when *Harbor Ice* was first published, I had no idea that it was the beginning of what would become such a fun and rewarding part of my life. Now, with *California Reckoning*, the tenth book in the Jack Beale Mystery Series, it just gets better. I hope you enjoyed this latest story as much as I did writing it.

If we're not already, let's become friends on Facebook. I am also on Twitter at @kd_mason and on Instagram at k.d._Mason. For news about the books, events I will be attending and whatever else I can think of that may interest you. Check out my website—www.kdmason.com and feel free to contact me by email at kd@kdmason.com with any questions or comments.

Thank you for your support,
KD

MORE RECIPES from the
JACK BEAL MYSTERY SERIES

To all my fans,
Whether it's a special cocktail, lunch or special dinner,
food and drink continue to play important roles in the lives
of my characters. Here are some of the recipes in this latest book,
California Reckoning, *for your enjoyment.*

Bon appétit . . .
K.D.Mason

Chapter 10

Edso inhaled deeply and studied what had been put in front of him.
In the bowl, on a thick cut piece of toated bread were large shrimps,
scallops, squid and clams, all in a tomato and wine broth.
"Zuppa di Pesce alla Napoletana," said Giles. "Neapolitan fish soup."

Neapolitan Fish Soup
Zuppa di Pesce alla Napoletana

Recipe by Mary Ann Esposito, host of PBS's *Ciao Italia*

4 pounds littleneck clams
1 cup dry white wine
¼ cup minced fresh flat-leaf parsley
4 cloves garlic, peeled and halved
¼ cup extra-virgin olive oil
1 large onion, chopped
1 cup chopped fennel

1 teaspoon red pepper flakes or ½ teaspoon red pepper paste

3 cups pureed plum tomatoes

1 pound squid rings

1 pound sea scallops cut in half

1 pound medium shrimp (26-30 count) peeled and deveined

Salt and freshly ground black pepper to taste

Juice of one large lemon

8 country-style bread slices, toasted

Scrub the clams in cold water; discard any with cracked shells or those that do not close when tapped. Place them in a large sauté pan with wine, parsley, and 4 garlic halves. Cover the pan and cook the clams over medium heat until they open; discard any clams that do not open.

Use a slotted spoon to transfer the clams to a bowl. Strain the liquid in the pan through a strainer lined with cheesecloth into a large glass measuring cup; you should have about 1 cup. Set the liquid aside. Remove the clam meat from the shells and set aside.

Heat the olive oil in a large soup pot over medium heat. Add the onion and fennel and cook until they soften; stir in the pepper flakes and cook for a minute or two. Add the reserved clam cooking liquid and the pureed tomatoes; stir well and bring to a boil over medium-high heat. Boil for 2 minutes, then lower the heat to medium. Add the squid rings and cook for 5 minutes; add the scallops and continue cooking for 3 minutes; add the shrimp and cook for an additional 3 minutes. Season with salt and pepper. Add the clams and heart slowly over low heat until hot; stir in lemon juice. Serve in large bowls over slices of toasted bread.

This recipe can be found in her new cookbook
Ciao Italia, My Lifelong Food Adventures in Italy - p.56
Peter Randall Publishers, Portsmouth, NH 03820

Chapter 13

A woman's voice came over the speaker,
"For dessert, I've made key lime pie."
"With the chocolate crust?"
"Is there any other?"

Nellie & Joes Famous Key Lime Pie

1 9-inch graham cracker pie crust
  (Nabisco Oreo chocolate crust preferred)
1 (14-ounce) can sweetened condensed milk
3 egg yolks (whites are not used)
½ cup Nellie & Joe's Famous Key West Lime Juice (no substitute)

Combine condensed milk, egg yolks, and lime juice.

Blend until smooth. Pour filling into pie crust and bake at 350°F for 15 minutes. Allow to stand 10 minutes before refrigerating.

Optional: Top with whipped cream and garnish with lime slices.

Chapter 18

Max was sopping up the sauce with a piece of bread. "Oh my god,
I love this sauce. The mussels are good, but . . ." Her words were muffled
by the sauce-soaked piece of bread she had just stuffed into her mouth.

Ben's Mussels
(served with good bread for sopping up the sauce)

NOTE: If making with fresh mussels in shells,
add mussels after fennel starts to sweat, and cook until they start to open.

8 ounces frozen mussels out of shells, thawed
  OR fresh mussels in their shells
1 tablespoon olive oil
1 cup fresh fennel, sliced

1 teaspoon fresh garlic, minced

¼ cup anisette liqueur (Anisette is what makes the dish.)

¼ cup cream

1 teaspoon turmeric

Sauté fennel in olive oil over medium heat until it starts to sweat.

Add the garlic and cook for 1 minute. (Adding it last makes garlic less bitter.) Add the anisette and flame off (carefully light it with a match and let the flame die down).

Add cream and turmeric. Add cooked thawed mussels and simmer until warm. Serve with bread to soak up the broth.

Chapter 51

"Come," said Giles, touching Edso's elbow
as if he were a date that required direction.
As they sat, Giles looked at his plate and said,
"This looks wonderful."
"It's Asian Salmon over rice with grilled asparagus," said Maria.

Asian Salmon

Serves 3-4

1 pound fresh salmon fillet

MARINADE:

4 tablespoons packed brown sugar

3 tablespoons vegetable or olive oil

5 tablespoons low-sodium soy sauce

4 tablespoons white wine (chardonnay is fine)

3 tablespoons orange juice

2 tablespoons minced garlic

2 tablespoons fresh gingerroot, minced

1 teaspoon hot red pepper sauce

⅓ cup minced white onion

2 or 3 scallions chopped for garnish

Combine all ingredients except the optional butter and scallions, and marinate salmon fillet for at least 1 hour. Transfer salmon fillet to a prepared baking sheet and reserve the marinade to use later in the sauce.

Bake salmon at 350°F until cooked through.

(15 to 20 minutes depending on the size of the fillet or until fish can be flaked with a fork)

Sauce:

While the salmon is baking, transfer remaining marinade to a small sauce pan and bring to a boil for at least 5 to eight minutes.

After plating the fish, spoon sauce over fish.

Garnish with the chopped scallions before serving.

NOTE: This dish is also delicious chilled.

Reality in the fiction of *California Reckoning*

Ch. 4 Maudsley State Park, Newburyport, MA
https://www.mass.gov/locations/maudslay-state-park

Ch. 6 Kona Kai Marina, San Diego
https://www.konakaimarina.com

Ch. 15 Drift, Portsmouth, NH
https://thedriftcollective.com

Ch. 19 John Wayne Airport, Orange County
https://www.ocair.com/default

In-N-Out Burger, Costa Mesa, CA
http://www.in-n-out.com

Sherman Library and Gardens, Corona del Mar
http://www.slgardens.org

Ch. 22 Voyagers, Newport Beach, CA
http://voyagersrentals.com

Ch. 23 Newport Beach Harbor, CA
https://www.newportbeachca.gov/Home/ShowDocument?id=5985

Ch. 29 Balboa Pavillion, Newport Beach, CA
http://www.balboapavilion.com

Balboa Pier, Newport Beach, CA
https://www.newportbeachca.gov/how-do-i-/find/beach-information

Ch. 31 Avalon, Catalina Island
www.catalinachamber.com

Mt.Ada, Catalina Islland
https://www.catalinachamber.com/visit/mt-ada/

Ch. 33 Catalina Flyer, Newport Beach, CA
http://catalinainfo.com

Green Pleasure Pier, Catalina Island, CA
https://www.catalinachamber.com

Scoops Ice Cream Shop
http://scoopscatalina.com

CH. 34   Chimes Tower, Catalina Island, CA
          http://www.catalinachimes.org

Ch. 35   Hotel Metropole, Avalon, Catalina Island, CA
          https://www.hotel-metropole.com

CH. 35   Metropole Marketplace, Avalon, Catalina Island, CA
          https://www.hotel-metropole.com

Ch. 38   Sunkissed, Metropole Marketplace, Avalon, Catalina Island, CA
          https://www.hotel-metropole.com

Ch.40   A Touch of Heaven Day Spa, Metropole Marketplace,
          Avalon, Catalina Island, CA
          https://www.hotel-metropole.com

Ch. 40   Bluewater Grill, Avalon, Catalina Island, CA
          https://www.bluewatergrill.com/locations/catalina-island

Ch. 42   El Galleon, Avalon, Catalina Island, CA
          http://catalinahotspots.com/el_galleon/

Ch.46   Del Ray Landing, Del Ray Marina, Los Angeles
          https://www.delreylanding.com

Ch. 47   Taco Loco, Laguna Beach, CA
          http://tacoloco.net

          Catalina Marathon, Catalina Island, CA
          https://runcatalina.com

Ch. 56   Alesso, Laguna Beach, CA
          http://alessalaguna.com

Ch. 70   Top of the World, Laguna Beach, CA
          https://www.visitlagunabeach.com/directory/top-of-the-world/

OTHER BOOKS BY K.D. MASON

HARBOR ICE (2009)

The winter has been brutally cold, leaving Rye Harbor frozen solid. Finally, the weather warms and the ice begins to breakup and drift out to sea. That's when a woman's body is found under a slab of ice left by the outgoing tide. Max, the bartender at Ben's Place recognizes that it is her Aunt's partner and that begins a series of events that will eventually threaten Max's life as well. It is up to her best friend, Jack Beale, to unravel the mystery.

CHANGING TIDES (2010)

Fate, Chance, Destiny . . . Call it what you will, but sometimes life chang- ing events begin in the most innocent and unexpected ways. For Jack Beale that moment came on a perfect summer morning as he stood overlooking Rye Harbor when something caught his eye. In that small space between the bow of his boat and the float to which it was tied, a lifeless body had become wedged as the tide tried to sweep it out to sea. That discovery, and the arrival of Daniel would begin a series of events that would eventually take Max from him. Who was the victim? Why was Daniel there and what was his interest in Max? Was there a connection? And, so began a jour- ney that would take Jack from Rye Harbor to Newport, RI and, eventually Belize, as he searched for answers.

DANGEROUS SHOALS (2011)

Spring has arrived in the small New Hampshire coastal town of Rye Harbor and all seemed right in the world. Jack Beale and Max, the feisty red haired bartender at Ben's Place, are back together after their split up the previous year and are looking forward to enjoying a carefree summer together. Then, someone who they thought was just a memory reappears, pursued by a psy- chotic killer. When he ends up dead, Jack and Max become the killer's new targets. What should have been an easy, relaxing summer for Jack, Max and his cat, Cat, becomes a battle of wits and a fight for survival.

KILLER RUN (2012)

Malcom and Polly were living their dream, running a North Country Bed & Breakfast they named the Quilt House Inn. The Inn was known for two things, the collection of antique quilts on display and miles of running and hiking trails for their guests use. Jack, training for his first trail marathon, The Rockdog Run, heard about the Inn and hatched a plan whereby he and Max could enjoy a romantic get-a-way and he could get in some quality trail training. For his plan to work, Dave and Patti joined them at the Inn. Meanwhile, in the weeks leading up to the marathon, a delusional antique dealer developed a fascination with one of the quilts on display in the Inn and It wasn't long before Malcom and Polly's dream and the four friends became forever entwined in a deadly mystery spanning two hundred years and 26.2 miles. Running a marathon is challenging enough by itself. Doing so on trails and starting before sunrise, in the dark, on a cold November day is even more daunting. When Jack trips and falls, landing on the lifeless body of an unknown runner, the race becomes a true "killer run."

EVIL INTENTIONS (2013)

Unseen forces at play may dramatically change the quiet seaside town of Rye Harbor forever. It's early spring, and one of the town's oldest homes, the Francis House, has just gone up in flames, revealing a badly burned body in the ashes. With help from an unexpected source, Jack and his friend Tom, the Police Chief, unravel the mystery fueled by a broken heart, a secret real estate deal, and a deadly double-cross.

UNEXPECTED CATCH (2015)

A summer heat wave blankets the New Hampshire seacoast. In an attempt to beat the heat, Jack's best friend, Dave, arranges for a day of fishing far off shore on the boat *Miss Cookie*. Even though they land only a few fish, they pronounce the day a great success—until Jack spots smoke on the horizon and they convince the reluctant captain to bring them to investigate. What they find will have a profound effect upon all of their lives as they deal with the consequences of an Unexpected Catch.

BLACK SCHOONER (2016)

Jack and Max hire a delivery skipper, TJ, to bring her catamaran from Belize to Rye Harbor, New Hampshire. TJ takes on a mysterious woman as crew in Florida, but after she jumps ship in Gloucester, TJ enlists Jack's help for the final leg of the delivery. In Gloucester, TJ, an incorrigible womanizer, reconnects with a former lover and crew mate, and that chance meeting triggers a search for a black schooner from his past—along with the chance it affords for closure and revenge. His search takes him through Kennebunkport, Boothbay, and Camden, Maine, and finally to the Isles of Shoals, where TJ and Jack's friend Tom, the police chief of Rye Harbor, become targets of an unknown killer.

JESSICA'S SECRET (2017)

On a starless night in 1942, New Hampshire fisherman Ben Crouse takes his boat, *Dorothy Kay*, out of Rye Harbor in the midst of a storm to patrol against the threat of German U-boats. What—and whom—he encounters that night will change his life forever. More than half a century later, his niece, Courtney, receives a series of threatening phone calls. As she struggles to run her late uncle's restaurant, navigate a new romance, and find answers to her family's secret past, she turns to her friends Jack and Max, who must solve the mystery of Ben's legacy and save her from the delusional children of the Third Reich.

CANCELED OUT (2018)

Best friends Jack and Dave get an unwelcome surprise at the local Thanksgiving Turkey Trot race when they meet Kim, an attractive runner who strongly resembles Sylvie, a mysterious woman from Jack's past. To the complete dismay of Max, Jack's girlfriend, the surprise intensifies when the real Sylvie contacts Jack just hours later. Having returned to New England after a long rest in Florida, Sylvie claims that Kim is a hired killer who is armed, dangerous, and has a contract to kill her. Sylvie asks for Jack's help, and despite his better judgment and Max's initial protests, he still feels compelled to give it. When the chase between Kim and Sylvie heats up over a series of frigid races, Jack and his friends get pulled deeper into their deadly game of cat and mouse, which can end with only one survivor.

Made in the USA
Middletown, DE
28 February 2019